"You have the most incredible eyes," Luke said softly. "Bluest I've ever seen."

Cassie felt her heart catch, then race, sending fire through her body. Her eyes widened as Luke watched her.

"I'm not a . . . I'm not gay," she finally stammered.

Luke laughed and snapped her fingers. "Damn! I keep forgetting that rule not to compliment straight women."

Cassie blushed crimson. "I'm sorry. I just thought I should . . ."

"Warn me? In case I had designs on you?" Luke laughed again, a deep, husky laugh that Cassie found enjoyable, despite her embarrassment. "You're perfectly safe. Trust me," Luke said.

Visit

Bella Books

at

BellaBooks.com

or call our toll-free number

1-800-729-4992

Artist's Dream

GERRI HILL

Bella
BOOKS

2005

Bella Books, Inc.
P.O. Box 10543
Tallahassee, FL 32302

Printed in the United States of America on acid-free paper
First Edition

Editor: Anna Chinappi
Cover designer: Sandy Knowles

ISBN 1-59493-042-2

Dedicated to my father, A. J., with nothing but fond memories.

Acknowledgments

After having a good, loving relationship with my own father, it was difficult to create Reverend Parker, as a father figure, that is. Thanks to those who shared their stories with me. Reverend Parker became a combination of them all. And although he is strictly conjured up from my imagination, sadly, I know there are men out there like him, pushing hate instead of love. On that note, I would like to thank Rosemary for her help with the Bible issues as I struggled through them. I appreciate your input, and your gentle scolding of my ignorance!

About the Author

Gerri lives in East Texas, deep in the pines, with her partner, Diane, of fourteen years. They share their log cabin and adjoining five acres with two labs, Max and Zach, and three cats. A huge vegetable garden that overflows in the summer is her pride and joy. Besides giving in to her overactive green thumb, Gerri loves to "hike the woods" with the dogs, a pair of binoculars (bird watching), and at least one camera! For more, visit Gerri's Web site at www.gerrihill.com.

Chapter One

"Why are you fighting this?"

Cassie looked at her best friend coolly over the rim of her coffee cup, then slowly lowered her lashes, dismissing the comment with an ease that surprised her.

"Why must we always have this discussion?" she asked.

"Because I can't stand to see you wasting away like this," Kim said.

"I'm hardly wasting away," Cassie replied, slowly pulling her eyes from Kim and glancing out the window at the approaching evening.

"You know what I mean."

"Yes, I know," Cassie said, letting out a long sigh. "I just don't know why it's so important to you. The whole world's not gay, Kim. I happen to like David."

"Oh shit! You can't be serious!" Kim jumped from her usual chair to stand in front of Cassie, blocking her view of the window. "He's a farmer, for God's sake! Not even organic. He probably votes Republican."

Cassie laughed, and tucked her legs more securely under her. "I'm sure he does," she said calmly. "I still like him."

"At least Paul was an artist. At least you had something in common with him," Kim continued.

"Yes, we had something in common. We both preferred men," Cassie said dryly.

"At least Paul was sincere enough to finally admit that. You're still living in denial regarding your own sexuality."

"Kim, I'm so tired of having this discussion with you. I'm perfectly capable of having lesbian friends without being a lesbian. I know you find this hard to believe," she added, "but not everyone is gay." She smiled at her friend gently. "I accept you like you are. Why can't you just accept me?"

"Because I know you, that's why. You're thirty-three years old and one of these days you'll stop trying to find Mr. Right." Kim looked at her for a moment. "Have you ever really looked in a mirror, Cass?"

Cassie put her coffee cup down, long weary of this discussion. "Shouldn't you be getting home? Lisa's probably worried about you," Cassie said, referring to Kim's partner.

"Lisa won't be back from the city until late," Kim said. "And don't change the subject. I've been there myself, Cass. God, when I found myself attracted to another woman, I nearly went crazy. I dated a dozen men, slept with half of them and convinced myself that I was in love with one of them."

"Yes. I went to your wedding, remember?"

"Yes. And why didn't you stop me?"

"I tried, if you recall," Cassie said, remembering how Kim had cried when she confessed that she had slept with a woman and how Kim had cried again when she told her that she was getting married. And Cassie was hardly the one to try to talk her out of it. What did she know about it? She just remembered how totally unhappy Kim was, and she told her to wait a few months before she decided anything. But Kim had been too scared to wait.

Now Cassie wished she had never told Kim about David. She knew Kim would only bring up this old argument. As sure as Cassie was that she would never enter into a lesbian relationship, she would never tell Kim that she found little attraction in men. Perhaps she was destined to live her life alone, without a husband, a partner, a companion. She was thirty-three years old and had never been in love. Had not even been close, she admitted. And Kim was right about David, they had nothing in common. He was just an attractive man who had asked her out, and she found his company acceptable. That was all. She would not sleep with him. She had not shared her bed with anyone in a very long time. That was something else she found unsettling. She had no desire for sex. She suffered through the few kisses she would allow her dates, but she always ended things when she felt the next step would lead to bed. This was something else she would not admit to Kim.

"It's all because of your father, isn't it?"

"Oh, Kim, please. We've already been down that road. A hundred times," she added.

"Just because he's condemned me, I hardly think he would disown his own daughter."

Cassie stared at her, picturing herself telling her father, the Reverend Parker, that she was a lesbian. It would send him to his death. Or hers. But that hardly mattered anymore. It wasn't like they were close. It wasn't like she relied on him for anything. He was just the only family she had.

"He's already condemned me just for living here. That and my profession."

Kim sighed and lifted her arms in defeat. "How long have we been friends?"

Cassie smiled. "Twelve years."

"Thirteen. We weren't even twenty."

"Both starving," Cassie added.

"Like we're famous artists now," Kim said sarcastically.

"We're hardly starving."

3

"No. We've done pretty well."

Cassie relaxed again, thankful the conversation was moving away from her personal life.

"How many pieces will you bring to the show next week?" Kim asked.

"I have seven or eight large pieces that are ready. At least that many more that I'm still working on, but I'll save them for the fair in October," Cassie said. "I didn't have nearly enough last year."

"Well, if you would quit doing the small trinkets and concentrate on the sculptures, you could have quite a showing."

"Yeah, but it's the small stuff that pays the bills," Cassie reminded her.

Chapter Two

Cassie stood for a long moment, staring back at her reflection in the mirror. She brushed the hair from her eyes and let out a deep sigh. As a child, she'd always wished for blonde hair, but she was still cursed with that in-between color. Too dark to be blonde but not nearly dark enough to be brown. She took both hands and ran it through the sides of her hair, tucking the short strands behind her ears. She kept it too short. Perhaps that was why she had a tendency to attract more women than men. And she had to admit, she fit the perfect stereotype—short hair, little or no makeup, casual, natural. But it wasn't a sexual statement she was making. She had always worn her hair short, and she had never been one for makeup, even during her college days when she actually thought about dating men.

Now, she simply didn't want the bother. Besides, she liked things natural. That was why she left most of her woodcarvings in their natural state. That was why she was a vegetarian.

But still, Kim's words haunted her. She should just come right out and tell her. Kim was her closest friend. If she couldn't confide in Kim, then who? But she had avoided the subject for so long, it had just become second nature to her. And it hadn't been that many years ago that she had finally admitted it to herself. Gay. A lesbian. She lifted humorless eyes and stared at her reflection in the mirror. Yes, she could admit it now. Why not? It wasn't like she was going to act on it.

It had been at least five years ago before she had actually been able to consider the possibility. She was always more comfortable around women, yes, but that didn't mean she was attracted to them. But she wasn't attracted to men, either. And she had several lesbian friends, it was true. Did she have any straight friends? But in this small community filled with artists, wineries, organic farms, and vegetarians, the lesbian and gay population was hardly closeted. And she knew a lot of them. Most of them. Despite her father's warnings.

She remembered that day so clearly, the day Kim had told her she was leaving her husband, that she wasn't going to live a lie any longer. Her father had been home. He had overheard. Poor Kim. Her father had whipped out his worn Bible and proceeded to quote from it with ease, his booming voice still able to send chills down her spine. He had sent Kim away, warning her to stay away from his daughter. Cassie stood up to him that day, one of only a few times that she could remember. Kim was her friend, she had told him, and he didn't pick her friends anymore. Guilt by association, he had boomed at her. They were all damned to hell and she best not be too close to them when the time came for God to clean up!

She lifted one corner of her mouth in amusement. She could smile now. The fear that her father instilled in her during her childhood was all but gone. She rarely saw him more than once a year. All they did was argue anyway. "An artist! By God, I raised you better. And living out here with them, thick as thieves, don't think I can't see it!"

She had bought her house in Sonoma County six years ago

when prices were still somewhat reasonable, and he had come exactly twice to see her. To preach to her, she corrected. But she didn't want to go there. Not tonight.

She reached up to turn out the light, but not before she caught the sad reflection in her blue eyes. She loved him, but only because he was her father and she was supposed to love him. But she knew without a doubt that she did not like him.

She lay in bed that night, her thoughts going to her mother, but she stopped them, as she usually did. Instead, she thought about the carving she had started that morning. When she found the piece of wood on the beach, she very nearly passed it by. It was small and she was looking for something much larger. But when she rolled it over, she saw that it was well weathered and very heavy. She had positioned it several different ways, trying to find something, an image that she could transform it into. Then she had looked out over the rocks and saw the seal, sunning itself, its wide eyes never leaving her, and she stood the piece of wood up, its sleek curves mirroring that of the seal. She knew instantly what the driftwood would become.

She still thought it amazing that she could see things in ordinary pieces of wood. She had perfected her craft by doing hundreds of small carvings and selling them to the shops in San Francisco, but her real love was creating the giant wood carvings that sometimes took a month to finish. She had been lucky, selling enough of them to get by, gradually able to command the prices that she felt her work was worth. She sold all eleven pieces at last year's county fair and was finally able to slow down and work mainly on the giant carvings that would each bring several thousand dollars.

She was finally satisfied with her professional life. Maybe that was why she could find little contentment in her personal life anymore. But she was used to being alone, and this period of self-pity would pass, as it always did.

Chapter Three

"Listen to this," Lisa said, pointing to the morning paper. "Says here that they are expecting the Labor Day Festival to draw nearly as many people as the County Fair this year."

"That's good news for us," Kim said. "Did I tell you Steve bought three more of my paintings for his store?" she asked Cassie.

"No. Good for you." Cassie put her coffee cup down and motioned for a refill. "I guess he's not having any trouble selling them."

"The seascapes always do well, although I'm getting bored with them," she said.

"Honey, take what you can get," Lisa said, reaching out a hand from behind the paper to rub her partner's knee. Cassie smiled at the unconscious affection Lisa displayed. Lisa was the only one with a normal job, but she knew full well the struggles of trying to make a living as an artist.

"I know, I just want to do something a little more exciting," Kim said.

"Then try it," Cassie encouraged. "The last thing you want is to get stagnant."

"Like you said, it's the small stuff that pays the bills. I am working on something that is a little abstract, though not without form," she said. "Very different from what I normally do."

"I can't wait to see it," Cassie said sincerely. She knew Kim had wanted to try different styles for years now but had been afraid. She had made a name for herself in natural seascapes and didn't want to damage that.

"She hasn't even let me see it," Lisa complained.

"That's because . . . good Lord, will you look at those legs," Kim whispered, staring down the sidewalk past the outdoor cafe.

"My, my," Lisa echoed quietly.

Cassie followed their gaze, her eyes locking on the back of tanned, muscled thighs. Khaki shorts prevented any other exploration, and she only glanced at the thin, white shirt tucked neatly inside. Dark, neatly layered hair reached to the collar of her shirt, and Cassie watched as the stranger stopped and casually shoved both hands into her pockets as she looked around. Cassie turned back to the table and picked up her empty coffee cup, embarrassed for having stared.

"I don't recognize her. Must be a tourist," Kim said.

"With legs like that, she should be a model," Lisa added.

"She's probably a dog," Kim said. "Wait until she turns around."

"Will you two stop," Cassie hissed under her breath. "Really, you'd think you're never around women."

"Come on, turn around," Lisa said softly, ignoring Cassie.

"Jesus, Mary, and Joseph," Kim whispered.

Cassie looked up and again followed their gaze. The woman had turned and was facing them. She was beautiful, staggeringly beautiful, and Cassie felt her breath catch in her throat as the woman walked toward them.

"You know, if we worked out, we could have legs like that," Kim said quietly.

"Yes, but that would mean we'd have to exercise," Lisa said.

Cassie tried to pull her eyes away, she wanted to pull her eyes away, but they refused to obey. Smooth, tan skin, full lips—Cassie stared. Then her eyes moved past the beautiful face and lingered briefly on small breasts, wondering crazily if she wore a bra, then locked again on legs before making the return trip. She gasped when her blue eyes were captured by dark brown ones, and she found she could not take a breath until the woman mercifully released her and looked away.

Hadn't she always known, and secretly feared, that this day would come? That she would see some woman and feel that attraction, that pull that she couldn't resist. She could lie to Kim all she wanted, but she couldn't lie to herself. She shuddered inwardly, acknowledging the fire that had started inside of her. For years, she had been able to keep these feelings away. She never allowed herself to think of any woman in a romantic way. She could control whatever impulses she may have. But one look at this woman and her carefully constructed wall had crumbled. Thank goodness she was a tourist, a stranger. At least it was a woman she would never see again. Walls could be rebuilt.

"Hey, earth to Cassie," Kim said, poking her arm playfully. "You still with us?"

"Hmmm?" Cassie blinked several times, embarrassed that her hand still trembled when she set her coffee cup on the table. "Sorry. What?"

Kim smiled and glanced after the woman who had now passed their table. "Nice, huh?"

Cassie nodded. "Yes. Attractive." She tried to convince herself that she had been looking at the woman with envy and not desire. It was a start to rebuilding that wall, anyway. She cleared her throat. "Perhaps we should take up jogging," she said lightly. "We could all stand to lose a few pounds."

"Perhaps we should take up something else," Kim said with a wink.

"Please don't start," Cassie said. "I'm not in the mood."

"Kim, leave her alone," Lisa warned.

"Thank you," Cassie said quietly. She rested her elbows on the table and stared at Kim. "Do I need to bring up David again?"

"Please don't," Kim said with a laugh. "I don't want to spoil breakfast."

But it was already spoiled for Cassie. She drove home with the windows open, wishing for a cigarette, something she had not done in years. The rolling hills sped by without notice as she stared straight ahead, her mind on only one thing.

How could one tiny, innocent glance at that woman bring such fear to her? Perhaps she wasn't as immune to her father's words of eternal damnation as she thought.

"I wasn't attracted to her . . . I was simply looking at a beautiful person," she said out loud. She shoved her sunglasses on to avoid seeing the truth reflected back at her from the mirror and drove on in silence, convinced she would be over this by evening.

But when she got home, she called David. They had not made plans this weekend. She had told him she would be too busy preparing for the upcoming art show, but now she wanted his company. She would invite him over to dinner, and she would let him kiss her and hopefully, she would feel something, anything to make her forget the way her pulse had raced earlier today.

Chapter Four

"I don't really miss the meat in here," David said, taking another piece of the lasagna.

"What's to miss?"

"Oh, come on," David said with a smile. "Don't you ever just want to plop a nice, juicy steak on the grill?"

Cassie eyed him coolly over her wineglass, then raised her chin. "I don't particularly care for dead cows bleeding on my grill," she said. "I prefer the smell of roasting vegetables."

David shook his head but smiled. "I don't think I could go without meat for too many meals, but once in awhile is fine," he said.

Cassie had told herself she would try with David, so she let that comment go unanswered. Instead, she filled both of their wineglasses and pretended to enjoy his company.

"How long have you been this way?" he asked as he swirled the Merlot.

She raised her eyes slowly. "What way is that?"

"Vegetarian."

She shrugged. "Since I was old enough to start cooking for myself."

"Why?"

"My father said I was going through a phase, and it would pass," she said. "Actually, one of my high school teachers described what a slaughterhouse was like, and that pretty much did it for me."

"Well, you just don't think about it."

"Well, we should think about it." She set her wineglass on the table, preparing to launch into a speech. "And not only for the cruelty to the animals, but what about all the agricultural land and water that is devoted solely to raising and feeding cattle when we should be growing food for human consumption."

"Whoa, now," David said, raising his hands. "I don't want to get into an argument with you. We have different opinions on this one, I'm afraid."

She leaned back and tried to relax. "Yes, I guess we do. I don't suppose you want to discuss organic farming?" she asked with a smile.

"Let's don't," he said. "In fact, I wanted to ask you about your work. You don't know how many times I've been to Potter's and have never thought to ask about the squirrel they have sitting on the counter. Then today, there was this woman asking who had done it, and I was surprised to hear your name. You said you did wood sculptures, and I guess I had no idea what you really did."

"I gave Carl that squirrel four years ago," she said. "I generally do larger pieces now."

She didn't want to talk about her work. She didn't want to share this with him, she realized. He would not understand how each piece became so very personal to her, even the small trinkets, as Kim called them.

"How is it that you've lived here six years and we've just now met?" he asked.

Just lucky, I guess. But she stifled her grin and answered tactfully.

13

"I doubt we have any of the same friends." They had literally run into each other at the grocery store, him knocking her flat on her backside as he had hurried into her aisle. His way of apology was to offer her lunch. Cassie was too embarrassed to decline.

"You hang out with artists, I guess?"

She shrugged. "I'm an artist. I do know some of the local farmers, though." She raised her eyebrows and forced a grin. "I hang out at farmer's markets, too."

"Buying only organic vegetables, no doubt," he said sarcastically.

She stared at him for a moment. "No doubt," she said dryly, realizing that she didn't like this man in the least. Why had it taken three dates for her to figure it out?

After dinner, she offered to make coffee, but he declined. He wasn't too fond of French vanilla, he said. She was thankful.

"We can sit and visit, if you like," he offered.

"Actually, I have some work to do, David. I hope you don't mind, but I'd like to call it a night."

"Oh, of course," he said immediately. "I'm glad we got to spend some time together. I know how busy you are."

He walked over and took her hands, and she steeled herself for the kiss she knew was about to come.

"Thanks for dinner. I enjoyed it." He lowered his head to hers, but she stepped back.

"Listen, David . . . I'm sorry," she said, pulling her hands away. "This isn't going to work."

"What do you mean?"

"Us. This," she said, motioning between them. "We're just . . . too different. And I'd like to be able to meet you on the street someday and consider you a friend and not an ex-boyfriend, you know what I mean?"

He sighed and shoved his hands in his pockets. "I guess. I feel kinda lost out there anyway. I mean, I'm nearly forty. I picked a hell of a time to start dating again. Half the women in this town are newly divorced and hate men, or they're gay, or they're into saving

14

the earth and picket my farm because I won't go organic, or they're vegetarian and despise me because I keep a few cattle . . . oh, I didn't mean you, Cassie."

She smiled. "It's okay. No offense. I haven't taken to picketing farms yet."

"Well, let me get out of here. I've enjoyed meeting you, if nothing else," he said.

"Thank you. I'm sure I'll see you around town." She waited politely beside the door until he had started his car and driven off.

She leaned against the closed door and shut her eyes. The only good thing to come of the evening was that she had not thought about the woman she had seen earlier that morning. She shoved away from the door. Not much, anyway.

Chapter Five

Cassie sat down and placed the piece of wood between her knees. She selected a palm chisel and began carving the wood, shaving off small pieces with each stroke. She found that people liked to watch her while she worked, and it helped sell the smaller carvings that she now had lined up on the table.

Her booth was roped off, a large ten-by-twelve area, with tables lining three sides. The fourth side was reserved for the giant carvings she had positioned there. She sat under the shade of an umbrella and looked around at the milling crowd, still small at this early hour but growing. She recognized a familiar figure walking toward her, and she lifted a hand in greeting.

Paul ducked gracefully under the rope after dodging a family of five.

"Quite a crowd already," he said after placing a friendly kiss on Cassie's cheek. "Jeff's worried he didn't bring enough."

Jeff did beautiful pencil sketches of wildlife and framed them using salvaged wood from old barns in the area. Jeff was the man that Paul had fallen in love with.

"So, things are still working out for you two?" she asked.

"Yes. Things are wonderful, Cass. I've never been so happy."

"Well, I was hoping that was the reason I hadn't seen you in awhile," she said.

"I'm sorry," he apologized. His face showed genuine dismay, and Cassie smiled and took his hand.

"Oh, I'm teasing, Paul. I know how happy you are. It's written all over your face."

"And how are you doing? The last time we talked, you seemed so down."

"Down? Did I? No, just preoccupied with my work, most likely," she said, trying to convince him as well as herself.

"Well, I better get back. I just wanted to say hello. Good luck today," he called.

She watched him go, smiling as he hurried back to Jeff. Now there was a man she had something in common with. He was an artist, a vegetarian, and he didn't get on with his parents, either. And so she had tried with him. There just hadn't been any passion between them. They were always the best of friends and could talk for hours, but whenever they tried to move their relationship to another level, it stalled. Their kisses were nothing more than affectionate. They were never in any danger of losing control. Actually, it was almost as if they had to remind themselves that they were supposed to be dating. Then he met Jeff. He finally confessed to Cassie that he had been suppressing his attraction to men for fear of alienating his parents even more. But Jeff had literally swept him off his feet, and Cassie had wished Paul nothing but the best.

When she thought about it now, it was almost a relief that Paul had met Jeff. If there was ever a man she thought she could be with, it had been Paul. He was a gentle, soft-spoken, kind man. But it was nearly exhausting trying to invent feelings where there were none. And they had maintained their friendship, although they didn't see each other nearly as often.

"These are beautiful."

Cassie raised her head, pushing her thoughts away and smiled at the young couple who had stopped to admire her carvings.

"Thanks. You're welcome to pick them up," she offered.

The woman touched a fawn, one of Cassie's favorites, and she saw her eyes light up, knowing instantly that they would buy it.

"How do you do it?" she asked Cassie.

Cassie stood and carried the piece she had been working on. "It starts like this," she said, holding up the wood she had just begun carving. "This is going to be a squirrel. At least, if I have enough wood left for the tail." She picked another piece out of the box under the table and showed it to them as well. "This was supposed to be a squirrel, too, but as you can see, no tail."

"How did you learn how to do this?" the man asked.

She shrugged. "Some people can paint . . . I carve." How did she tell someone that it just came naturally?

Out of the corner of her eye she glimpsed a woman admiring the large golden eagle standing nearly three feet tall from its base. She turned to watch the woman, to see her reaction to her work, and she actually felt her breath catch in her chest. *It's her.*

"I really like the deer. How much is it?" the woman asked.

Cassie swallowed with difficulty and made herself turn back to the couple, smiling. "Seventy-five. All of these smaller ones start at seventy-five and go up to one twenty-five." Then she pointed to the end where an assortment of larger squirrels sat. "Except them. The larger squirrels there are all two hundred."

"Is seventy-five too much, Mark?"

"No. If you like it, we'll get it," he said.

Cassie turned again to watch the woman squatting beside the eagle, unmindful of the sign that warned her not to touch. Her sunglasses were shoved casually on top of her dark head, and her sleeveless shirt showed off well-muscled arms. Cassie's eyes traveled from her thick, dark hair to smooth cheeks tanned a golden brown, on down to small waist and . . . *perfect legs.* Cassie had the same reaction to her the second time around. Heat assailed her body, and she was afraid. "You do take checks?" the man asked.

"Hmmm?"

"Checks?"

"Oh, yes." Cassie forced herself to wait patiently while the man wrote out a check. "I'll wrap that for you, if you like." She wrapped the fawn gently in newspaper and taped one of her cards on the side.

As they left, she turned and was startled to find the woman watching her.

"Your work is exquisite."

The voice was not what Cassie would have expected. It was softer, gentler than the imposing woman standing before her with only a hint of the huskiness Cassie imagined. Words refused to form, so Cassie kept quiet.

"You are Cassandra Parker, right?" the woman prompted.

"Cassie, yes." Cassie paused only briefly before taking the woman's offered hand, daring to meet her dark eyes for only a moment.

"Luke Winston." The woman released Cassie's hand much too slowly.

Cassie frowned slightly, and the woman paused, as if waiting for Cassie to question the unusual name. She pressed her lips together, refusing to ask the obligatory question. It wasn't any of her concern, she told herself.

"I'm looking for a couple of pieces for a client," Luke explained. "One outdoors, one in."

Cassie motioned to the remaining six that she had. "Only the two largest eagles have been finished for the outdoors, I'm afraid. And the totem. I can put a finish on one of the others, though, if there's one you like."

"No," the woman said, moving away from Cassie, again circling the smaller eagle. "This one belongs inside, anyway."

"I'm working on another eagle," Cassie said unexpectedly. "In flight, six foot wing span," she explained. At the woman's expression, Cassie smiled. "It just sort of happened, and I have no idea how I'll transport it, if I even want to sell it."

"That may be more of what they're looking for," she said, again

19

turning toward the golden. "This one is beautiful, really." She looked up and caught Cassie's eyes and her voice softened. "I want it. I have the perfect spot for it."

"For you? Or your client?" The thought of this woman having one of her pieces was causing all sorts of emotions to sift through her body.

"I feel drawn to this one. Like it was meant for me," she said quietly. "Do you ever get that feeling?"

Cassie nodded, her eyes locked with this stranger. She opened her mouth, hoping her voice would follow. "Most of my work is from driftwood, small and large. I see a piece and it pulls me, tells me exactly what it needs to be." Cassie's voice was equally as quiet.

The woman was staring at her, as if she wanted to say something, and Cassie raised her eyebrows.

"What?"

The woman looked away and shook her head. "Nothing," she said, almost to herself. Then she looked back and their eyes held, and Cassie was powerless to look away as they stared at each other.

"Hey, girl," Kim called, breaking the spell. "Oh, I didn't know . . . *oh*," she said again, seeing the woman. "Well . . . I'll let you finish with . . . whatever you're doing," she said and grinned wickedly at Cassie.

Cassie glared at Kim, although she was thankful for the interruption, and she moved away from the stranger. She watched as Kim shoved her hand toward the woman.

"I'm Kim Monroe. Just a friend," she said pointedly and Cassie winced.

"Luke Winston."

"Luke? Parents wanted a boy?" Kim asked the question that Cassie had not.

Luke smiled at Cassie before answering. "My mother wanted a Lucinda." She opened her waist pack and pulled out her checkbook. "You do take out-of-town checks?" she asked.

"Yes, of course," Cassie said.

"With all proper identification," Kim added.

"Don't you have your own booth to run?" Cassie asked under her breath.

"Lisa's got it under control."

"I guess I should ask how much it is," Luke said.

"Two thousand," Cassie said confidently.

Luke smiled and met her eyes again. "I would have paid at least four."

Cassie gave a smile that didn't reach her eyes. *Four?*

After boxing it up carefully, Cassie offered to get help to carry it, thinking of Paul.

"No, not necessary," Luke said. "I think two of us can manage. I'm parked fairly close," she said.

Cassie looked at Kim with pleading eyes, but Kim smiled and rubbed her lower back before sitting down.

"I'll hold down the fort. You run along," she said to Cassie.

"Thanks a lot," Cassie murmured, then bent to take one end of the box.

"I hope you put one of your cards in there," Luke said as they made their way through the crowd. "I think I can get you a sale on that eagle. Money is no problem, by the way."

"That's nice to know. Maybe I should let you price it then," Cassie said lightly. "I have no idea what to ask for it."

"They've just built a home over on Russian River. Logs, totally natural. They have this enormous deck that reaches nearly to the water's edge. They'll love your stuff," she said. "There's a perfect spot for one of your large eagles."

Luke was watching Cassie, so she tried not to labor as she helped carry the cumbersome box. Finally Luke grinned.

"Do you need to take a break?"

"Please," Cassie panted.

"Sorry about that."

They sat the box down, and Cassie rested her hands on her hips, trying to catch her breath, noticing Luke didn't seem winded in the least.

"You work out," Cassie stated unnecessarily. Her eyes moved

21

over Luke's upper body, resting on her biceps. Luke shifted her weight and casually crossed her arms, watching Cassie watch her. "The most exercise I get is carrying driftwood back to the house," Cassie admitted to this stranger.

"It started out as a relief to . . . my life, I guess. It became addicting," she said. "But then, it beat the alternative."

Cassie waited for her to explain but Luke didn't and Cassie was polite enough not to ask.

"You're really very talented," Luke said unexpectedly. "I'm sure you hear that all the time."

"Mostly from people who can't afford to buy my work." Cassie shifted from one foot to the other nervously, making a pretense of scanning the crowd. "But I do okay here."

"Surely you've tried the city," Luke said, casually resting her hands on her hips, her shirt straining across her chest.

"Yes," Cassie said, pulling her eyes away from Luke's shirt. *Her breasts.* "I started out in San Francisco. I still have several shops that carry my carvings and they do quite well there, but I find I work much better out here," Cassie managed. "It's peaceful. I don't feel like I'm always in a hurry anymore."

"Yes, I know what you mean. It's nice out here. Hard to believe we're only an hour or so from the city."

Cassie nodded, again looking into the crowd to avoid having to look at Luke Winston. It wasn't fair, she thought. No one, especially a woman, should have the power to affect her so. She took a step back, suddenly feeling crowded by this woman's nearness.

"I'm ready if you are," Cassie said, wanting nothing but for this encounter to be over and done with.

"Okay. On three." Luke bent easily and grasped her corner, waiting for Cassie to do the same.

Cassie watched as Luke bent. Against her will, her eyes were drawn to those tan legs and she completely forgot their task as her eyes ventured higher.

"Cassie?"

Cassie jerked her head away and met dark eyes that held just a hint of amusement. She blushed crimson.

22

"Sorry," she murmured and hurried to pick up her end, silently cursing herself.

Luke smiled, flashing even, white teeth. "It's okay," she said lightly.

Cassie kept her eyes averted as they made their way to the parking lot, and Luke was true to her word. She paused beside what appeared to be a new Lexus SUV, as black as the woman's hair. With a push of the remote, the back opened while they waited.

"I appreciate you helping me." Luke slid the box carefully inside, then slammed the door shut.

"No problem. It was worked into the price," Cassie said as lightly as she could manage.

Luke flashed her a grin. "Well, I'll let you get back. Your friend is probably waiting."

Again she placed her hands casually on her hips and again Cassie had to drag her eyes away. She raised them to meet Luke's and forced a smile, which faltered only slightly when Luke extended her hand.

"It was nice meeting you, Cassie. I feel like we've met somewhere before though. You look so familiar."

"No. I don't think so." Cassie took her hand briefly, then pulled away. "I would have remembered. And thank you. I hope you enjoy the eagle."

"Oh, I will. It's very beautiful." Luke's voice softened to nearly a purr, her eyes never leaving Cassie's. "I hope we run into each other again."

Suddenly Cassie didn't want to leave, and she hesitated as the woman's voice enveloped her. She swallowed, willing her feet to move, willing her eyes to pull away. *Do something!*

"Well . . . good-bye, then." She turned and made herself walk, not run, her back positively burning where she assumed dark eyes were looking.

She ran both hands through her hair in frustration as she faded into the crowd. Why was Luke Winston able to make a mockery out of her life without even trying?

Luke Winston. Such an odd name for a woman so beautiful. She closed her eyes tightly. Not beautiful. Just an attractive woman. Just a stranger that she would never see again. *With any luck.*

"Hey, about time," Kim called. "I'll need commission, I think." She pointed to the empty spot where the small totem had been.

"You sold the totem?" Cassie asked, her eyes wide. She had been trying to get rid of it for three years. "How did you know what to ask?"

Kim bit her lower lip. "How much did you want for it?"

"A thousand," Cassie said.

Kim broke into a smile. "Good. I got fifteen hundred."

"Jesus Christ! How?"

"Well, I knew to ask less than the eagle."

"The eagle took me twice as long to make," Cassie explained. "I dropped the price to eight hundred last year, just in hope of getting rid of it. It takes up space in my shop."

"Hey, so post signs next time," Kim said. "It was an older gentleman with four teenagers in tow. He wanted it for a lodge or something. Now, the details." She lowered her voice and grinned. "That woman is gorgeous, with a body to go with it. God! Her check says she's from the city. What's she doing here two weekends in a row?"

"How should I know," Cassie said crossly, looking away from Kim.

"She didn't offer and knowing you, you didn't ask."

"Why would I ask? It doesn't concern me," Cassie said.

Kim tilted her head and grinned. "In all the years I've been doing this with you, that was the first time you've ever offered to help carry one of those out of here," she stated, waving at the remaining pieces.

"I'm sure you're mistaken. I've done it . . . several times." *Damn!*

But Kim only smiled. "Sure you have. Did she make a pass at you?"

"Of course not! Why would she?"

"Oh, come on. Surely you could see the way she was looking at you," Kim teased.

24

Cassie turned cool blue eyes to Kim. "Don't," she said quietly. "I will not have this discussion with you here."

"I'm just teasing."

"Yes, well don't."

Kim placed her hands on her hips and stared at Cassie. "Can't you just let go for once? Must you always have this shield around you?"

"I don't know what you're talking about," Cassie said, searching for her piece of wood, something, anything to appear busy.

Kim handed her the wood silently.

"You're never going to enjoy life," she said, raising her hands around her, "if you're so goddamned afraid of having feelings."

Cassie faced her squarely. "I don't know how to have feelings," she said quietly.

Kim shook her head. "Just let go for once, Cass. What are you afraid of?"

"I'm afraid of life. It comes from years of living with my father," she said.

"Oh, I'm sorry," Kim said. "I didn't mean . . ."

"No, I know I have a problem. I can't seem to feel anything for anyone," Cassie said. Her expression softened. "I don't mean you. You're my best friend. I feel that," she said, touching her chest. "I just can't seem to find anyone . . . for me. And yes, maybe I am afraid. I'm afraid of men because my father warned me about them my whole life, how they're only after one thing. And I'm certainly afraid of women, because I'll rot in hell from that kind of love for sure," she finished, tears now brimming in her eyes.

"Hey, I'm sorry," Kim said gently, giving her a quick hug. "I'm sorry."

Cassie brushed an errant tear from her cheek and smiled slightly. "I need a good therapist, I know."

"Maybe you just need a good lay," Kim said, and Cassie laughed with her.

Chapter Six

Cassie studied the two bottles of wine in her basket, then reached for one more. Another advantage of living in Sonoma County was the wine selection. And after spending two weeks of forced solitude in her workshop, she was ready to break loose a bit. She felt like cooking, too. She had barely taken time to eat, much less cook, and cooking was her one means of escape.

She had spent nearly every waking hour working on the eagle in flight. As she had told Luke Winston, it just happened. She and Kim had struggled with the huge chunk of driftwood for hours, finally getting their friend Carl to assist them. His truck had barely held the wood and the three of them had managed to carry it into her workshop where it laid for months. She knew it would be an eagle, it could have been nothing else. The eagle was her favorite subject. But it had grown and grown, until its magnificent wings stretched out six feet. Now, after two months of lovingly chiseling and carving, it was finished. And she hated to part with it. But she had worked painstakingly the past two weeks on the off chance that Luke Winston would call, or at least the clients she had spoken of, and offer her an outrageous amount of money for it.

Now, she just wanted to relax. And the weather forecast seemed perfect. A storm was coming. Heavy rain was due by this evening, and it would linger through tomorrow. She planned to cook and curl up with a good book and read, something she had not taken the time to do in months.

But she was surprised at the dark clouds overhead as she loaded her groceries. The rain was not supposed to hit until later but already the first fat drops were wetting her face as she hurried inside her van. She rubbed her hands together quickly to warm them before pulling away, a smile breaking her face. The rain was as good an excuse as any to stay inside and avoid company. Mainly Kim. She had spoken to her only a few times in the last two weeks. Their conversation on the day of the festival still hung between them, and Cassie knew that Kim wanted to talk about it. But Cassie, however, did not. She had grown accustomed to hiding her feelings. A trait that caused many to call her cool and aloof. In reality, she was anything but that. But it was a facade that grew on her, and she had perfected it over the years. So much so, that she rarely shared her true feelings with anyone. In fact, she wasn't sure she even knew what her true feelings were anymore.

She headed down the rural road which would take her to the acre lot she had purchased nearly six years ago. The house hadn't been in the best of shape, but the large work shed had been in nearly perfect condition. That and the eight mature apple trees had sold her on the place. Over the years, she had remodeled the tiny house more to her liking, redoing most of the kitchen, her favorite room, and knocking out a wall and making the two small bedrooms into one large room for herself. She rarely had company, and on the two occasions that her father had come to visit, he had made do with the sofa.

She had moved to Sebastopol for two reasons. One, because Kim had moved in with Lisa and had left a terrible void in her life. She found herself making the trip nearly every weekend to stay with them, and she had fallen in love with the area. And two, because it was filled with artists. And art shows. So, she had saved every penny and bought the farm nearly a year after Kim had moved. She never regretted her decision. If nothing else, it had enabled her to escape her father. At least physically. Mentally, his words and preaching still haunted her.

"Those boys only want one thing, Cassandra. I will not have a daughter of mine seen out *dancing*, of all things. It will only lead to trouble, girl. You mind my words. Don't you *ever* let one of them touch you!"

She was lost in thought when the rain hit with dizzying speed. Her wipers could not keep pace with the downpour, and she strained to see the road, leaning closer to the windshield and rubbing the now foggy glass with her hand.

The sudden jolting of the van made her grip the steering wheel tightly to keep it on the road, and then she heard the unmistakable sound of a flat tire.

"Oh shit," she hissed. Cassie slowed, her eyes wide, trying in vain to find the side of the road, hoping she didn't drive off too far and land in the ditch, but far enough so that she wouldn't be hit by another car. It was impossible to see through the pounding rain, and she eased off the road just a little farther.

Turning in her seat, she searched the back for the umbrella, cursing when she remembered leaving it beside the kitchen door the last time it had rained.

"Shit . . . shit, shit," she muttered. She then looked for something, anything to shield her, wondering why she still believed the so-called experts. The storm wasn't supposed to hit for hours yet. She was totally unprepared.

She shook her head, then on a silent count of three, threw open the door against the wind, and went out into the downpour. Shielding her eyes from the rain, she surveyed the very flat tire on the passenger side, now sinking lower into the muddy earth as water ran off the road at an alarming pace.

"Well, shit," she said again under her breath, her soaked clothes clinging to her chilled body. How was she to attempt to change the tire in this weather? Providing she even knew how to change a tire.

She had just passed one of the many dairy farms in the area. She supposed she would have to attempt to walk there. She shook her head, wondering why she did not have a cell phone like most normal people. Probably the same reason she didn't have a computer, she mused.

The blast of a horn startled her and she looked up, shocked to find a black Lexus easing to a stop. The passenger door swung open and Cassie stared inside.

"Get in before you drown," Luke Winston yelled as the storm raged around them.

Cassie hurried to the door, then hesitated, glancing at the leather seats.

"I'm soaking wet," she said unnecessarily.

"No kidding. Get in."

Cassie hopped in and slammed the door as water ran from her wet hair into her eyes and down her face. The sound of the storm subsided somewhat as Luke pulled in front of her van and stopped.

"Are you okay? What happened?" she demanded.

"Just a flat," Cassie said. "Do you have a phone? Can you call someone?"

"Yes, I've got a phone, but I doubt you'll get anyone to come out in this storm," Luke said. "Where do you live?"

"About another five miles," Cassie said, finally wiping at her rain soaked hair and daring to look at her rescuer. "But this storm . . . I hate for you to have to drive in it."

Luke bent her head and looked out at the weather, frowning. "I live just ahead," she said. "You can come home with me until this lets up some. Then we can see about getting your tire changed."

"You live . . . here?" Cassie asked, the surprise evident in her voice.

"I have a house here, yes," Luke said, starting to pull away.

"Wait," Cassie said, her hand reaching out lightly to grab Luke's forearm. "I mean . . . I hate to impose," she said lamely. She most definitely did not want to go to this woman's house.

"You're not imposing."

"I've got food . . . I've been shopping," she stammered.

Luke gave her an amused smile. "I wasn't expecting payment."

Cassie gave a short laugh. "No. I mean, I've got things in the van that need to be refrigerated."

Luke cocked her head and raised an eyebrow. "Well, lucky for you, I have a refrigerator."

She leaned between the seats, and Cassie pressed herself against the door, her nerves on edge, this woman's nearness immediately causing her senses to reel.

Luke turned back around with an umbrella in her hands and offered it to Cassie.

Cassie stared at it silently for a moment, then looked up into dark eyes. "I don't really see the point," Cassie murmured, lifting one corner of her mouth in a smile as a raindrop ran down her nose. She hurried back into the storm, putting into one bag the things that would spoil and rushed back to Luke.

"I'm so sorry . . . your seats," she said, trying to wipe the rain off of the leather.

Luke took the canvas bag from her and put it in the back. "Don't worry about the seats. Now, strap in," she said, motioning to the seatbelt.

Luke turned down a dirt road only a few hundred yards past Cassie's stranded van, a road Cassie had passed hundreds of times before. Luke wiped at the windshield with her hand as they splashed through the mud, jarring them in their seats.

"Hell of a storm," Luke said, almost to herself.

Cassie nodded silently, wondering what in the world she was doing riding with Luke Winston, going to her house, no less! She kept quiet, hoping that Luke could see the road because she could not. The wipers tried frantically to keep pace with the rain, and Cassie glanced at the woman beside her, noting how strong her hands seemed as they gripped the steering wheel. Her fingers were long and smooth with neatly kept nails, and Cassie's eyes were glued to them. She felt a strange sensation travel through her body as she watched those hands. She pulled her eyes away, closing them briefly as she listened to the rain pound the vehicle.

She was surprised when the sound subsided, and found that

they were under what appeared to be a carport of sorts. Luke cut the engine, and they sat for a moment, staring at each other.

"I didn't know you lived out here," Cassie said carefully. "I've never seen you around town."

"I've been building," Luke explained. "I just recently started staying here."

It wasn't actually a carport, Cassie noted when they got out. It was more of a covered shelter built into the side of the building. She looked around as Luke reached in the back for her bag. It looked more like a barn than a house.

"Come on."

Cassie followed her inside, pausing to remove her muddy shoes by the mat before entering the most unusual house she had ever seen. She stood there, arms wrapped around her chilled body, and glanced at the large expanse of the building.

"You need to get out of those wet clothes," Luke was saying and Cassie brought her eyes back to the woman standing before her.

"In there," she said, gently pushing Cassie toward a door. "Take a hot shower. I'll bring you some clothes. Afterward, I'll give you the nickel tour if you want."

Cassie nodded silently and opened the door to the bathroom, much larger than her own. She slowly turned a circle, looking at the impeccably clean room, wondering if it had ever been used before. Then she faced the mirror and groaned. Her hair was plastered to her head and her wet shirt and shorts clung to her body. She looked frightful.

She turned from the mirror and stripped off her wet clothing, putting them all in a neat pile on the floor. The walk-in shower had no door and she stood at the back of the tiled enclosure, looking at the three shower heads with a slight frown. There was only one knob. She turned it, surprised that water fell from all three shower heads. *Neat.* She stepped into the hot spray, thinking that Kim would find all of this very amusing. She smiled. Actually, she found it quite amusing herself. Here she was, calmly showering at the house of a woman that she had secretly prayed she would never see again. A woman whose mere presence sent her pulse racing.

31

When she stepped out of the shower, she was surprised to find her wet clothes gone, replaced by a pair of gray sweats and an Oakland Raiders jersey. She had not heard Luke enter the bathroom. A thick towel hung beside the shower and Cassie reached for it, quickly drying herself. As she pulled the sweats over her naked body, she groaned with embarrassment. Luke had not only taken her wet clothes, she had taken her bra and panties as well.

She found a comb in one of the drawers and brushed her wet hair back. It would dry soon enough and she stood there, in clothes one size too big, delaying her departure from the sanctuary of the bathroom. She met her eyes in the mirror and tried to smile. She would have to go out eventually. She could get through this, she told herself. *Right?*

"Of course you can," she murmured quietly. "She's just a woman."

Cassie's stomach rumbled as soon as she stepped out. Luke was apparently cooking. She found her at the opposite end, the kitchen separated from the rest of the house by a ten-foot long bar. As she walked toward Luke, she looked around, astounded by the unusual house. It was simply one very large room, the ceiling reaching up some twenty feet or more. Floor-to-ceiling windows covered the entire back wall, and Cassie watched the rain splatter against them, wondering at the view on a clear day. Opposite from the kitchen on the far side of the building were stairs going up into a loft. The bedroom, Cassie assumed. It, too, was full of windows facing west. Tucked neatly under the loft was a large stone fireplace. Two leather sofas formed a semi-circle, encompassing both the fireplace and the patio. Beside the fireplace, looking out toward the patio, was her eagle.

"Feel better?" Luke called.

"Much. Thanks for the clothes."

"I put yours in the dryer," she said. "Feel free to look around."

The only area of the room that was not impeccably neat was a desk, complete with a computer, printer and fax. Blueprints were strewn about and Cassie looked back to Luke.

"You're an architect," she stated.

"Yes."

Cassie looked back at the room. "And this . . ."

"I like space," Luke said. "I can't stand being crowded by walls and low ceilings." She stirred the pot one more time and put on the lid, then joined Cassie. "I finished it about six months ago, but I was too busy to move in. Actually, I'm not all the way moved in yet. I still have a house in the city that hasn't sold so I haven't had to clean it out. I'll probably do that within the next few weeks, though. My realtor says she thinks she'll have a contract on it by the end of the week."

"This is beautiful," Cassie said. "It's most unusual."

"I like it. I've been working on it for nearly two years. I was more than ready to have it finished." Luke pointed to the loft. "I'd take you up and show you the bedroom. The view is incredible, but we wouldn't see much today." She walked back into the kitchen. "Something to drink?"

"Yes," Cassie said, walking into the spacious kitchen for the first time.

"Nonalcoholic, I'm afraid." She opened the refrigerator and peered inside. "I have juice—apple-strawberry. Club soda, a nice sparkling apple cider made right here in Sebastopol, and plain old Coke," she said, looking at Cassie expectantly.

"How about the nice sparkling apple cider?" Cassie pulled out one of the barstools and sat down, watching Luke as she reached for two wineglasses, her eyes drawn to Luke's flat stomach as her shirt pulled up. Luke had changed her clothes, too. Gray cotton shorts replacing her jeans. Cassie swallowed and pulled her eyes away, feeling a hot blush on her cheeks as Luke handed her a glass. She took it quickly and shrank back away from her.

"Wineglasses but no wine?" Cassie asked. "You'll be run out of Sonoma County if anyone finds out," she said with a smile.

"Yes. A bit like moving to Santa Fe and not liking Mexican food." Luke paused, as if deciding whether to continue or not. "Not liking it wasn't my problem," she said. "Beer, whiskey, wine . . . I liked it all. Too much. So, I quit."

"Totally?"

"Totally, yeah. That's when I started working out. I ended up trading one addiction for another." Luke's face broke into a smile. "And it's become that. I've got a small gym out back. Just the basics, but enough to keep me satisfied."

"How long now?"

"Since I've had a drink?"

Cassie nodded.

"I was thirty-two. Six years now, I guess," she said. She pulled out a stool at the opposite end of the bar, and Cassie's eyes followed her. They studied each other for a moment, silently.

"You have the most incredible eyes," Luke said softly. "Bluest I've ever seen."

Cassie felt her heart catch, then race, sending fire through her body. Her eyes widened as Luke watched her.

"I'm not a . . . I'm not gay," she finally stammered.

Luke laughed and snapped her fingers. "Damn! I keep forgetting that rule not to compliment straight women."

Cassie blushed crimson. "I'm sorry. I just thought I should . . ."

"Warn me? In case I had designs on you?" Luke laughed again, a deep, husky laugh that Cassie found enjoyable, despite her embarrassment. "You're perfectly safe. Trust me," Luke said.

"I'm sorry," Cassie said again, now totally humiliated. "You probably have a . . . someone . . . in the city."

"Actually, no. I'm just not looking." She got up to stir the pot again and Cassie forced her eyes to remain on her empty wineglass. "Usually it just screws up a good friendship," Luke said. She turned back around to Cassie. "But I thought you were . . . you know, gay."

"No, I'm not," Cassie heard herself say, surprised at the ease that statement came to her.

Luke shrugged and put the lid back on. "A good day for chili," she said. "Vegetarian, though. I hope you don't mind."

Cassie's lips parted in surprise. She was a vegetarian, too? She shook her head. "No, I don't mind at all."

Chapter Seven

Cassie got up to get a second bowl of chili and carried it to the bar. Luke apologized again for not having a dining table.

"It is supposed to go over there," she said, pointing to an open spot. "But now I'm not sure I want one. I've gotten used to having the space."

"Unless you entertain a lot, I find they're a waste," Cassie said. The chili was wonderful, thick and spicy and she dipped the home-made bread into it.

"How long have you lived out here?" Luke asked.

"About six years. Kim, the woman you met at the fair, moved out here when she met Lisa. I came to visit them all the time." Cassie laughed. "I'm sure Lisa was glad when I finally moved here. I was becoming a permanent fixture in their spare room."

Luke grinned. "I thought you were going to tell me Kim wasn't gay either."

Cassie smiled. "No, Kim is definitely gay. She thinks the whole world is gay, they just don't know it yet."

"Meaning you?"

Cassie nodded. She wasn't about to discuss this with Luke, however. "This chili is delicious," she said.

"You've already said that. Twice. But I can take a hint," she said. "We'll change the subject. I saw an adorable little squirrel you did. It's at the grocery store in town. That's how I found out your name."

"Carl had a pet squirrel. Not really a pet. Just tame enough to sit in his hand and eat," Cassie said. "It just disappeared one day. Carl likes to think that it ran off for some wild sex or something," Cassie said with a laugh. "Most likely he became dinner for some owl or hawk, though. Anyway, I gave that to him as a remembrance of Chester."

"I offered him several hundred dollars for it," Luke said. "But he said it absolutely was not for sale."

Cassie laughed. "No. He's become quite attached to it."

"That's why I came out to the festival that day. He told me who you were and that you had a lot of little critters for sale." Luke met her eyes then, and Cassie got warm all over from her stare. "But I fell in love with your eagle. I never even looked at your smaller carvings."

"I feel something for eagles, I think," Cassie said. "They're my favorite subject, by far. So powerful, their stare so intense," she said quietly. She turned and followed Luke's gaze to the eagle standing guard by the windows.

"I would love to see the one you're working on now," Luke stated. "The one in flight."

"I've finished it," Cassie said. "Though it will be difficult to part with. I want someone to have it who loves it for what it is. I don't want someone to just fork over a bunch of money and put it on display somewhere because it looks good."

Luke laughed. "All artists are the same. I've become that way myself. At first, I would design a home just as ordered, plowing down all the trees and making a nice, flat area to build. But I can't do that anymore. Homes should blend with the environment and be a part of the land and add to it, not merely sit upon it as if they're some sterile structure that doesn't really belong there."

"What was the house that Frank Lloyd Wright designed? Falling waterfall something or other?"

Luke stared at her again. "Fallingwater," she said. "1936, in Pennsylvania. Totally unbelievable. He was the master, of course. But that house is what inspired me to design as I do. In the summer, when the leaves are all out, you can hardly tell there is a house there. It's built nearly on top of the waterfall, and it appears the water is coming right out of the house."

Cassie smiled. "You love your work," she stated.

"Yes. As do you."

Cassie again felt warm from her stare, and she had to look away. She carried her bowl to the sink, just now noticing how dark it was outside, but the rain had slowed to a steady drizzle.

"I think the storm's let up," she said.

"Yes," Luke said from directly behind her. Cassie jumped, startled. She had not heard Luke get up. Cassie turned, their arms brushing and Cassie's skin burned where they had touched. She moved away as Luke set her own bowl in the sink.

"I can run you home, if you like. Or you can sleep here, and I'll take you to get your van in the morning," she suggested.

"Oh, I couldn't," Cassie said quickly. "I've imposed enough."

Luke watched her intently. "You really are scared of me, aren't you?"

Cassie swallowed. "Of course not," she lied. But yes, she was afraid. Afraid of Luke, afraid of herself. Afraid that this time, she wouldn't be able to ignore this attraction? *Afraid? How about terrified?*

"Okay. Let's see if we can get you home, then."

Cassie sighed with relief. The sooner she left her company, the better. Her relief was short-lived, however. The tiny creek they had to cross, normally just flowing at a snail's pace, was now a raging river out of its banks and Luke's headlights locked on the rushing water as it flowed across the road, carrying small limbs and branches with it.

"Wow!"

"Shit," Cassie murmured. "I didn't realize it had rained that much."

Luke turned in her seat and Cassie could see her smile in the soft glow of the lights. "Well, guess I'm stuck with you for the night."

Cassie clutched her neatly folded shorts and T-shirt to her and watched as Luke carefully turned them around and headed back to her house. Cassie stared straight ahead, not daring to look at this woman whose nearness affected her so.

She sat on the rug beside the fire and watched quietly as Luke stirred the logs, sending sparks up the chimney. The fire gave off a cheery glow, and Cassie found herself relaxing, really relaxing for the first time that day.

"So, a minister, huh? Must have been tough." Luke laid the poker on the stones and sat down beside Cassie, although not too close to make her uncomfortable, Cassie noted.

"You don't know the half of it," Cassie finally replied. "He would have been perfectly at home in the Deep South. He was all fire and brimstone, for sure, and could definitely put the fear of God in you." She smiled slightly. "That was the problem, although he could never see it," she said. "I was so afraid of doing something that would send me straight to hell that I never learned what I could do to get me to heaven."

"What do you mean?"

Cassie leaned back on her elbows and stretched her sock-clad feet out to the warm fire. Kim was the only other person she had ever told about her father, but Luke was looking at her intently, and she found she wanted to talk.

"I was eighteen before he would let me go out on a date. It was my senior prom and I had to beg for that." She tried to laugh, but it came out as a choked cough. "I don't know if it was so much that I wanted to go or that I was supposed to go. He agreed only if he could take us and pick us up and if I promised no dancing."

"Eighteen?"

This time she did laugh. "I was so afraid of boys and what would happen to me if they touched me, kissed me, that I was secretly thankful he was picking us up. You have to understand, from the time I was old enough to remember, he was telling me what they were really after, although he never said what they were after, just that they were after it. I would catch something and become very sick if they kissed me, maybe even die. I would get pregnant if they touched any part of my body. And heaven forbid if I touched them. Blindness would strike me immediately!"

"Jesus," Luke whispered.

"Yeah. Really." Cassie took a swallow from her juice before continuing. "Of course, as I got older, I knew those things wouldn't really happen, but I was terrified nonetheless. I guess that was the reason I had no interest in boys." She glanced at Luke and smiled. "I was twenty-two before I slept with a guy. And it wasn't that I wanted to, really. I wasn't in love with him or anything. In fact, I don't think I even liked him all that much. But I was tired of being the oldest virgin at school."

"I see you still have your eyesight."

"Yes. I came out unscathed. Physically, at least. Emotionally, I felt . . . empty. I felt nothing," she said quietly. "I've never been able to feel anything," she added softly.

They were quiet for a moment, then Luke stirred, leaning forward to nudge the logs again. Cassie watched her in the warm glow, watched her hands as they lightly gripped the poker. She had a momentary glimpse of those hands touching her, and her chest tightened. She wished she could feel nothing now.

"You haven't mentioned your mother," Luke said.

Cassie slid her eyes from Luke to the fire. "She left us when I was five. I know now that she left my father, but at the time, it was me that she left behind."

"I'm sorry," Luke said quietly. "You don't have to tell me."

"No. I'm okay about it now. I don't blame her in the least. I left as soon as I could, too."

"Do you see her?"

Cassie shook her head. "I haven't seen her since the day she hugged me and walked out. I have no idea where she is."

"Your father never said?"

"She may have tried to contact me, I don't know. I would like to think that she did. But her name was never mentioned in our house." She paused again, then spoke softly. "I remember the first Christmas after she left. Her parents, my grandparents, came to the house. My father sent me to my room, and he wouldn't let them in. They had presents for me, they said. But he sent them away, and we never talked about it. I never saw them again either."

"That's so very sad," Luke murmured. "But you still see your father?"

"He's been up here twice in the last six years. I don't go see him. Well, I went one Christmas a few years ago, but that turned into one big 'Let's Save Cassandra' weekend. We talk on the phone occasionally. Briefly. That's about as much as I can take of his preaching."

"What about Kim? How did you meet her?"

"I met her in an art class my second year in college. We just hit it off right away. Kim's been my therapist all these years. She knows all about my father. First hand."

"What do you mean?"

"When Kim discovered she was . . . a lesbian, she came to the house, she needed to talk."

"You still lived at home?"

"I lived at home until that week, yes. She had gotten married six months before. Just to prove to herself that she wasn't gay, I think. But, it didn't work out. She came over to tell me that she was leaving him, that she couldn't live a lie anymore, that she was ready to accept what she was. My father was home, listening. He nearly brought the house down with his Bible quotes that day," she said, managing a laugh. "Kim's eyes were so big," Cassie remembered, smiling. "I thought she was going to pass out. He sent her away, forbid me to see her. That was the first time I had ever stood up to him. I moved out that week 'over his dead body,' and Kim and I lived together for nearly a year."

At Luke's raised eyebrows Cassie laughed. "No. We were just friends. Always."

"I take it your father never came to your house," Luke said.

"No. Never. He assumed I was living in sin. That I had become *one of those*. And when I moved up here with all these 'unnatural people, thick as thieves'—that's one of his favorite sayings—he vowed he would never see me again. I think that's one reason I moved. I was perfectly happy having a long distance relationship with him over the phone. It's been two years since he was last here."

Luke was shaking her head and smiling.

"What?"

"We grew up so differently. At opposite ends of the scale, I think."

"Tell me."

"You'll be shocked," Luke warned.

"No more so than you were hearing about my life."

Luke sat back down, folded her legs and faced Cassie. "My mother was fifteen and pregnant when she ran away from home. Oklahoma. She made it to Berkeley, got a job as a waitress and lived in a run-down apartment building until I was born. She named me after her grandmother," Luke said. "But I'm no Lucinda."

"No, you're not."

"My mother was a flower child," Luke said.

"Flower child?"

"Yes. A real hippie. In the late sixties, early seventies, we lived in a commune of sorts. Grew our own food and lived royally," she said and laughed. "They were all vegetarians and war protesters. They would load up the vans, kids and all, and go to peace rallies, protest marches, demonstrations. We hit them all."

Cassie smiled delightfully. "Go on," she said.

"Neal, that was my mother's man, he's the one that started calling me Luke. One day after a rain, I wanted to help in the gardens. I came back home covered head to toe in mud. As he was spraying me off with a hose, he asked what I had done with Lucinda. There

41

couldn't possibly be a little girl under all that dirt, he said. I must be her brother, Luke." Luke shrugged now. "The name stuck. Thankfully."

"You don't know who your father is?" Cassie asked.

"No. He was just some farmer's son that my mother lost her virginity to. She didn't love him. That's why she ran away. Her parents wanted her to get married."

"Have you ever wanted to know?"

"Not really. Neal was all the father I needed. They're still together, living in sin," she said lightly.

"They never married?"

"Oh, no. They wouldn't even consider it."

Cassie stared at her for a moment, jealous of the freedom Luke seemed to have had as a child. "Does your mother know about you . . . about your life?"

"Does she know I'm a lesbian? Yes. She's the one who told me."

Cassie's eyes widened. "What do you mean?"

"I was like you. Never went out on dates, never had any interest in boys. But there was this one guy who kept asking me out. He was the quarterback, Mr. Popularity, and I was seventeen, thinking that it was time I started noticing them. So, I told my mother that I was going to go out with him. She wanted to know why. I remember looking at her for the longest time, wondering that myself. Then I told her that was what I was supposed to be doing at that age."

"Then what?"

"Then she took me to see Aunt Susan and Aunt Darlene," Luke said.

"I don't understand," Cassie said.

Luke smiled and stood. "They weren't really my aunts. They weren't really sisters. They had lived at the commune with us, always together. They were lovers," Luke said. She walked over to her bookshelves and took down two framed pictures.

"Oh."

"And then it all made sense. I didn't have to go out with the quarterback." She handed Cassie the pictures before sitting down again. "That's us back then. I must have been five or six, I guess. The other one was taken four years ago at a reunion."

Cassie smiled at the small, dark-haired girl in the picture, surrounded by an odd group of . . . well, hippies. The second picture showed Luke as Cassie knew her today.

"That's my mother and Neal," Luke pointed out. "That's Susan and Darlene."

Cassie compared the pictures, the carefree smiles of the first picture captured again some thirty years later.

"So, you've never been with a man, then?" Cassie asked, thinking of Luke's earlier comment about the quarterback.

"No. Why would I?"

"But . . . how can you know for sure if you've never tried it?" Cassie asked.

Luke laughed softly, then leaned forward. "How can you be sure you're not a lesbian if you've never been with a woman?"

Cassie leaned back, away from Luke, away from her heat. "Point taken," she said quietly. She felt Luke's eyes on her, but Cassie refused to look. She stared into the fire, telling herself that was the only heat she was feeling.

"I think I'm ready to call it a night," Luke finally said. "Will you be okay on the sofa?"

"Of course," Cassie said quickly.

"I'll go find you a sheet and blanket, then."

Cassie watched her climb the stairs, then heard her shuffling in the loft and shortly she came back carrying a pillow along with a blanket and sheet. "Good enough?"

"This is fine," Cassie said, tossing them to the couch. "Thank you for . . . everything. Rescuing me, feeding me, everything."

"You're welcome," Luke said lightly. "I've enjoyed your company. Feel free to put another log on, if you want."

She left her without another word, and Cassie busied herself making up a bed on the sofa. The fire was inviting, so she did lay another log on before crawling under the blanket. She lay on her side, staring out at the rain, now only a fine mist. She thought she saw the moon breaking through and got just a glimpse of the patio beyond the windows, then darkness again. She snuggled deeper into the pillow and her body warmed. She caught a scent that was becoming familiar. Luke. It was her pillow from her bed, Cassie knew instantly. She breathed deeply, pushing her face into the softness before she could stop herself. Then she groaned and rolled over onto her back, her arms folded across her chest.

This is insanity, she thought. But that didn't stop her heart from pounding in her chest.

Chapter Eight

Cassie's van was just as they left it, the tires now sunk low in mud. She stood with her hands on her hips, mentally going over her choices.

"I can pull it out," Luke said, interrupting her thoughts.

"You can?"

"Sure. It's not really stuck. We'll just pull it out on the road and change the tire there."

Cassie felt like a helpless female as Luke tied a thick rope she had produced from her Lexus to each of their vehicles' bumpers. In a matter of minutes, her van sat limply on the road, leaning slightly from the flat tire but no worse for wear. Of course, Cassie had never changed a tire before. She told Luke as much.

"It's past time you learn then," she said. "Suppose you're stuck on a deserted road, late at night and suppose a group of women came along—lesbians, no less—and they've been drinking and they see you, standing helplessly beside your van. Bet you wished you had known how to change the tire then."

Cassie laughed. "Oh, stop. If that were the scenario, they would all hop out and have my tire changed in no time and I'd be on my way, thankful it wasn't some farmer's son that had stopped."

Luke laughed, too. "No doubt."

Cassie supervised as Luke lifted the tire with ease and fifteen minutes later was wiping her hands on a rag Cassie had found in the back of the van.

"All set," Luke said.

"I don't know how to thank you," Cassie said, then blushed as Luke raised a mischievous eyebrow.

"How about showing me the eagle, then?"

Cassie hesitated only a second before agreeing. What harm would that do, she thought. She found herself glancing in her mirror frequently, feeling oddly comforted by Luke following her. She liked her, she admitted. They certainly had not lacked for conversation, last night or this morning. Which was unusual for her, Cassie knew. She was a loner, always had been, and it usually took awhile for her to warm up to people, but she had thoroughly enjoyed Luke's company. And if she could just get past this silly attraction she was feeling, she thought she and Luke could possibly become good friends. Luke had not even hinted that she thought of Cassie as anything but that. In fact, she had said that she wasn't looking for anyone. Cassie smiled. It could be the start of a new friendship. And it had been awhile since she'd added one of those to her life.

"My God. This is . . . *incredible*," Luke said a short time later as they stood in her workshop. She glanced at Cassie, then back at the eagle. "Words fail me," she said quietly. She reached out a gentle hand, as if afraid to startle the eagle and cause it to take flight. Cassie watched those fingers stroke the head lovingly and she drew in a quick breath. Again, she had the briefest image of those hands touching her that way and she shivered.

"Beautiful. So absolutely beautiful," Luke was saying, and Cassie turned away, trying to busy herself. She was always embarrassed when she showed her work, afraid they wouldn't like it nearly as much as she did.

"So you like it?"

"Are you kidding? I love it. It's . . . magnificent. You have such a talent."

Cassie blushed at her praise, secretly pleased that she liked it.

"You do want to sell it?" Luke asked.

"I can't very well keep him in here," Cassie said. "What do you think I could get for him?"

"I wouldn't take less than ten thousand, maybe twelve," Luke said as she walked around the eagle.

Cassie nearly gasped.

"That much?"

Luke nodded. "I saw a bear. It was bigger than this but not nearly as detailed. A lodge out near Yosemite has it. They paid fifteen for it, they said." Luke turned and met her gaze. "I have a buyer for it," she said suddenly.

Cassie's eyes widened. "It's a little cumbersome, with the wingspan and all. He'll be hard to move."

Luke nodded. "I have a buyer."

"I've become attached to him. I'm not sure I'm ready to have him displayed somewhere with strangers touching him. Probably out front of some building with kids trying to climb on him. I don't think I could stand that."

Cassie walked to her eagle and brushed off a speck of dust from his wing. She was being silly, she knew. Luke probably thought she'd lost her mind.

But Luke was looking at her in an odd way, her smile gentle.

"What if I promise there won't be strangers touching him? And he won't be at a public place. He'll be at someone's home, guarding their backyard."

Cassie slid her eyes from Luke back to her eagle. "You really think you can sell it for me? Your friends on Russian River?"

"Oh, they would love him."

Cassie nodded. "Okay then. I mean, I can't keep him here, that's for sure."

Luke looked around the shop for the first time, and her lips parted in surprise. "You've got tons of stuff here," she said as she walked over to a beaver that was chewing happily on a log. "This one is great, too."

"I want to take at least ten pieces with me to the County Fair next month. These are all but finished. They just need touch-ups here and there," she said, waving at the animals that stood in varying positions around the shop.

Luke walked to the workbench and gently picked up a fawn. "This is so delicate," she said softly. She glanced up and met Cassie's eyes. "You have incredible talent."

"Please stop," Cassie said, blushing again. "You're starting to embarrass me."

Luke turned the fawn around in her hands, then set it back down. "With the type of homes I design, I meet a lot of woodworkers, mostly men. They make beautiful cabinets, furniture, railings. Anything the homeowner wants." Luke paused. "Do you ever work on commission?"

Cassie nodded. "I have on a few occasions."

"If you're interested, I could probably get you more business than you could handle. Most of the homes I design are totally natural." Luke waved a hand at Cassie's workshop. "These pieces would fit perfectly."

"The problem I've found with commissions is that the customer wants something other than wildlife, and I'm not at all comfortable producing that." Cassie wrinkled her nose. "Or fish. They always want carved fish stuck on a board. To me, it just looks like a dead fish." She, too, waved at the pieces scattered about. "I like to think that my animals are very much alive, all with different looks and personalities."

"Well, that is one good thing about working for commission. You can always say no. Of course, if you agree, that will really limit the time that you can devote to regular art shows and county fairs and such."

"You're right, but the people who frequent those places usually can only afford the small carvings. Fortunately, it doesn't take me long to make them."

"Well, right off the top of my head, I can think of three or four clients who would be interested in your work. If it's okay with you, I'll give them your business card."

Cassie hesitated only a moment. Did she want to be indebted to Luke? It didn't matter. She was no fool. It would be insane for her to turn down an opportunity like this.

So she nodded. "I would appreciate it."

"You have great talent," Luke said again. "And you should be getting paid for it. Truthfully, the eagle I bought from you was practically a steal. It was worth twice what I paid."

"Yes, but I wouldn't sell any if I priced them that high."

"No, probably not at the county fair." It was Luke's turn to hesitate. "I know it's really none of my business, but have you tried the Internet?"

Cassie blushed. "I don't even own a computer."

Luke rolled her eyes.

"I know what you're thinking," Cassie said. "How can people exist without a computer? I hear it from Kim all the time. I just . . ."

"You're afraid?"

"I wouldn't know where to begin."

Luke laughed. "Gotta start somewhere, sweetie. Next time we've both got a free evening, I'll show you my Web page. You could fix one up like that for yourself. It'd be great advertising."

Cassie nodded uncertainly. "We'll see."

"Okay. We'll take baby steps with this then."

When they walked back outside, the rain was starting again. Before Cassie had time to reconsider, she invited Luke in for coffee.

Luke flashed a quick grin and nodded.

"I'd love a cup. I'm usually a bear without it in the mornings, but I knew you were anxious to get your van so I didn't bother at the house."

As Cassie opened the kitchen door to her small, modest house she had an overwhelming urge to take back her invitation. After spending time at Luke's spacious home, her own seemed tiny in comparison. She wondered what Luke's reaction would be. But she needn't have worried.

"This is great, Cassie." Luke moved into the kitchen, her architect's hands and eyes moving over the cabinets that had been built well before either of them were even born. "How old is this?"

"It was built in the thirties, they tell me. And he wasn't even a cabinetmaker, he was a farmer. He and his son built the entire house. It's been remodeled a few times, me included, but no one's touched the cabinets," she said.

"Who would dare? I can't believe all the detail," she murmured as she bent for a closer look. "Custom cabinets, sure, even back then they had fine cabinetmakers." Luke turned back to Cassie. "You had them refinished?"

"They were painted when I bought the house."

"*Painted?*"

Cassie tried to hold back her laugh, but the look of total disgust on Luke's face was too much.

"I know. You must be completely appalled. I couldn't believe it myself," she teased.

Luke smiled good-naturedly.

"It was a sin, whoever did it."

"Yes, I agree."

Cassie poured water into the coffeemaker, then pulled out several varieties of coffee.

"I hope you don't do decaf," she said.

"Of course not. But I do tend to tamper with it a bit," Luke cautioned.

"Sugar?"

Luke nodded.

Cassie made a face. "And cream?"

Luke lifted one corner of her mouth wryly. "I add enough sugar and cream to disguise the coffee, I'm not sure why I drink it."

"Well, you'll have to make do with soy milk. I don't have any cream," Cassie said as she turned back to her task. She felt Luke move close behind her, peering just over her shoulder.

"Smells good," she said. "Do you mind if I look around?"

"No. It won't take you but a minute, though. The two bedrooms are now one and then the living room," Cassie explained, relaxing a little as Luke moved away from her. She returned a short time later.

"I like it," she said. "It's . . ."

"Quaint?" Cassie supplied.

"I was going to say cozy," Luke said. "I like your bedroom."

Cassie managed not to blush, but she turned back quickly to her coffee, making a production of pouring two cups.

They sat at her small kitchen table and she watched, horrified, as Luke put an outrageous amount of sugar and milk into her cup. She sipped her own, enjoying the rich flavor but smiled as Luke made a satisfied moan at her own first sip.

"Perfect."

"Sure you have enough sugar?"

Luke ignored her with a flick of one eyebrow.

"Tell me what you've done here. The sliding door to the patio is obviously new. What about in here?"

"The laundry room is through there," Cassie said, pointing to a door at the opposite end of the kitchen. "When I bought it, that was a large storage room, I guess. The connections were outside so I brought them in and remodeled that room and extended the patio. In here, just new flooring."

"Was your workshop here?"

"Yes. That's the main reason I bought this place. The workshop was perfect. And I just remodeled a little at a time. The bedroom wall was the first to go," she said.

"I guess having one bedroom cuts down on company. Of course, that can be a good thing sometimes."

Cassie stared into her coffee, wondering why she was even considering confiding in Luke. Her relationship with her father was something only Kim knew about, and even then, Kim knew only what Cassie wanted her to know.

"I've never admitted this to anyone before," she said quietly. "I think the main reason I knocked out the bedroom wall was so that my father wouldn't come stay with me." She looked up and met Luke's gentle gaze. "Is that terrible?"

"I don't think that's terrible. I guess that was easier than just telling him you didn't want to see him?"

Cassie sighed. "How do you tell your father that you don't like him and you don't want to see him? He's the only family I have," she said. "And I'm all he has."

"But?" Luke prompted.

"But it's very hard for me not to hate him. I don't have any pleasant memories of my childhood. None. I can't recall a time of just being a kid and laughing and playing. Everything was always so serious. It was like I was being punished for something I had yet to do."

"Did you have friends in your neighborhood? At church?"

"Not really. He wouldn't allow me to play with the neighbors and the few kids at church, well, I think they were too afraid of my father. He sent more than one off crying."

"I'm sorry," Luke said quietly.

A ghost of a smile appeared on Cassie's face, then it was gone just as quickly. Something she had never told Kim now surfaced. Something she thought was better kept buried, but the memory emerged now.

"Every night before dinner, we would read a chapter from the Bible. Sometimes short ones, sometimes not. But I had to memorize it, word for word, before I could eat. Some nights, it would be hours before I could do it. Some nights, I couldn't do it at all. So instead of dinner, he would lock me in his office and tell me not to ask to come out until I had it memorized."

"Cassie, I'm so sorry," Luke whispered.

"I never could do it," Cassie said. "I would sleep on the floor,

52

crying for my mother, wondering why she had left me there with him." Cassie brushed at an errant tear, unable to stop the pain and loneliness that suddenly enveloped her.

Luke reached out and captured her hand, squeezing lightly.

"And you ask me if I think it's terrible that you don't want him to visit?"

"Do you think he even remembers doing that to me?"

"Why don't you ask him?"

Cassie pulled her hand away from Luke's warm one and shook her head. "I'm sorry. I don't know why I told you all that. Kinda ruins a good cup of coffee," she said lightly. "Except yours. It was already ruined."

Cassie stood, intending to refill their cups, but Luke stopped her with a firm grip on her arm.

"If you need to talk, I'm a good listener," she offered.

Cassie met her eyes and attempted to smile. "Why on earth would you volunteer for that?"

"Because talking about past pains is the only way to heal," Luke said gently. "And I'm guessing you've not talked with anyone. Maybe your friend Kim?"

"Kim knows a lot but she doesn't know about that. I've never told anyone about that. I was too ashamed. I don't know why I told you now," she said.

"You can talk to me anytime, Cassie."

Their eyes held, and Cassie knew that Luke was being completely sincere. And it would be so easy to unburden herself, to dump it all on Luke and have her sort through it. But right now, she didn't want to think about it anymore, much less talk about it.

"Thanks. I'll keep that in mind."

"Okay. Well, thanks for the coffee, but I need to get going. I'm meeting a new client this afternoon in Sacramento."

They both looked up at the same time as thunder rolled outside.

"Thanks again for your help," Cassie said. "For rescuing me and all."

"No problem." Then Luke grinned. "It was my pleasure."

Cassie watched her drive away, arms wrapped securely around herself as the rain fell softly. Luke was so very different from any woman Cassie had ever met. Perhaps that was why she found herself attracted to her. And yes, she could admit that now that Luke was safely out of sight.

Chapter Nine

After unpacking the groceries from her van and the ones she had brought from Luke's, she put on a pot of lentils to simmer, then spent the afternoon in her shop, finishing up on the beaver and another much smaller eagle. She would put off calling Kim until after dinner. There had been two voice mails from her. One from last night and one this morning. Knowing Kim, if she had even the slightest clue that Cassie had spent the night at Luke Winston's house, she would not let it rest until Cassie relayed every detail of the evening and every word spoken between them. But Cassie wasn't ready to share her new friendship with Kim. Kim would turn it into something it wasn't. So Cassie swore Kim would never know that she had not spent last night in her own bed. It was just easier that way.

And she tried to push Luke from her mind, but still, she stayed. It was her hands, Cassie thought, that drew her. She had lovely hands. Long, strong fingers. Neatly trimmed nails. Soft hands, although she had not actually felt them. Cassie dipped her own into the soapy water at the sink to avoid thinking of Luke Winston's hands. Her own were nicked and callused from working with wood all day long. She applied lotion constantly, but to no avail.

After three days of working nonstop, Cassie was finally able to get through the hours without constantly thinking of Luke Winston. It was progress. She told herself that eventually, if she were to be around her more, she would lose this infatuation she seemed to have for her, and she could concentrate on the friendship they had started. And that was really all she wanted.

After five days of neatly avoiding thinking about Luke and avoiding talking to Kim for more than a few minutes at a time, she felt that she was back to normal. Her days became routine again, and she was certain that she would finish all of the pieces before the fair. She was just sanding down the beaver's tail for the last time when she heard a noisy truck approach. She frowned. She was not expecting company. She stood and brushed the wood chips from her bare legs and went out into the sunshine.

It was a truck she did not recognize, pulling a flat bed trailer. She did, however, recognize one of the passengers. Her breath caught instantly at the smile Luke flashed her, and she smiled in return, cursing her traitorous body as it melted under Luke's stare.

"I would have called but I couldn't find your card and I was too lazy to call information," she explained. "These are friends of mine. Jack and Craig. They live over in Guerneville." She pointed to first one, then the other.

"Hi." She shook their offered hands and said to Jack, "I think we've met. You look familiar."

"Yes. I told Luke we had one of your carvings. Nothing like the eagle she's described, though. Just a small one. A Steller's jay," he said.

Cassie's eyes widened, and she turned to Luke. "You've come for him?"

"Yes. I've got a cashier's check for twelve thousand. How does that sound?"

"Twelve? Are you kidding?"

Luke shook her head. "I told you I had a buyer."

They stood facing each other, and Cassie forgot about Jack and Craig. "I don't know that I'm ready," she said. "I mean . . ."

"The longer you hold onto him, the harder it will be," Luke said quietly.

"You're right, I know," Cassie said, unable to pull her eyes from Luke. "It's just that . . . this one has become kinda special, you know? He's got his own personality."

Luke smiled gently and nodded. "He'll be well taken care of, I promise. No strangers touching him or climbing on him. Promise."

Cassie looked at Jack and Craig, feeling embarrassed. "Okay then," she said. "I guess I can't turn down twelve thousand dollars." At least she wouldn't have to worry about paying her bank note for awhile. Then she smiled. "I can't believe they paid that much."

"It's well worth it," Luke assured her.

Cassie stood by while they loaded her eagle onto the trailer. Again, she felt very much the helpless female as she watched Luke lift her end. Her eyes lighted everywhere, finally landing on the biceps of Luke's arms as she strained to carry him. The gently rippling muscles on Luke's shoulders did nothing for her, she told herself, but still she stared. Then her eyes landed on Luke's thighs as she stood, every indentation of muscle outlined as they walked cautiously with her eagle. She mentally shook herself, dragging her eyes away and focusing instead on Jack as he walked backward toward the trailer. *But she felt nothing.* She let out a heavy sigh and allowed her eyes to again settle on Luke's lean form, watching with envy, she told herself . . . not . . . well, certainly not with desire. *Admiration.* Much better. They wrapped her eagle with blankets before securing him with ropes, and she was finally able to move, offering suggestions as to where to tie the ropes.

"You'll need to let me know where he'll be," Cassie told Luke. "In case I want to drive by and look at him."

"Well, perhaps I'll take you there myself," she said. "I'm sure you can have visiting rights."

Cassie smiled. "You think I'm being silly."

"Not at all. You created him. You love him."

Jack and Craig were already in the truck, ready to go as they stood there facing each other. Cassie folded her arms across her chest as Luke shoved hers into her shorts.

"How have you been?" she asked.

"Okay. Working."

"I wanted to call, but . . . well, I didn't want to impose. I thought . . ."

"You probably didn't want to call because you were afraid I'd take you up on your offer," Cassie teased.

"Not at all. But I haven't been around that much. I've been in the city."

"That's okay. Maybe we can get together for lunch or dinner or something," Cassie heard herself say.

"I'd like that."

Cassie nodded, not knowing what else to say. As she looked into Luke's eyes, she thought she had been mistaken by their color. With the sun shinning on her face, her eyes weren't dark at all. They were nearly golden and Cassie found herself again being pulled to this woman. She nearly shivered from the heat that passed through her.

"What?" Luke asked as Cassie stared.

"Hmm?" Cassie blinked, trying to focus, trying to clear her head.

Luke took a step toward her and stopped, just long enough for Cassie to take a nervous step backward. She clasped her hands together and turned to the truck, making a show of telling the guys good-bye. Luke watched her for a moment, then walked around the truck and opened the door. Before getting in, she looked back at Cassie.

"You're okay, right?"

"Yes, of course. I'm fine," Cassie said. "Drive carefully with him."

"We will. Later," Luke called, and Cassie watched them drive away with her eagle.

Well, so much for putting Luke Winston from her mind for the past week. Just one look had brought back all of the feelings she had been trying to suppress. Heat . . . desire. She groaned and turned away. Not desire, she told herself. She wouldn't allow those feelings to surface.

"Just friends," she murmured. "Just going to be friends."

Chapter Ten

"What do you see?" Kim asked anxiously.

Cassie stared at her painting, so different from the natural seascapes that Kim normally created. She unconsciously rubbed her chin and turned her head to one side, studying it.

"I see the ocean. And cliffs." She turned to Kim with a smile. "It's like an abstract seascape," she said.

Kim smiled broadly. "You're good."

Cassie laughed. "We took the same art classes." She turned back to the painting. "I like it. Something new for you."

Kim crossed her arms and studied the painting, too. "Yes. Different. But still a seascape."

"There's nothing wrong with that. You love the ocean. It would be like me not carving eagles anymore. They're my favorite." Then she turned back to Kim. "Think of Cezanne. He must have painted the same mountain a hundred times. It was what he saw every day from his home."

Kim nodded. "Mont Sainte-Victoire," she said quietly. "You're right, of course."

"But Kim, it's good. Don't be afraid to try different styles. When our art stops being an expression of ourselves and is done solely for commercialism—"

"It's a sad day for us all," Kim finished with a smile. It was a quote they had heard many times from art professors.

"And it keeps us fresh," Cassie added. "If I did nothing but eagles, they would all begin to look alike. There has to be some variety."

"Yeah. That's really why I did it. I couldn't muster up my usual inspiration anymore, and I've wanted to try an abstract for awhile, I've just been afraid. I mean, what if it sucked?"

Cassie laughed. "It doesn't suck, Kim. It's just different for you. Try it at the fair. Put an outrageous price on it and see what happens," Cassie suggested.

"It took me forever to finish. I guess I could ask more than I usually do."

Cassie took another look at the painting. She normally wasn't too fond of abstract. She preferred things in their natural state, which meant a seascape should look like a seascape. But Kim had captured the colors of a sunset perfectly.

"You may have found a new niche."

"You think so? Really?"

"I really do," Cassie assured her. "Now, let's eat. I'm starved."

They settled around the table as Lisa brought out a dish from the oven. She had her favorite apron tied around her waist and looked every bit the homemaker. Cassie and Kim looked at each other across the table, waiting for Lisa's standard announcement before each meal.

"It's lentil casserole, and I have no idea how it'll taste. It doesn't look too appetizing, if I say so myself."

"I'm sure it will be great," they said in unison, as they always did. And Lisa stuck her tongue out at them, as she usually did. Lisa had a penchant for trying new recipes. Whether they turned out good or bad, she seldom tried the same thing twice.

And actually, it was good. Cassie spread butter on the hot rolls and helped herself to seconds. She was hardly a guest in their home anymore, and she would do the dishes afterward while Lisa and Kim sat at the table and filled her in on the latest gossip. It was a routine that Cassie had come to love. After spending nearly every weekend with them after Kim had moved, they had all become accustomed to this time together. Once she had made the move, too, they continued to invite her to dinner at least once a week.

"Oh Cassie, you'll never believe what we heard," Kim said. "You remember that gorgeous woman at the fair? The one that bought your eagle?" Then she laughed and shared an amused smile with Lisa. "Luke Winston is her name. You know who I'm talking about?" she asked again.

"I know who you're talking about." Cassie gave her a wry glance before shoving the roll in her mouth.

"Know why we've seen her around lately?"

Cassie stopped chewing for only a second. It had been nearly two weeks since she had seen Luke, and she had spent that time trying to forget the way her body reacted when she was around her. When she reached for her glass of wine, she was pleased that her hand did not shake.

"She's moved out here," Lisa said before Kim could.

"Really?"

It was ironic, wasn't it? Here they were, dropping this bit of news, Kim probably hoping that she could play matchmaker now, and Cassie not only knew Luke lived here, she had spent the night at her house. Wouldn't they be surprised?

"Yes. Carl says she's an architect," Lisa said.

"Really?" Cassie murmured again.

"Caters strictly to the wealthy, from what I hear," Kim added. "She's supposedly loaded."

"How nice," Cassie said. But then, she had already suspected that, judging by her home. And her casually dropping two thousand dollars at the festival for her eagle. "Well, maybe you'll become friends," she said.

"And just maybe . . ."

"Don't start, Kim," Cassie said, pointing her fork at her. "If you do, I'll be forced to call up David and ask him out."

"Oh, please. You no more want to go out with David than I do," Kim complained.

"You're right. I don't. And I don't want to go out with Luke Winston, either," she said.

"Kim," Lisa warned. "Let her be."

Cassie did the dishes, only half listening to their conversation behind her. She had been hoping they wouldn't find out that Luke lived here. At least, not for awhile. But it shouldn't matter. It wasn't like they would see her out much. Artists tended to hang together, and she didn't think that Luke knew anyone here. Their paths might not cross too often. At least, that's what she told herself. Since Luke had not called her, Cassie assumed that she had changed her mind about wanting to get together. Perhaps it was for the best.

Chapter Eleven

She was tempting fate, she thought, as she sat at a table at the local gay bar in Guerneville that Saturday night. Kim had talked her into it, as usual. And it wasn't like she hadn't been out with them before. In fact, she had many times. But when she saw Luke walk in with Jack and Craig, her heart fell into her stomach and she actually felt faint. She had missed Luke, missed talking to her, but running into each other at a gay bar was not how Cassie wanted to resume their friendship. She glanced quickly away, hoping Kim and Lisa had not seen her. She ran her suddenly damp palms across her jeans, then just as quickly, ran her fingers through her hair, nervously tucking the short strands behind her ears.

"Oh, God," Lisa gave an exaggerated moan and rolled her eyes. "Teresa's here."

"Searching out her next victim, no doubt," Kim added.

Cassie only half listened. Normally, she would be joining in. Teresa never failed to ask Cassie to dance, and Cassie hated having the encounter with her. She never said yes. She never would. Teresa frightened her. She was over six feet tall, built like a truck and rode a Harley. But right now, there was someone else here that scared her more.

Kim stood and pulled Lisa with her. "We're going to dance. Will you be okay?" she asked. "You know Teresa will be making the rounds."

"I'll be fine," Cassie said, and motioned for them to go. She looked around, trying to find Luke. Apparently they had taken a table at the opposite end of the bar. She was thankful.

She watched Kim and Lisa as they danced close. She gave a silent laugh and smiled. They really were a perfect match and about as different as you could get. Kim's hair was cut very short, bleached nearly white on top where gel held it sticking straight up. Lisa's conservative brown hair reached to her shoulders, her natural curls tamed somewhat tonight. Kim was thin as a rail. Lisa, like Cassie herself, had to watch everything she ate or she ended up fighting an extra five or ten pounds before she knew it.

Cassie's gaze followed her friends across the dance floor, and she was lost in thought. That's why the deep, husky voice startled her.

"What's a pretty girl like you doing sitting here all alone?"

Chills ran down Cassie's spine, and she turned her head slowly, not at all prepared for the warm welcome she found in Luke's eyes. Her bones turned to jelly, and she found herself returning the smile as their eyes locked. Luke pulled out a chair and turned it around, her back to the table. Then she leaned her elbows on her knees and grinned mischievously.

"You know, if you hang out at gay bars like this, people will start to talk."

Cassie laughed. "Kim made me tag along," she explained.

Luke nodded. "Me, too. I had dinner with Jack and Craig. They thought I needed a night out."

"Did you?"

Luke nodded. "I've been busy. How about you?"

"Working, yes. Getting ready for the County Fair."

Cassie pulled her eyes from Luke and focused on the woman approaching. "Oh, no," she groaned. She reached out without thinking and wrapped her fingers tightly around Luke's forearm, ignoring the sharp thrill that ran through her. "Stay where you are, please," she whispered as she locked eyes with Luke.

"If you insist," Luke murmured.

"Hey, doll. Let's dance."

Cassie raised her eyes to the puffy face of Teresa and shook her head. "Can't." She motioned to Luke. "Busy tonight."

Teresa shook a finger at Cassie, her cigarette dancing in Cassie's face. "One of these days, doll. It'll be my turn."

"I seriously doubt it," Cassie whispered as Teresa walked away. She turned to Luke. "That woman scares me."

Luke gave an exaggerated shudder. "Shit, she scares me, too. Could be the handcuffs on her belt," she said and they laughed together.

Cassie looked past Luke again, this time to Kim and Lisa as they made their way back to the table. The fates were definitely not in her corner tonight.

She turned quickly to Luke. "Listen . . . Kim . . . she doesn't know that we're . . . that we've talked. That we know each other . . . at all," she stammered. "And I just can't deal with it . . . right now." She didn't expect Luke to understand her hesitation, but Luke was nodding.

"She would think . . . that you're . . . that we . . ." Luke said, pointing to first Cassie, then herself.

Cassie nodded. "Yes. You don't know Kim," she whispered hurriedly. She realized she was still clutching Luke's arm, and she reluctantly released her.

"Then your secret's safe," Luke said quietly. "Although I was hoping we'd have a chance to visit. Maybe . . ."

"Well, I thought that was you," Kim said, interrupting them. "Luke, isn't it?"

Cassie rolled her eyes and watched as Luke and Kim shook hands.

"And this is Lisa."

"Good to see you again, Kim. Lisa, nice to meet you," Luke said pleasantly.

"Join us," Kim invited. "I'll get you a drink."

Cassie opened her mouth to say that Luke didn't drink then closed it just as quickly, but Luke was already standing.

"Thanks, but I'm here with friends. I just saw Cassie and thought I'd say hello." She turned to Cassie and touched her shoulder lightly, giving her a quick wink. "Glad I ran into you again."

"My, but she's attractive," Lisa murmured.

"Don't start, Kim," Cassie warned without even looking at her. Her eyes were glued to Luke's retreating back.

"I wasn't going to say a word," she said and chuckled. "Not a word."

Cassie tried to pretend that her shoulder wasn't on fire where Luke's hand had so casually rested, but it positively burned. She wanted to touch it, but she didn't dare. And it wasn't fair, she thought again for the hundredth time. There was no logical reason for her to have such a reaction to Luke. Well, there was a logical reason, but Cassie refused to name it, refused to accept it. It was just something about Luke. Something that she couldn't explain. Something that she wouldn't dare explain.

Oh, but she liked her. She really did. Luke was charming. Luke was attractive and likable. Luke was a woman and a lesbian. Cassie sighed. A woman and a lesbian that she was insanely attracted to.

"It was nice of her to come over to talk, though," Lisa said, interrupting Cassie's thoughts.

"Yes," Cassie said. "She seems nice." Cassie scanned the dance floor occasionally, hoping to see Luke dancing, thinking she could watch her unobserved. She did see Jack and Craig dancing once, but never Luke.

It was nearing midnight, and Cassie gave Kim 'The Look' that said it was time to go. Kim had learned long ago not to argue. Cassie would simply refuse to go out with them the next time.

"Had enough?" Kim asked.

"I think so. Besides, Teresa is giving me the eye again," Cassie said lightly.

"I see someone else giving you the eye," Kim teased, motioning with her head.

Cassie looked up in time to catch the smile on Luke's face as she approached. Her heart fluttered, like an idiot, she chided herself.

"We're about to go, but I thought I could steal one dance from you," Luke said.

Dance? Cassie's eyes widened and her mouth dropped open. "With me? Oh . . . I don't . . . I mean, I'm not very good," she stammered.

Luke reached for her hand and pulled her up before Cassie could object. "Well, we'll be not very good together," she said. "I haven't been dancing in years."

"But . . ."

"Just one." Luke's strong fingers locked around her own, ignoring her protest.

Cassie was amazed that her legs supported her. She was having a hard time breathing, and when Luke turned and slipped an arm around her waist, she was certain that she was going to pass out.

"Okay?"

Cassie nodded, afraid to speak, and her body turned rigid.

"Relax. You're all tense," Luke said.

"I am relaxed."

Luke smiled and pulled away a little. "You have this very large space around you, don't you?"

"What do you mean?"

"You know, personal space. Some people don't need very much, like me. Others need a lot of space."

"Yes," Cassie nodded. "I tend to require a large personal space." In truth, she never allowed anyone close, maybe Kim. Another side effect of her childhood, she suspected, and Luke was much too close.

But Luke pulled her closer again. "Kinda hard to do when dancing, though," she teased, and Cassie could hear the amusement in her voice.

Cassie's feet slid along with Luke's. She was on automatic, she realized. She didn't want to think. She didn't want to think about the arm around her waist or the warm hand holding her own. *Soft.* She didn't want to think about the strong shoulder that her own hand rested upon. And she certainly didn't want to think about the breasts that were only inches away from her own. Oh, dear Lord, she thought, I'm going to faint. *How embarrassing.* Her face was flushed, and she felt as if her skin were on fire. She felt perspiration trickle down her back, and she breathed deeply, her feet still moving along without a care in the world.

"We didn't get a chance to talk," Luke was saying, and Cassie managed to nod at her. "I didn't want to make you uncomfortable in front of Kim," she teased. "Seeing as how we hardly know each other."

Cassie smiled and felt herself relax. She was thankful for the conversation. It beat the thoughts running through her head.

"I wanted to invite you over for lunch tomorrow," Luke said.

"Lunch?"

"I have something to show you." Luke spun her around quite nicely and Cassie managed to step on her foot only once.

"I sold my house, by the way. I've been in the city on and off the past two weeks, cleaning and moving stuff out here. In between that, I'm trying to squeeze in work. That's why I haven't had a chance to call you."

"So you'll finally move in all the way, then?"

"I brought a few pieces of furniture with me and the rest of my clothes." Luke spun her around again. "So, lunch? About one?"

If Cassie had any sense at all, she would decline. Maybe seeing Luke and attempting a friendship was more than she could handle right now. Maybe she just needed to get her feelings under control before she saw her again.

"Okay," she heard herself say.

"Great." As the song ended, she pulled Cassie in close and whispered in her ear. "You're a very good dancer, by the way. And," she added mischievously, "you appear to still have your eyesight."

Cassie nearly broke speed records pulling out of Luke's arms, murmuring thanks for the dance, and hurrying back to her table. She thought her legs would fail her at any moment. She could still feel Luke's hot breath on her ear, still feel her breasts as they brushed against her own.

But she slowed and took a deep breath as she approached the table. She hoped her face showed none of the emotions rolling around inside of her. Cassie smiled pleasantly at Kim and Lisa, then waited for their teasing.

For once, Kim appeared speechless.

"What? Nothing to add?" Cassie asked.

"God, she's cute," Lisa said.

"Yes," Cassie said, wagging her finger at Lisa. "But she's gay, and I'm not, so it doesn't really matter how cute she is." She tried to sound firm and convincing, but her voice cracked with nervousness. Thankfully, neither Kim nor Lisa commented further.

As they walked to the car, Kim put her arm around Cassie affectionately, ignoring her immediate stiffening, as she always did.

"I think you should invite her to the wine and cheese party next weekend," Kim said.

"And why would I want to do that?"

"She probably doesn't know many people out here. It would give her a chance to meet someone."

"Well, if I happen to see her again, I'll mention it," Cassie said, although she knew she shouldn't. If for no other reason, Luke did not drink wine.

Chapter Twelve

Cassie spent a fitful night. Her father's voice boomed at her constantly. "Unnatural!"

She tossed in her sleep, fighting off the soft hands of a woman that kept coming to her again and again. Then she wasn't fighting anymore. She was welcoming the hands upon her. She welcomed the soft caresses and the promise of passion that she had only dared to dream about.

"Unnatural!"

She struggled out of her dream, pulling out of strong arms and away from too tempting lips that sought to capture her own. Her pillow was soaked with sweat, and she sat up, her body still hot, her heart still pounding. She tossed off the covers and walked through the dark house, sitting silently in the living room while she got herself under control.

"Just a dream," she murmured. "Doesn't mean anything."

She wished she still smoked. Her fingers itched to hold a cigarette, and she thought that this was the second time since she had met Luke Winston that she longed for a smoke. She leaned back finally and closed her eyes. It was just the dance, she told herself. Having Luke hold her like she had, just set her off.

No, she admitted. That wasn't it. She was . . . attracted to her. Sexually. She cupped her head with both hands and squeezed her eyes shut. She tried to muster up her usual attitude of indifference, but it wouldn't come. The walls weren't creeping back up. Instead, they lay shattered at her feet, exposing her to feelings she was certain she would never experience. And most likely, it was totally one-sided. Luke had never done or said anything to make her think differently. And the dance . . . she had simply been teasing her. *Right?*

No, she wasn't in any danger. She just . . . had to deal with this. A test, her father would say. She didn't actually believe it was a test, but still, she felt frightened by what she was feeling. She had nothing to compare this to. In all her thirty-three years, no one person had ever affected her so, had ever haunted her dreams. But deep in her heart, she always knew that if someone were to come to her, it would be a woman.

She crawled back into bed just hours before dawn and slept soundly until nine. It was a beautiful October day, and she took her coffee out onto the back porch and sat in the sun. She was still tired, she realized a short time later when her eyes closed heavily.

She made herself get up and she moved to her workshop. As was her custom, she put in a CD, skipping her usual selection of soothing guitar music and choosing instead an early Tracy Chapman. She turned the volume up and selected a newly sharpened chisel from her assortment of tools, intending to work on the sleek back of the seal she had started. She soon lost herself in her work, only stopping at the last possible minute to allow enough time to shower. She thought that maybe she should call Luke and cancel lunch, but that would hardly be fair. Cassie decided she was being silly. After all, Luke had done nothing wrong, and the seal would be here when she got back.

But still she was nervous as she drove down the long drive to

Luke's house. She wished she could be more nonchalant about their lunch date. She certainly did not want her uneasiness to show. She wanted to be friends with Luke, she really did.

Luke opened the door even before she could knock and all her plans fell right through the roof. Luke was wearing short shorts and a tank top. Cassie's eyes burned as she pulled them away from her muscled legs and arms and tried to match Luke's lazy smile with one of her own.

"I'm glad you came. Come in," Luke invited and she stepped aside to let Cassie pass. Cassie tried not to breathe as she walked past her, but she did. She caught the scent of her, the scent she remembered from last night, the scent she remembered from Luke's pillow, and she felt chill bumps on her skin. How funny, she thought, when her skin felt so hot.

"I'm sorry. I just got through working out, and I haven't had a chance to shower yet."

It was only then that Cassie noticed the light film of perspiration on Luke's skin and her slightly flushed face.

"It's okay. Am I early?"

"No, of course not. I'm just running late," Luke explained. "Make yourself at home while I take a quick shower."

Cassie nodded and looked away, suddenly extremely nervous.

"I'll finally get to see your . . . oh my *God*!" she gasped. She turned and clutched Luke's bare arm tightly, forgetting her nervousness. "You've got him!"

She had glanced out the windows toward the patio, curious as to the view Luke had on a sunny day like today, and there he was. Her eagle.

"I told you I had something to show you," Luke said.

Cassie followed numbly behind her, her eyes locked on the beautiful bird ready to take flight.

"But you said you got it for a client," Cassie accused.

"No. I told you I had a buyer," Luke reminded her.

Cassie nearly shoved her out of the way, and she went out onto the patio, hands clutched to her chest.

"God, he's so beautiful. He belongs out here, not inside some stuffy building," Cassie said quietly, almost to herself.

"And, he's in love," Luke said.

Cassie turned around and looked where Luke was pointing. The first eagle that stood guard inside seemed to be watching.

"They stare at each other all day," Luke said, her face breaking into smile.

"He's perfect here, Luke. He really is." Then Cassie turned on her. "How dare you pay me twelve thousand dollars! If I had known it was you, I would never have taken it," she said.

"I know. That's why I didn't tell you," Luke said easily. "Don't underestimate your work, Cassie. He's well worth every penny."

Cassie turned back to the eagle, then pulled out a chair to better watch him. Luke laughed. "I guess you'll want to eat out here."

"Do you mind? It's such a nice day and . . . God, your *view*!" For the first time, Cassie looked past the eagle. Luke's house sat on a rise, and falling down the slope was a beautiful meadow, giving way to forest which eventually gave way to vineyards. It was as if she could see all the way to the Pacific. "How much land do you have?"

"Just ten acres," Luke said. "Part of the forest is mine, the rest belongs to the recreation area."

"No wonder you don't have any curtains or drapes in your house," Cassie said.

Luke smiled. "To quote Thoreau, 'it cost me nothing for curtains, for I have no gazers to shut out but the sun and moon, and I am willing that they should look in,'" she said quietly.

Cassie met her eyes as she spoke and their gazes held for a quick moment. Long enough for Cassie to feel the heat down to the bottom of her toes.

"That's . . . beautiful," Cassie said softly.

"Well . . . let me shower, and I'll get lunch," Luke said, and Cassie watched her walk away, wishing with all her might that she did not like Luke Winston. But she did. She liked everything about her.

74

While she was gone, Cassie inspected the deck, walking around her eagle. Her eyes slid along the natural wood railing, following the steps to the second level, lingering on the hot tub for only a brief moment before continuing past the deck. Luke had only begun landscaping. Small fruit trees, apple she thought, were planted close by. Flowerbeds were designed and built, but not planted, and only the planters on the deck held flowers. But still, it was very nice and inviting. She could tell Luke had spent many hours planning the deck and surrounding gardens. Once everything was planted and flowering, it would be a feast for the eye. Cassie wondered if Luke would have it finished by next spring— and if she would be around to see it.

"I went to the farmer's market yesterday," Luke was saying as she pushed open the sliding door with her elbow. "This salad has a little bit of everything in it." Her arms were loaded with salad and two bowls and Cassie stood to help her.

"I've got it," Luke said. "But there's pasta in the kitchen, if you could bring that out."

Cassie was glad to escape Luke's presence, if only for a moment. It allowed her time to collect herself. Luke's hair was damp from her shower, but her legs and arms were still bare, still tempting Cassie's eyes.

Luke followed her back inside and took a pitcher of tea from the refrigerator.

"Is this okay?"

"Tea's fine," Cassie managed as she grabbed the bowl of pasta from the counter.

They brought everything out from the kitchen, including hot French bread, and Cassie settled at the table, her eyes alternating from the eagle to the view, anywhere but Luke.

"I wouldn't be able to get any work done if I lived here," Cassie said, determined to lose her nervousness with conversation.

"I know. That's why I put my desk against the back wall." Luke tore off a piece of bread and handed it to Cassie. "Actually, I do most of my real work at night." Then she smiled. "I've started painting again. Whenever the sun's out like this, I haul all my stuff down the meadow and find something interesting to paint. That's why I'm running late today. Inspiration struck this morning."

Oh, God. An artist and a vegetarian? Cassie swallowed with difficulty, washing down the bread with tea.

"You paint? Just a hobby?" Cassie choked out.

"Oh, God, yes," Luke said. "They're for my eyes only. Stress relief."

"I'd love to see some of your work," Cassie said.

Luke shook her head. "I'm what your art classes would have called naive art."

Cassie raised an eyebrow. "There's a fine line between naive art and impressionism."

"Monet was the impressionist. And trust me, mine's naive," she said, but she smiled at Cassie. "I don't mind really. My talent is architecture. That's where the pressure is. My attempt at art is solely pleasurable."

"You mean if I snooped around your house, I wouldn't find anything you've done?" Cassie asked.

Luke grinned wickedly at her. "Not unless you're nosing around my bedroom."

Cassie felt herself blush even though she tried her best not to. She shoved a fork loaded with pasta into her mouth to avoid speaking.

Luke laughed. "I've embarrassed you. Sorry," she said.

Cassie shook her head. "No. I just embarrass easily. Must be my upbringing," she said lightly.

"And did I embarrass you when I asked you to dance last night?"

Cassie looked up quickly, catching amusement in Luke's eyes. "No, you didn't. Well . . . maybe a little," she admitted.

"And your friends? Did they tease you?"

Cassie laughed. "Actually, I think Kim was quite startled by the whole thing."

"Do they know you're here today?" Luke asked.

Cassie shook her head. "I didn't say anything, no. They did tell me to invite you to a party next Saturday. That is, if I saw you."

"Really?"

"I'm sure you wouldn't be interested," she continued, wishing she had not brought it up at all. "It's a wine and cheese party and all."

"Ahh. I remember those," she said. She stared at Cassie for a second longer. "So, are you inviting me or what?"

Cassie hesitated, her eyes being held captive by Luke's. "Would you want to go?"

"Would it make you uncomfortable if I was there?"

Cassie shook her head. "No, of course not," she lied.

Luke flashed her a smile, making Cassie hate herself for wishing she had not mentioned the party. "Then I accept. It'll be nice to meet some people here. And I'll sneak in a bottle of apple cider."

"It's at . . . her name is Deborah . . . a friend of Lisa's. It's in town, I'm not really sure of the address," she stammered.

"Well, I'll get it from you sometime this week. Or I could pick you up, and we could ride together." Luke motioned to Cassie's plate with her fork. "How's the pasta?"

"Delicious," Cassie said around a mouthful. *Ride together?*

Cassie found that they had lingered over lunch when she glanced at her watch and saw that it was past three. The entire loaf of bread was gone as well as most of the salad. The conversation had alternated between Luke's work and Cassie's carvings. Luke seemed genuinely interested in Cassie's art and asked intelligent questions. Cassie found she enjoyed telling Luke about her creations. Luke had her elbows propped on the table, resting her chin in one hand, watching her as she talked.

Cassie was suddenly all too aware of the eyes upon her. She fidgeted with her napkin nervously.

"I didn't realize the time," Cassie finally said. "Let me help you clean up before I go."

"I enjoy your company," Luke said unexpectedly. "I wasn't sure that I would."

Cassie looked up, surprised. "What do you mean?"

"You seemed so reserved when I first met you. Quiet. Nervous, almost." She stood and began gathering their plates.

"I'm sorry," Cassie said. "I'm not real good with strangers, I guess."

"You're not afraid of me anymore, are you?"

Cassie avoided her eyes as she picked up the salad bowl. "No. I'm not afraid of you," she said. "Should I be?"

"Of course not. I'm harmless," Luke said. "Besides, I really hope we can be friends. Like I said, I don't really know anyone out here. Jack and Craig are the only ones I'd really call friends. Others that I know in the area are just acquaintances."

"Well, they're really all friends of Kim and Lisa. I just always seem to get invited."

"Women?"

"What do you mean?"

"The party. It'll be women? Lesbians?"

"Oh. Well, yes, mostly."

"But they're really only friends of Kim and Lisa?" Luke asked with only a hint of amusement in her eyes.

Cassie cleared her throat nervously before answering. "They're my friends, too, I guess," she allowed. Then she smiled. "They don't really know what to make of me, I suppose."

"Because you're straight and all?"

"Something like that," Cassie murmured.

She helped with the dishes despite Luke's protests and left quickly thereafter with a promise to call about the party. Luke had written her phone number on the back of one of her business cards, and Cassie shoved it in the pocket of her jeans.

As she drove home, she had the strangest feeling that her life was no longer hers to control. She was acutely aware of Luke's card in her pocket, and if she had any sense whatsoever, she would tear it to pieces and not see her again.

Chapter Thirteen

Cassie filled her wineglass for the third time, consciously aware that her eyes were searching for Luke but powerless to stop them. She rode to the party with Luke, despite her protests to herself and to Luke. Kim would jump to conclusions, she knew. Kim was already curious as to when Cassie had seen Luke to invite her. Cassie had been evasive, simply saying she had run into her and mentioned the party, but Kim's eyebrows shot to the ceiling when they walked in together. Luke apparently noticed Cassie's discomfort and politely kept her distance. Cassie spotted her several times talking with different people, seemingly carrying on conversations as if they were old friends.

Now, Cassie found Luke talking to Trish, the only person to always arrive alone at parties. She never left alone, however. Cassie couldn't see what all the fuss was about. Trish was cute enough, she supposed, with thick blond hair flowing well past her shoulders. But she wore too much makeup for Cassie's liking. Not that she had a preference when it came to women, she added firmly. Now Luke was laughing at something Trish had said and Cassie felt a jolt of jealousy as she watched Trish lightly grasp Luke's arm and gaze adoringly at her.

Cassie looked away, embarrassed for having been staring and totally dismayed for what she was feeling. *Jealous?* She gulped down her glass of wine without tasting it and reached again for the bottle. *Why should I be jealous?* She was drinking too much, she knew, but it beat being completely sober and totally aware of what she was feeling.

"I see Luke's met Trish. Shall we take bets on Trish's next conquest?" Kim walked up beside Cassie and took the bottle from her hands, her eyebrows raised.

"I haven't been the only one drinking out of it," Cassie lied.

Kim drained the last of it and set it aside. "It was nice of you to invite Luke, Cass. But I'm kinda surprised that you rode together."

"Yeah, well, I'm kinda surprised myself," Cassie said dryly.

"You may have to find your own way home though," Kim said, motioning with her head to where Luke and Trish stood talking. "Or maybe Luke will just let you take her car. I don't think anyone's ever turned Trish down before."

Cassie shrugged, as if uninterested. Trish's list of conquests was as long as her arm and if she wanted to add Luke Winston to it, it certainly was none of Cassie's business. But then, when Luke looked up and caught her eye, Cassie was unprepared for the warmth in Luke's smile. Her body went warm instantly, and she took in a deep breath, trying to still her racing pulse. *Damn the woman.*

"Then again, this may be a first," Kim murmured as she witnessed the look that passed between Luke and Cassie.

Cassie opened her mouth to protest, then closed it again. She didn't want to get into it with Kim. Not here, anyway. Instead, she swirled the wine around in her glass before taking a sip.

"I think I'll find another bottle," she said to Kim. "Excuse me."

She felt Kim's eyes on her as she walked away, but she was much more aware of the dark eyes that followed her across the room.

She found solitude in the kitchen and rested her hands on the counter for a moment. She shouldn't have come. She had no business being here, really. Just because she was Kim's friend, she was automatically invited, and she had long ago stopped feeling self-conscious about being the honorary lesbian at these gatherings. But still, she shouldn't have come. And least of all with Luke Winston.

She pushed away from the counter, and reached for the corkscrew and a bottle of merlot at the same time. This was a wine party, after all. Why not try a new bottle?

"Need some help?"

Cassie very nearly dropped the bottle, but she refused to turn around.

"No. Thanks," she said, again trying to manage the corkscrew. Warm hands closed over hers and gently took the bottle and corkscrew from her.

"Are you all right?" Luke asked as she expertly pulled the cork from the bottle.

"Of course. I'm fine," Cassie said, ignoring the way her body trembled from Luke's touch.

Luke slid the bottle along the counter to Cassie, then stood with her arms folded until Cassie dared to look up and meet her eyes. She saw concern and . . . puzzlement in Luke's eyes. Cassie forced a smile.

"I'm fine, really. I just felt like . . ."

"Drinking tonight?" Luke finished for her.

"Yes, actually." Cassie turned away and filled her glass. "You don't mind, do you?"

She knew Luke was watching her, but she wouldn't turn around.

"I don't mind. You're not driving, and I won't be the one with the headache tomorrow."

81

Cassie turned around quickly, her eyes flashing. "Look, it's none of your business." Cassie motioned to the door. "Why don't you just go back out and . . . and finish whatever you've started with Trish. Don't leave her alone for too long or she'll move on to her next victim."

Luke's eyebrows shot up and she cocked her head to the side, watching Cassie for a second before taking a step toward her. Cassie stepped back until she was pressed against the counter, her heart beating painfully in her chest at Luke's nearness. Luke stopped, but not until their thighs were nearly brushing.

Luke spoke very quietly, her eyes never leaving Cassie's. "There's not really anything to finish with Trish. She's not at all my type." Cassie's breath stopped entirely as Luke lowered her eyes to Cassie's lips. "Besides, somebody has to take you home."

Cassie's lips felt burned from Luke's stare, and her tongue came out to wet them as she waited for Luke's eyes to capture hers again.

"Don't feel obligated to me," Cassie said. "I can manage."

"I'm sure you can," Luke said and finally stepped away, giving Cassie room to breathe again. "Well, I'll go out and mingle and leave you to your drinking."

She turned to go, but Cassie called her back.

"Luke? Are you having . . . a good time?"

"Yeah. I'm having a great time," she said. "Thanks for inviting me."

When she left, Cassie pressed her fingers to her lips, feeling as if Luke had touched them with more than just her eyes. *Oh, you are such a fool!*

Why had she brought up Trish? It wasn't any of her business who Luke chose to talk to and . . . flirt with. The last thing she wanted was for Luke to think she was actually jealous of Trish. Cassie forced a laugh. As if she would be jealous!

She was thankful, actually. Maybe Luke and Trish would hit it off, maybe they would start dating. Then maybe Cassie could be satisfied with just a friendship with Luke. Maybe that would be enough.

She cursed herself when her hand trembled as she filled the wineglass again. She couldn't very well hide in the kitchen the rest of the night. She took the bottle with her and went back into the living room. She avoided Kim and Lisa, instead squeezing in next to Shelly on the sofa. She tapped her foot to the music and drank her wine, listening to the conversations around her but contributing little. She wondered where Luke was. For that matter, she wondered where Trish was, too. Perhaps they had gone somewhere quiet, where they could talk . . . or whatever.

When her bottle was empty, she accepted a glass of chardonnay from Shelly with only a nod, her head already beginning to pound. She was well past her limit and knew she must stop. She had no idea what time it was, but she was ready to go home and get into bed.

Luke materialized just as her eyes were sliding closed. She squatted down in front of her, took her nearly full glass, and Cassie let out a weary sigh.

"Had enough?" Luke asked quietly, with only a hint of teasing.

Cassie nodded. "More than enough," she whispered painfully. "And I've got to pee."

Luke grinned and stood, holding out her hand, offering it to Cassie. Cassie stared at it, wondering again how it could look so strong and soft at the same time. She finally took the offered hand and let Luke pull her to her feet. She was dizzy from her touch and the wine and would have fallen if Luke had not grabbed her with both hands. They rested lightly at Cassie's waist and Cassie gripped Luke's strong forearms hard.

"I'm not used to drinking this much," she murmured.

"It's okay," Luke assured her. "I've got you."

"Yes, that's what I'm afraid of," Cassie whispered.

Luke laughed softly, the laugh that Cassie was growing to love, and then lifted up one corner of her mouth. "Now, don't tell me you're afraid of me." She pulled Cassie closer, the hands at her waist tightening. Her breath whispered in Cassie's ear and Cassie felt faint all over again. "I told you, I'm harmless."

83

Cassie realized she was breathing hard . . . but at least she was breathing. She stepped back from Luke and managed a smile. "You're making me crazy, you know that?"

"I'm sorry. You're just so damn adorable," Luke whispered.

"Adorable, huh? I don't feel very adorable right now. I've had too much wine and I really, really have to pee."

"Okay. I'll wait here."

Luke gave her a push down the hall.

Cassie was afraid to walk, afraid she would fall. She still felt dizzy, although she wasn't sure if it was from the wine or Luke's presence. She wanted to think it was only the wine. "Maybe you could just . . . walk with me?"

Luke chuckled slightly and nodded, leading her slowly toward the hall and the bathroom.

But Kim intercepted her progress with a worried look on her face.

"Hey, Cass. Are you okay?" Kim looked first to Cassie then Luke, who had a light grip on her arm.

"I'm perfectly fine," Cassie said sharply. "Just a little dizzy."

Kim looked at Luke. "Wine?"

Luke nodded. "A lot, from what I can tell."

"I'm fine," Cassie said again. "I may have had one glass too many, but I'm just going to pee and then we're going home."

"Do you want us to take you home?" Kim asked.

"I'm fine, Kim," Cassie insisted. Then she glanced at Luke. "Unless Luke would rather stay."

"No. I'm ready to go myself. I'll take you home."

"Are you sure?" Kim asked Luke. "Because I can do it."

"Kim, go find Lisa. It's okay."

"Are you sure you don't need some help?" Kim asked as Cassie fumbled with the doorknob.

"Of course not. I can manage perfectly." She escaped inside the bathroom, now totally embarrassed. She heard Luke and Kim talking quietly outside, and strained to hear what they were saying. For some reason, Kim didn't want her going with Luke. This surprised her. She would have thought Kim would be pushing them together.

When she stepped out, Luke was alone, leaning against the far wall, waiting. Cassie closed the door and leaned against it, allowing herself to stare. There was no one watching. And God, Luke was attractive. Her hair was nicely layered against her face, thick and dark, and Cassie's fingers itched to touch it. She clenched her hands at her side, afraid of what they might do. They stood there watching each other for what seemed like an eternity, then Luke pushed off the wall and moved just in front of Cassie, a lazy smile and warm eyes relaxing Cassie more than wine ever could.

"Better?"

"Yes, thanks." With Luke so close, she lost all her inhibitions as a traitorous hand reached out to brush at Luke's hair just over her ear. "I'm sorry. If you'd rather, I can get Kim to run me home."

"I think I can manage. I've had lots of experience with drinking too much wine."

"And who took care of you?"

Luke smiled but didn't answer.

"Come on. Let's get you home."

They managed a quick exit through the kitchen door. Once outside, Luke's arm came around her shoulders, and Cassie leaned her head against Luke, if only for a moment. She closed her eyes, wanting nothing more than to snuggle against Luke's soft breasts, and this realization made her feel all the dizzier. She finally stopped walking, breathing deeply instead, trying to clear her head but unable to stop her body from trembling

"You're shivering. Are you cold?" Luke asked.

Cold? Could Luke not feel how hot her body was?

"I'm okay."

"Sure?"

"Yes." Cassie held both her hands against her flushed cheeks and shut her eyes. "I'm so sorry," she whispered.

"Don't worry about it." Luke took her arm and guided her slowly to the Lexus. "Let's get you to bed."

It was a perfectly innocent comment, Cassie knew. And had her own thoughts not been running in that same direction, she could have taken it at face value. But her stomach rolled, and she was afraid she was actually going to be sick. She swallowed hard, gulping in fresh air, wishing she had a glass of cold water. Luke's hands were warm on her skin as she helped her inside and Cassie leaned against the cool leather and closed her eyes. She felt like hell. She would feel worse tomorrow, she knew. And God, she was embarrassed. What must Luke think of her?

"Are you okay?"

Cassie nodded and slowly rolled her head to face Luke, finding concerned eyes looking back at her.

"Actually, I feel like crap," Cassie admitted as her eyes slid shut.

She heard Luke chuckle and managed a small smile of her own. It faded quickly when a warm hand cupped her cheek. It took all her strength not to rub against that hand, to move her lips over the soft palm. She heard a low moan and was mortified when she realized it had come from her. That same hand slipped behind her neck and strong fingers rubbed gently, relaxing her.

She leaned her head forward, giving Luke better access and she was unable to stop another low moan from escaping. She didn't care. The impromptu massage felt too good. The throbbing in her head subsided somewhat and she felt herself drifting, her last conscious thought that she wanted to lay her head down in Luke's lap and sleep.

A nudging of her arm woke her, but her eyes refused to open, and she snuggled closer against the warmth, her face touching warm skin.

"Come on, Cassie," a voice penetrated the haze in her brain. "As much as I'm enjoying this, you'd be more comfortable in bed."

Cassie groaned and tried to lift her head. "No. This is fine, really," she murmured. Then a husky laugh in her ear brought her around, and she opened her eyes, only to find her face snuggled securely in Luke's neck.

She pulled back, Luke's arm sliding off her shoulder, and she sat back in her own seat. How had she managed to cross the console and end up practically in Luke's lap? Her eyes widened and she felt a deep blush creep up her face.

"I'm so sorry," she whispered.

Luke laughed again. "Please don't be sorry. It was rather nice."

Cassie blushed a deeper red and turned away, trying to open her door.

"Don't stand up just yet," Luke was saying, but Cassie was already swinging her legs out. She would have fallen to the ground if Luke hadn't run around the Lexus to catch her.

"I speak from experience," Luke said. She pressed Cassie against the trunk, holding her there, and Cassie was aware of every place their bodies touched. "I don't ever . . . do this," she said. Her thighs burned where Luke pressed against them, and she shut her eyes against the fire. "I hardly drink more than a glass or two at a time."

"Then why tonight?"

Luke's voice was barely a whisper, her mouth just inches away, and Cassie couldn't pull her eyes away from Luke's lips.

Cassie shook her head. Her body seemed to have a life of its own, and she felt it pull away from her and pulse toward Luke. "Please, I'm just having a really difficult time . . . with some issues right now," she whispered. She finally raised her eyes to Luke's. "You confuse me."

"Oh, no. *You* confuse *me*," Luke countered.

"I confuse myself," Cassie admitted.

They were standing too close together, and Cassie knew they should move. She was aware of her uneven breathing, her rapidly beating heart. It was only then she noticed the pulse throbbing in Luke's neck and her own quickly drawn breath. It would be so easy, Cassie thought. Luke's lips were there, so close and inviting and all Cassie had to do was . . .

"Cassie?"

Cassie pulled herself out of her daze, daring to meet Luke's eyes. It was a mistake. Eyes darkened with desire looked back at her. She lost herself in those eyes. In that one moment, she knew that if Luke had taken her hand and led her inside, she would have been powerless to resist. Their eyes locked, both seemingly searching for answers to questions not yet asked. Then Luke mercifully moved away from her, breaking the spell.

"Where's your key?"

"Pocket," Cassie said, and then she laughed when Luke grinned mischievously.

"Oh, well, allow me to get it," Luke teased, reaching for her.

Cassie playfully slapped her hand and produced the key.

In the short walk to the front door, Cassie's head began to pound again, and she handed Luke the key while she leaned against the wall. She watched Luke in the moonlight as she struggled to fit the key in the lock. She wanted to touch her, she realized. She wanted to touch her face, her hair. Cassie had never been an overly affectionate person, never had the desire to be physically close to people. That was another wall Luke had managed to take down, she thought.

"I'll just see you in."

Luke stepped aside and Cassie walked past, not stopping until she walked into her bedroom and lay down sideways on the bed. She should at least see Luke out, thank her, but Cassie was suddenly too tired to take another step.

"Can I do anything?"

"Make the bed stop spinning," Cassie whispered. She heard Luke chuckle, then felt her weight as she sat down on the bed beside her. Cassie rolled her head toward her slowly. "Luke, why did you start drinking?"

Luke shrugged. "A woman. What else?"

"What do you mean?" Cassie asked, trying to ignore the warm hands that brushed the hair away from her forehead.

"She was married. We were having an affair. She was going to leave her husband," Luke explained. "After a year, I started drinking a little bit more. After two years, I was drinking a lot. And as we started on three, I was drinking all day long," she said quietly.

"But she didn't leave her husband?" Cassie asked softly.

Luke shook her head. "No. I finally realized that she had no intention of leaving him, and I was slowly killing myself. Physically, I felt like crap. Professionally, I was close to losing my job." She looked away for a moment, staring off. "She was . . . playing with me, I guess. Experimenting," Luke said, almost to herself. She turned back to Cassie. "I ended things with her, went home and poured out all the booze in the house and spent a couple of weeks at a health club soaking up carrot juice and fresh fruit," she said. Then she smiled. "I sort of became a health nut. Beat drinking," she shrugged. "Dove into my work with both feet, finally starting my own company. I guess I can thank her for that."

"And the woman?" Cassie asked.

"Still married, I suppose," Luke said.

"Are you still in love with her?"

Luke smiled. "No. Not even a little bit," she said. "That was a long time ago."

"And why don't you have someone now?"

"Because that one just about killed me," Luke said.

Cassie let her eyes slide shut. "Well, she was no good for you," she whispered. She felt Luke get off the bed, and she tried to open her eyes.

"I'll get you some aspirin."

"And water," Cassie murmured.

"And water," Luke agreed. "Why don't you get out of these clothes? I'll bring you a wet cloth for your forehead."

Cassie rolled her head toward Luke again and forced her eyes open. "Luke? Thank you. I was rude to you earlier tonight, in the kitchen. I'm sorry."

"And why was that?"

"Trish," Cassie whispered. "I don't like her for you. Don't get involved with her. She's not a nice person. And you are." She looked up at Luke then. "Have I told you that I think your eyes are beautiful?"

"No, you haven't."

Luke's low chuckle sent shivers through her, but she continued anyway. "They are beautiful. They're not always so dark, though. Sometimes they're almost golden."

She saw Luke smile at her, and she smiled back before closing her eyes.

"Why Trish?" Luke asked. "Why don't you like her?"

Cassie just shook her head. "Never mind," she whispered. "I just meant to tell you about your eyes."

"You've had way too much to drink," Luke stated unnecessarily. "You know, there's this rule about straight women complimenting lesbians. It could be very dangerous."

"I thought it was the other way around," Cassie whispered, and she felt herself drifting off to sleep. "I'm not really straight, you know." Cassie didn't know if she had spoken the words or not. As her eyes shut firmly, she prayed she had only thought them.

Dream hands came to her, unbuttoning her jeans and pulling them down. She helped them, wanting those dream hands upon her. Then they came to her blouse, and she waited patiently as they unbuttoned it slowly. Hurry, she was thinking, but the dream hands took their time. She grabbed them once, entwining their fingers before pulling the dream hands to her breasts, but they resisted and she whimpered, rolling toward the dream hands, searching for them again but they left her, left her body on fire and wanting.

Then she sighed as the dream hands gently touched her face and she felt the briefest caress as dream lips brushed her cheek, then her own lips. She turned toward them, seeking, but they were gone.

Chapter Fourteen

Cassie rolled her head very gingerly to the side and pried one eye open, trying to see the clock. Only six. She groaned. She was a habitual early riser, and her internal clock had not taken a break.

"Oh, Christ," she whispered. She saw the empty water glass and thought that at some point during the night, she remembered swallowing the two aspirins.

She stretched out her legs and groaned again. Through the pounding in her head she realized that she was naked. She sat up on one elbow and frowned. She didn't remember getting undressed. At least, not alone. She had a vague memory of hands on her, pulling her jeans down, but that had been a dream. Surely, just a dream.

She lay back down, trying to remember what had happened. Luke had been here, she had taken her home . . . yes, she had come into her bedroom. She was going to get her aspirin and water. Cassie saw her clothes folded neatly in the chair and her mouth dropped open.

"Oh, dear Lord," she murmured. What had happened last night? She touched her lips with her fingers, then touched her cheek. She had a vague memory of lips brushing hers, of hands touching her, but . . . she had been dreaming. *Surely.*

After a silent count to three, she sat up, her head feeling like a bass drum during a very long parade. She grabbed her head with both hands and groaned.

"Okay, I swear," she whispered. "I'll never drink again." She stood on shaky legs, her head about to explode, and made her way to the bathroom. If she could just get through this day, she would be all right. And on the heels of that, *if I could just remember what happened last night . . .*

Chapter Fifteen

"Look, correct me if I'm wrong here, but I get the feeling that you and Luke are more than just casual acquaintances," Kim told her as she paced behind the beaver.

Cassie tried to ignore her. She got down on her knees and brushed off the dust and wood chips from the carving.

"Why are you not answering me?"

Cassie sat back on her heels and placed her hands on her hips. "What do you want me to say?"

"You claim to barely know her, yet she seeks you out at the bar and asks you to dance. Then, you show up together at the party. You get drunk on your ass, and she takes you home, and you have nothing to say?" Kim faced her with her own hands on her hips. "Give me a break. I wasn't born yesterday. I've seen her type."

"Her type?"

"Yes. Her type! My God, look at her! She's like the high school quarterback, and you're the last virgin in school." Kim bent down and looked Cassie in the eye, her tone deadly serious. "She's trying to win the toaster oven."

Cassie burst out laughing, falling down on the floor as she laughed. "You're incredible," she gasped. "I don't think Luke Winston is the type to go around converting women!"

"Why are you laughing? I'm completely serious!"

Cassie sat and folded her legs and wiped at the smile on her face. "I thought you'd be happy that some woman was paying me attention. After all, you're convinced I'm a lesbian. It wouldn't really be converting then, would it?"

"She's not what I had in mind," Kim said. "She's too . . . just too much."

"Too what? Too attractive?"

"No. Yes. She's . . . Cassie, just look at her. She could have any woman she wanted, any time she wanted. I'm sure she's been around the block a time or two."

Cassie laughed again. "Kim, Luke Winston is not interested in me. Nor I her," she added, hoping she sounded convincing.

Kim stared at her, and it was her turn to laugh. "You surely aren't going to tell me that I imagined those looks between you and Luke?"

Cassie's smile vanished and her chin rose. "I most certainly am," she said. "We're only friends and hardly that," she insisted. "I'm sorry if you think otherwise."

"Honey, I know her type," Kim said again gently. "I worry about you. I don't want her to take advantage of you."

Cassie took Kim's hand and brought it to her lips. "I love you, Kim. You're the best. But don't worry about me. I can handle this." She waved one hand above her head. "Whatever *this* is," she said. "Luke is a really nice person, and I do like her a lot. But as a friend," she insisted.

Kim looked at her silently for a long moment. "If you need to talk . . ."

"I know. You'd be the first."

"Okay." Kim stood and walked away, feigning interest in a small nuthatch that Cassie had recently finished. "So, one more week until the fair. You'll be ready?"

Cassie nodded with relief. Work, she could talk about.

After Kim left, Cassie spent the afternoon cleaning up her workroom. She arranged all her tools again, which would soon be scattered about, but for the moment looked neat. She even brought the vacuum out and cleaned in all the corners. Her carvings were all ready, save two. She only had to box them up for the move to the fairgrounds. She piddled in the workroom, trying not to think about Luke Winston and Kim's words to her. She actually was feeling much better about the whole thing. It had been four days since the party, and she had only spoken to Luke once, briefly, the day after.

Absently, she picked up a delicate fawn, admitting to herself that she had been intentionally rude to Luke on the phone. In truth, she had been totally embarrassed and didn't have a clue as to what to say to Luke. Of course, it would help if she could actually remember everything that had happened that night. She only had her imagination and a faintly remembered dream to rely on. Both of which she would rather forget. *Hands.* Always hands coming to her, touching her. Luke's hands. But it was just a dream, she told herself. She didn't want to think about how she managed to wake up naked.

But now, she needed to apologize. Luke had done nothing wrong, and she certainly didn't deserve to be treated as if she had. And Cassie felt like a total ass for being short with her on the phone.

She reached for the phone beside her workbench, one hand still clutching the fawn and dialed Luke's number from memory. It was answered on the second ring.

"It's me . . . Cassie."

There was only a brief moment of silence before Luke spoke.

"Hey. I was hoping you'd call."

Cassie smiled. She should have known Luke wouldn't be mad, and she wished she'd called sooner.

"I need . . . I need to apologize," Cassie said. "I never meant to
. . ."

"No. You don't need to apologize. Forget about it," Luke said.
"I should have waited to call, I was just making sure you were
okay."

"I know you were. I appreciate it. But still, I was rude, and I had
no right to be."

"Okay. You've apologized. I accept."

Cassie smiled again. She had missed Luke, she realized. And
she felt comfortable enough to ask her the question that had been
gnawing at her for the last few days.

"Luke, I didn't . . . you didn't . . . I mean, I was naked when I
woke up," she said quietly. She had to know what had happened,
no matter how embarrassed this was making her. She couldn't
stand not knowing any longer. But Luke's low chuckle sent chills
over her body.

"You don't remember a thing, do you?"

"Not much, no," Cassie admitted.

"You mean, even when you ravished me by the front door?"

"Luke! Please . . ."

Luke laughed again. "Don't worry. You were quite the lady . . .
and I was a perfect gentleman," she said.

Cassie sighed with relief. "I thought . . . well I was worried . . ."

"That I had taken advantage of you?"

"No! Of course not," Cassie said. Is that what she thought? "I
was just hoping that I wasn't . . . well, I never act like that. I'm sorry
you had to witness it."

"It's okay. Really. And I'm glad you called. I was actually going
to call you. If you don't already have plans, I was hoping you'd
come over for dinner Saturday evening."

"Dinner?"

"Yes. You know, cook and eat," Luke said with just a hint of
teasing in her voice.

Cassie smiled, knowing she was crazy to even consider it but also knowing she would agree. She seemed to be powerless when it came to Luke.

"I don't have plans."

"So . . . that means you accept?"

"I accept," Cassie said.

"Great. Come about six, and I'll put you to work in the kitchen."

When they hung up, Cassie still stood by her workbench with the fawn resting lightly in her hand. It was crazy, she knew. The one person who might be able to break down her carefully constructed walls, and she was going to her willingly. That's a laugh, she thought. What walls? There didn't seem to be any walls where Luke was concerned. She tried to tell herself it was just the friendship she craved, but her body told her something else entirely.

Chapter Sixteen

As Cassie drove down the long drive to Luke's house, she wished she had worn something a little more casual. She looked like . . . well, like she was going on a date. Her usual jeans had been replaced with soft, khaki pants and the comfortable T-shirt she had started with lay crumpled on her bed. Instead, a crisply ironed blouse was neatly tucked inside and she chided herself for being so foolish. It wasn't a date. It was just dinner with a new friend. *Right?* She met her reflection in the mirror, her eyes refusing to lie to her. She wanted it to be a date, she realized.

"Great," she murmured. "Wanna start dating? Sure. Let's not start with someone safe. Let's start with Luke Winston!"

She stood at the door for a minute, rubbing her damp palms on her slacks before knocking. She felt as nervous as a schoolgirl, and she almost wished she hadn't brought the fawn. But Luke wasn't like most people. You couldn't just grab a bottle of wine. And flowers would be just . . . too much. *Flowers? What are you thinking?*

She raised her hand to knock just as the door opened. She stood face to face with Luke for the first time in a week, and she wasn't prepared for the slow roll of her stomach when Luke gave her that lazy smile of hers.

"I thought I heard you." Luke stepped back, her eyes traveling slowly over Cassie. "You look great."

Cassie blushed, and glanced down at her slacks, again wishing she'd left her jeans on. Luke's own faded jeans were baggy and hung low on her hips.

Luke motioned with her head. "Come in. It's good to see you again."

Cassie stepped inside, the fawn still clutched in her hand, offering her a bit of comfort. She finally lifted her hand and offered it to Luke.

"I wanted you to have this," she said, her voice thick.

"It's the fawn," Luke said quietly. "You didn't have to do that."

"I know. But I knew you liked it."

"I love it. It's so . . . delicate, fragile almost. It's beautiful." Luke placed it on the mantle over the stone fireplace then turned to face Cassie. "Thank you. I'll treasure it."

Cassie nodded, then shoved nervous hands into her pockets. "Well, I didn't want to come empty-handed, and I couldn't very well hand you a bottle of wine."

"Cassie," Luke smiled, and walked up and grasped her arms with both hands. "Relax, will you."

Cassie tried to laugh, but her skin burned where Luke's hands still rested. "Is it that obvious?"

"Yeah," Luke nodded. "It is." She finally released her, and Cassie was able to breathe again. "Are you embarrassed about the other night?"

"Yes. I'm terribly embarrassed," Cassie admitted. "That was just so . . . not me," she said. "And I feel terrible, with you having to . . . take me home."

"I've been there many times." Then she smiled, and Cassie relaxed a little. "Just don't make a habit of it."

"No. Not ever again." Cassie followed Luke into the kitchen, her eyes following the sway of Luke's hips as she walked.

"Good. Now, maybe you could help me with the egg rolls."

Luke stopped, turned and caught Cassie staring. Cassie rolled her eyes to the heavens, secretly hoping to be swallowed up, but thankfully, Luke made no comment.

Cassie finally cleared her throat and attempted to speak. "You make your own egg rolls?"

"Yeah. You like Chinese, don't you?"

"Love it."

Cassie pushed her sleeves to her elbows, watching as Luke brought out a platter of egg rolls ready to fry. Cassie was in charge of them, but she watched in amazement as Luke fried rice in one pan and stir-fried vegetables in another and had some sort of sweet and sour tofu concoction going in a third without so much as one mishap.

"Wow!" Cassie exclaimed. "You're good."

Luke raised her eyebrows and grinned. "Yep. I know my way around a kitchen," she said good-naturedly, and went back to her pans.

Soon, the smells of Chinese food filled the entire house, and Cassie's earlier discomfort had vanished, replaced by the warm, pleasant feeling you got simply by cooking a meal with a friend. Cassie found herself singing along with the Indigo Girls as she and Luke shared the kitchen, side-stepping each other with ease. They each made heaping plates and carried them to the new table Luke had brought in.

"I like it," Cassie said of the table. "Not too big. It won't get in the way."

Luke shrugged, then nodded in agreement. "Well, I thought it would be uncivilized if I didn't have one." She sat down, then stood just as quickly. "Wait, I forgot the candles." She hurried back to the kitchen and brought out two brass candleholders, then rushed back into the kitchen for matches.

Cassie watched her with a small smile, thinking how pleasant the evening had been so far. When Cassie cooked, she didn't want anyone else in her kitchen, but Luke had made her feel welcome, and they had shared the space with quiet companionship, Luke occasionally shoving a spoon in her mouth for a taste test.

"There," Luke said as she stood back to survey the table. "Perfect."

Cassie took her first bite of the egg roll and groaned. "God, this is good," she said around a mouthful.

"Mmmm," Luke agreed. "My mother's . . . well, really Aunt Susan's recipe. We used to all get together and chop veggies for what seemed like hours, then we had an assembly line to roll them." She laughed. "I bet we used to make hundreds of them at a time."

"In the commune?" Cassie asked.

"Yeah. And Susan could really cook. Back in those days, you couldn't just go to a bookstore and find vegetarian cookbooks. Lots of trial and error," she said. "But, I got my love of cooking there. She taught all of us, really."

"So you've always been a vegetarian? I mean, even when you were a kid?"

"Pretty much," Luke said. "I wasn't even a year old when my mother moved us there."

"And your Aunt Susan? Do you ever see her?"

"Not that often," Luke said. "She and Darlene still live in Berkeley though."

"I can't believe they're still together," Cassie said.

Luke nodded. "They had a breakup about fifteen years ago or so. Middle-age crisis for both of them, Susan likes to say. They're both almost sixty, I guess."

"Do you see your mother?"

"I see her some, yes. We talk on the phone more, though," Luke said.

Cassie could feel Luke watching her, and she looked up. "What?"

"Is this time of year hard for you?" Luke asked quietly.

"What do you mean?"

"Well, it's almost November," she said. "Thanksgiving, then Christmas. Do you miss that family thing?"

Cassie smiled. "No. Not at all. It's hard to miss what you've never had," she said. "I was too young to remember a Christmas with my mother. Just vague memories, really. And my father, well, he was more interested in his Christmas sermon than Santa and presents and all that," she said.

"Christmas was a great time when I was growing up," Luke said. "Just one big extended family. But the last few years, I've just enjoyed being alone or with good friends. My mother and Neal still get together with some of the old gang, but I'm just so far removed from that now," she said.

"I usually have dinner with Kim and Lisa," Cassie said. "They still put up a tree, but I haven't had one in years."

"I always put up a tree, no matter what," Luke told her. "I have to have something to remind me of the time of year. And it makes me feel good," she continued. "I like to turn off all the lights, put a few candles out and just have the Christmas tree lights on and music. I could sit for hours," she said softly. "Just sitting. And thinking."

"I get . . . I get depressed around Christmas," Cassie finally admitted. "I always put on this brave front, especially in front of Kim, but when I get home, it just hits," she said quietly. "I think about my mother and wonder who she is, where she is. I think about my life, and I feel so terribly alone." She leaned her elbows on the table and tried to smile. "I'm sorry. I'm not usually so sentimental."

Luke reached across the table and took her hand, and Cassie let her fingers entwine with Luke's. She had a brief flash of dream hands, and she knew that they were Luke's.

"I'm sorry I brought it up," Luke said gently. "You've got good friends, Cassie. That can be better than family sometimes."

"I know." Cassie allowed herself to squeeze Luke's hand before pulling away. "But how did we get off on this conversation?"

102

"My fault," Luke said. She waved her fork at Cassie. "How's the meal?"

"You're a fabulous cook, but I'm sure you've been told that before."

Luke laughed and Cassie looked up and caught her eyes, thinking again what a great laugh she had.

"A couple of times, but they were just flirting with me," she said. "What's your excuse?"

Cassie felt herself blush, and she pulled her eyes away. "I was starving, not flirting," she managed. "And I like to eat."

"And I like to tease," Luke said. "So relax, will you?"

Cassie helped with the dishes, then went out on the patio while Luke made coffee. She ran her hands slowly over the eagle, so glad that he was here and not at some stranger's house. But Luke had been a stranger once. Now, they were . . . friends. Yes, they were friends. Cassie felt comfortable around her. Well, she would feel a lot more comfortable if her pulse didn't race so when Luke looked at her with those dark eyes, but still, she was comfortable around her. And it had been awhile since she had made a new friend.

"Do you miss him?"

Cassie turned in the darkness, startled to find Luke standing just behind her.

"I think about him some, always wondering where he was. I'm really glad you have him," she said sincerely.

Luke stood with her hands in her pockets, looking past Cassie to the eagle. "Me, too."

Cassie allowed Luke to catch her eyes, but just for a moment. She was having trouble breathing, and she pulled them away, wishing they weren't standing alone out here in the dark.

As if sensing her discomfort, Luke motioned back inside. "Coffee's ready."

Cassie settled on the floor in front of the fireplace. It was too pleasant a night for a fire, so Luke brought candles and placed them in front of the screen instead. Luke sat on the floor, too, her back leaning against the stone of the fireplace, and Cassie watched her as she poured their coffee, wondering again why she felt so drawn to this woman.

"Cream only, right?"

"Please."

The coffee had a light vanilla flavor to it, and Cassie nodded her approval. Then she watched, again horrified as Luke added not one but two spoonfuls of sugar to the perfectly good coffee. She grimaced as Luke took a sip.

"What?" Luke asked and Cassie realized she had been staring.

"Nothing. I just . . . nothing." She sipped her own cup quietly, painfully aware of the silence surrounding them. Then Luke picked up a remote and soft piano music replaced the silence.

"I've got other CDs if this isn't to your liking," Luke offered.

"No, this is fine." Cassie was suddenly very aware of the intimate setting—candles and music—and wondered why panic had not yet set in. But she felt completely at ease. It was almost as if in a dream, she realized.

"Do you remember the day we met?" Luke asked quietly.

Cassie smiled. "Yes. At the festival."

"You looked so familiar to me. I was certain that we had met before," she said. "Then I remembered. The night of the party, I looked up, and you were watching me."

Her voice was quiet, soft, and Cassie was entranced, wondering where this was leading.

"Just like that day on the sidewalk. I thought then that you had the most beautiful blue eyes I had ever seen."

Cassie trembled and struggled to bring her coffee cup to her lips without spilling any. She had hoped, really hoped, that Luke would not remember that day. Cassie had been staring, yes. And when their eyes met that day, it was as if Luke were looking into her very soul.

"I've embarrassed you yet again," Luke said. "I'm sorry."

"No." Cassie made herself look at Luke, and she ignored the flame that ignited in her body. "I was with Kim and Lisa. They were commenting on how attractive you were." She smiled at Luke. "And I was . . . looking, too," she admitted.

"And when I caught you looking . . ."

"I was embarrassed," Cassie finished for her. After all, she was supposedly straight. What business did she have staring at another woman the way she had been? What business did she have to be sitting here right now with that very same woman?

"Why were you looking at me like that?" Luke asked and she held Cassie's eyes captive until she answered.

"I thought . . . I thought you were . . . *beautiful*." Cassie's voice was barely a whisper. There. She had admitted it. And she apparently surprised Luke with her admission. Luke cocked her head to the side and raised one eyebrow, the candlelight now reflecting golden in her dark eyes. And as those eyes stared into hers, Cassie felt the fire spread quickly through her body, yet she shivered from the heat of it.

"Your eyes . . . turn golden . . . sometimes," Cassie whispered before she could stop herself, and she was unable to pull her eyes from the golden flames.

"You told me that before."

It was Cassie's turn to stare, her eyebrows furrowed, questioning.

"When I took you home that night," Luke explained.

"I don't remember," Cassie said. Then she leaned forward and rested her arms on her knees. "I woke up . . . naked," she said quietly, and she turned again to meet Luke's eyes. "I don't remember getting undressed."

"You don't?"

"No. Did you . . . undress me?" she finally dared to ask.

A slow smile appeared on Luke's face and she nodded. "But I kept my eyes closed the whole time. Promise."

Cassie remembered the dream, hands unbuttoning her jeans, her own hands helping to push them down. Hands unbuttoning her blouse, hands that she reached for, hands that she wanted to touch her. She stared at Luke now, her mouth opening slightly as she realized that it had not really been a dream at all.

"It wasn't a dream," Cassie murmured.

Luke stared at her for so long, Cassie thought she would melt from the fire inside of her. When Luke reached out a hand to cup her face, Cassie didn't pull away. She closed her eyes and, against her will, turned her lips into the soft palm, ignoring the warning bells sounding in her mind.

When Cassie opened her eyes again, Luke was there, mere inches away.

"I want . . . to kiss you," Luke whispered.

"Yes," Cassie breathed. "I want you to."

Cassie could not have said no, and she watched in fascination as Luke's mouth came toward her. But still, she was not prepared for the feel of Luke's lips against her own. She shuddered. She didn't know what she had expected, but she felt totally out of control as strange sensations traveled through her body. She could feel herself trembling, and she could not breathe. Her body felt hot, so hot, and when Luke cupped her face with both hands and brought soft lips to Cassie's, Cassie felt her skin melting away. She heard a low moan and realized that it had come from her own lips.

Luke pulled back, but Cassie's mouth still burned from her gentle kiss. When Cassie looked into Luke's eyes, she saw that Luke wanted much more than just the brief kiss they had shared. With those soft lips so close to her own, Cassie realized that she, too, wanted more. Before she could stop herself, she pulled Luke to her, her lips seeking, meeting Luke's hungry mouth.

And then she was falling, falling away, and she grabbed Luke and held on. Her fingers dug into strong arms, and she felt the soft cushion of carpet beneath her back, then Luke's lips were on hers again. At the gentle push of tongue, her mouth opened fully, the groan starting low in her throat, and she cried out softly when she felt Luke's tongue brush against her own. For one insane moment, she knew what she wanted, what she needed, and she let herself slip a little farther into the whirlwind of passion that Luke had created. Her mouth opened to Luke, and she kissed her back, her own tongue slipping shyly into Luke's warm mouth, her groan mingling with Luke's as they let their passion carry them, if only for a moment.

But the warning bells clamored to be heard and with great difficulty Cassie pulled away from Luke, knowing she was extremely close to losing complete control. Her chest heaved as if she'd been running, and Luke, too, was having a difficult time catching her breath.

The tears came without warning, and Cassie covered her mouth, her insides feeling like they would burst at any moment.

"Shhh, no . . . I'm so sorry," Luke whispered urgently. She pulled Cassie into a sitting position and wrapped both arms around her. Cassie's tears turned to sobs and she buried her face against Luke's neck, letting her tears fall as they may.

"Please don't cry," Luke urged. "I'm so sorry, Cass."

Cassie tried to stop. She squeezed her eyes shut and took deep breaths, but the explosion of emotion was too much. It was as if a dam had broken and she again buried her head, feeling Luke's hands in her hair as she tried to calm her.

"Shhh, it's okay," Luke murmured. "It won't happen again. I promise."

Cassie shook her head. Luke thought it was her fault, thought Cassie was crying because she'd kissed her. How could she explain her tears to Luke when she could barely understand them herself?

"I'm sorry," she finally whispered, her voice hoarse.

When she raised her head, Luke brushed lightly at the remaining tears, her eyes cloudy with worry.

"No, I'm the one who should apologize, Cassie. I never should have . . ."

"You don't understand," Cassie said, stopping Luke's apology with a soft finger on her lips. "I've lied to myself for so long, told myself that I could never have feelings for a woman." Cassie swallowed hard and reached out a hand that trembled only slightly as she touched Luke's soft face. "It was just too much," she said quietly. "I felt like I was going to explode," she admitted.

"I still shouldn't have pushed you," Luke insisted.

A small smile touched Cassie's lips. "I wanted you to kiss me."

Luke entwined her fingers with Cassie's, then brought Cassie's hand to her lips.

"So . . . you want to . . . pretend this never happened?" Luke asked, her eyes searching Cassie's. "Or maybe . . . see where it goes?" she asked shyly, finally looking away.

Cassie shook her head. "From the moment I saw you on that sidewalk, I knew if I was to get to know you, you'd be the one that could break down all the walls I've built around myself. I don't want to pretend it didn't happen," she said. "But where it'll take us, I don't know. It's taken me years to work up to a kiss."

Luke smiled and nodded her understanding.

"It's been a very long time since I've wanted to get to know someone, since I've wanted to be around someone," Luke said. "I don't want to let this pass us by, Cass. I can be as patient as you need me to be."

"You may regret those words," Cassie murmured.

"No, I won't."

Luke pulled her gently into her arms, and they sat together with their backs against the sofa and watched the candles flicker as the piano music played on around them. Luke was apparently content just having Cassie near, so Cassie settled deeper into her embrace, her mind still filled with a hundred questions. But right now, she didn't want to think. She just wanted this . . . closeness, something she'd never had with anyone.

Later, as Cassie settled into her own bed, alone, she allowed her thoughts to return to the evening. Panic had set in as she drove home, and she'd nearly convinced herself that she shouldn't see Luke anymore, that she should go back to her safe, solitary, lonely life. Luke had left it up her, simply telling Cassie to call her when she wanted to talk.

She really didn't know why she was shocked by what had occurred. Hadn't she known this would happen? Hadn't she felt desire from the moment she looked at Luke that day on the sidewalk? Hadn't she known that if anyone were to bring her around, it would be Luke?

She rolled over and faced the wall, willing the desire to go away. She didn't need it, she told herself. She was perfectly happy with her life the way it was. Safe and boring and lonely. She squeezed her eyes closed and tried to shut out her father's booming voice.

"Living here with them, thick as thieves. You'd think you're one of them, the way you flock to them. It's unnatural, I tell you!"

Chapter Seventeen

Cassie smiled at the family as they looked over her pieces, then scowled at the little boy as he picked up a squirrel and shoved it at his sister.

"Stevie, stop that," the mother said. She threw a glance at Cassie. "I'm sorry. He knows better," she apologized.

Sure he does, Cassie thought, as she reached for the deer he had just picked up. "They're breakable, Stevie," she muttered under her breath.

She was irritable, she knew. She shouldn't be. The fair was going well, and there wasn't a cloud in the sky. People packed the fairgrounds and she knew she would be nearly out of her small carvings by the end of the weekend. That is, if this brat didn't break them first.

"Stevie! Put it down," the mother said. She turned to her husband with pleading eyes. "Please take him somewhere. I really want to look at these carvings." She turned to Cassie again. "Sorry. He has abundant energy today," she apologized again.

And I hope you have him on some sort of medication, Cassie thought. But she smiled sweetly. "Look all you want," she said.

"These are how much?"

"The smaller ones are seventy-five. The larger ones go up to one twenty-five."

"How much are the big ones?" she asked, pointing to the giant carvings.

Cassie followed her eyes to the eagle. "They vary. Anywhere from two to four thousand. Except the seal and the beaver. They are both five."

"Oh, my," she said. "Out of my range." She picked up the deer Stevie had been holding and turned it in her hands. "Seventy-five is reasonable," she murmured.

"There you are!"

Cassie turned at the sound of the unfamiliar voice and frowned.

"Cassandra Parker, right?"

"Yes," Cassie nodded. She guessed him to be in his late fifties, although his skin was nearly wrinkle-free. Perhaps it was his shiny bald head that aged him, she thought, but she didn't have a clue as to who he was.

He smiled and stuck out his hand. "I'm Weldon Arnold. A dear friend of mine has a couple of your carvings. You do exquisite work, and I'm in the market," he said quickly, his eyes darting to her carvings.

Cassie let her hand fall after Weldon Arnold had given it a gentle squeeze. She motioned to the wood carvings behind her. "You're welcome to come back here for a closer look," she offered.

"Oh, my," he said, his hand going to his throat. "Luke said you did much more than eagles."

Luke? Just the name sent shivers across her skin, and she folded her arms at her sides. One week. One week since Luke had kissed her, and she could still feel her, taste her as if it were only minutes ago. She closed her eyes tightly for a moment, trying in vain to block out the images that she knew would come. Butterflies slammed against the walls of her stomach, and she took a deep breath, swallowing hard before turning back to the woman holding her deer.

"Sorry," Cassie apologized. "Do you like it?"

"Yes. I think I want this one. Checks okay?"

"Of course," Cassie said.

"Ms. Parker?"

Cassie turned back to Weldon Arnold. "Yes?"

"I really like the beaver for the patio. You even have flakes of wood chips here where he's chewed the log," he said. "It will make a great conversation piece. Will it weather?"

"Yes, it's been finished for the outdoors," Cassie said. "Most of the larger ones have, except the smaller eagle there."

"Great, great," he murmured. "I love it." He turned back to the eagle.

Cassie took the woman's check and hurriedly wrapped the deer. A seventy-five dollar sale could not compare to the beaver. "Thanks," she said. "And tell Stevie to be careful with it," she added.

She turned back to Weldon Arnold as he studied one of the eagles. It was similar to the one that Luke bought that first day, just smaller, and she could tell Weldon wanted it very badly.

"You like the eagle?" she coaxed.

"I offered Luke fifteen thousand for the one she has on her patio, the eagle in flight," he said.

Cassie's mouth dropped open. *Fifteen?*

"She wouldn't even consider it," he said. "I don't suppose you have another like that?"

Cassie shook her head. "No. That was definitely one of a kind."

He smiled. "Oh, well. I probably shouldn't, but I can't leave this beauty behind. I'll take them both," he said.

"Both?" Cassie asked, and he laughed at her shocked expression.

"Yes, both. You don't have a limit, do you?" he asked lightly.

"Of course not. The eagle won't weather," she explained. "I can put a finish on for you if you plan to keep it outdoors."

"Thank you but that won't be necessary. I've got a spot for her by the fireplace."

She smiled broadly at him, trying to keep the excitement from her voice. The two pieces totaled nine thousand dollars. "Well, Mr. Arnold, you've made two excellent choices."

"I'll get them both tomorrow before I leave. Is that okay?"

"Of course. You live in the city?" Cassie asked. She accepted his platinum credit card with only slightly shaking hands.

"Oh, no. Out on Russian River. We've just moved into a log home that Luke Winston built. But we're from the city, and this is our first county fair," he explained.

This must be the client Luke was telling her about that first day. "Well, I hope you're enjoying it," Cassie said as she waited for his receipt to print.

"Very much. My partner and I just recently retired, and we were so ready to get out of the city." He rubbed his neatly trimmed mustache then flicked his eyes again to her carvings. "Could I have some of your business cards? If you don't mind, I have a good friend up at Lake Tahoe that has a shop. Your eagles would go over so well up there."

Cassie's breath caught, but she kept calm. "Woodcarvings in the mountains are everywhere. I doubt this would be anything special."

Weldon Arnold dismissed her comment with a wave of his hand. "Chainsaw art, if anything. A dime a dozen, you're right. But this, hand carved from driftwood, your detail is spectacular," he said, running his fingers lightly over the eagle's head.

"You have a good eye," Cassie commented. "Were you in the business?"

He smiled. "We owned an art gallery, yes. And I know good work when I see it. How is it you've been hiding away out here in the country?"

Cassie shrugged, remembering her struggles of trying to find shops in the city that would carry her carvings. Of course, back then, she seldom had the time to devote to her large carvings.

"I haven't been doing this that long," she explained. "The giant carvings, only about five years now, but I have a couple of shops in San Francisco that sell the smaller ones."

"Our gallery was in the Union Square area. Your work would have done wonderful at the Union Street Spring Arts Festival."

Cassie's eyes widened and she laughed. "I'm afraid I was never good enough for Union Square."

"Oh, honey, trust me, you're good enough. You just didn't have the right contacts." He paused, as if considering, then continued. "Luke says you two are friends, and any friend of Luke's is okay by me. I still have a few contacts there. If you're interested, I'd be happy to make a call for you," he offered.

Cassie was speechless. Any local artist would kill to have their work displayed in Union Square. Suddenly, things were moving too fast, and she was stunned. Mr. Arnold seemed to notice her discomfort and patted her hand.

"My dear, I can see I've dropped a bomb on you, and I have no idea what your inventory is like. If you decide, just let Luke know. She can contact me directly."

"I really, really appreciate the offer, Mr. Arnold, but it is a bit overwhelming. I've gotten used to these county fairs and local art shows, I'm afraid."

"I understand. If you would at least allow me to call my friend at Lake Tahoe?"

"Of course, if you think he'd be interested."

He smiled and pocketed the business cards she handed him. "After thirty years in the business, I do miss discovering new talent. Think about my other offer. It would be my pleasure to introduce your work."

"Thank you. I will." Then she motioned to the carvings he had bought. "And I'll have these ready for you tomorrow," Cassie assured him.

"Wonderful. It was so nice doing business with you." He took her hand, kissed the back of it, and left as quickly as he had come.

She sat down in a daze after he had gone. Two pieces just like that. And just because Luke Winston said she did exquisite work. She owed Luke a very big thank you, but wondered when she'd have the courage to call her.

Luke. Why did the mention of her name call up memories of them on the floor . . . kissing? They came to her with such vividness that she felt her stomach roll and pulse quicken. She had spoken to Luke only once in the past week, but had not seen her. Luke had gone to San Francisco on Wednesday and Cassie had not heard from her since.

And she was fine, she told herself. She didn't need to see Luke, to talk to her. It was better that they took some time. She took a deep breath, staring out over the crowd, seeing nothing. It wasn't better, she finally admitted. She missed Luke. She didn't want to miss her, but she did.

She stood quickly, pacing in her small, roped off area, trying to forget about that night, wishing it still didn't come to her with such vividness. All these years, she thought. All these years of pretending she was something she wasn't. All it had taken was one kiss. One kiss and she could no longer pretend.

She heard someone call her name and saw Kim making her way through the crowd. She groaned silently. She had been avoiding Kim all week, afraid she would see through the facade. She would have to tell her sooner or later, she knew.

"Hey," Kim called before stepping over the rope. "How's business?"

Cassie avoided Kim's eyes, making a show of going to the beaver and eagle, a broad smile on her face.

"Say good-bye to these two," she said.

"Two more? It's barely noon," Kim said. "You only have five left."

"Yes. Isn't it great? Some guy came in and just like that," she said, snapping her fingers, "He bought both of them. He's coming back tomorrow to pick them up," Cassie said. She did not mention that Luke Winston had sent him. She cocked her head to the side with a grin. "How about you?"

"You were right about the abstract," Kim said. "I got rid of it first thing this morning. The guy let me keep it until this evening, and I had at least six other offers for it."

"Well, it'll give you something to do this winter," Cassie said.

Kim nodded, then stood with her hands on her hips.

"Have you been avoiding me?"

"Of course not."

"I've barely talked to you all week. What's going on?"

"Nothing."

"Are you okay?"

"Of course I'm okay," Cassie insisted.

Kim stared at her for a long moment, long enough to make Cassie uncomfortable.

"You sure?"

"I'm sure."

"Okay. Well, I better run. I'm just taking a pee break. Great crowd, huh?" She stepped over the rope, then called back, "Don't forget about the party tomorrow night," and was gone.

The party. She had forgotten. It was a tradition that had started long before Cassie had moved here. Each year, the artists got together for a party after the fair ended on Sunday, just to brag about good fortunes or lament the sale that got away. Paul and Jeff were hosting it this year, and Cassie was thankful she would have someplace to go instead of her empty house where flashes of Luke's kiss seemed to be hiding in every shadow.

She had to stop this, she knew. It was slowly driving her crazy, these feelings raging through her body at just the slightest thought of Luke Winston.

She wanted, needed to see her again. She missed Luke. But maybe Luke was giving her time to adjust. Their conversation on the phone had been brief, Luke simply making sure she was okay and to tell her she would be in the city the rest of the week.

With difficulty, she pushed thoughts of Luke from her mind, and instead, replayed the conversation with Weldon Arnold. It was too good to be true, really. Union Square? God, she would be the

116

envy of the locals, that was for sure. Even Kim, who had had showings in the downtown galleries, never made it to Union Square.

But did she have enough pieces? Five left here. A handful more in her workshop in various stages of completion. If she did that, she would only be able to concentrate on the bigger pieces. No more sitting on the porch in the evenings, carving small birds and squirrels. Did she want to give that up? Then she grinned. She wasn't a total fool. No artist in their right mind would turn down an offer of Union Square.

Chapter Eighteen

Cassie waved at Kim briefly, then let herself be pulled into the kitchen by Paul.

"You haven't been here since I moved in," Paul complained.

"I was here at the Christmas party last year," Cassie said.

Paul scowled then shook his finger at her. "Cass, you and I came together for that one. That was only the second time Jeff and I had met."

Cassie grinned and punched Paul in the arm. "And we all know what happened that night, don't we?"

"I fell in love," Paul said dramatically, and Cassie laughed.

"Yes you did," she said. "And I got dumped."

Paul grasped her hands. "It could have been worse."

"Yes. You could have left me for another woman," she said lightly.

Paul ignored her comment and pulled her in close. "And what about your love life?" he asked quietly.

Cassie looked away quickly. "What love life?"

"I thought you were seeing some farmer."

She dismissed his comment with a wave of her hand. "Oh, that. I wouldn't actually call it dating," she said. "There was nothing there," she said.

He stared at her for the longest time, and she grew uncomfortable under his gaze.

"What?" she asked finally.

He smiled and stared at her for a second longer, then shook his head. "Nothing," he said lightly. He filled a wineglass for her and handed it to her after a quick kiss on the cheek. "Now, how was the fair? The last time I checked, you only had five pieces left," he said.

"I still have them. And I guess the seal will stay with me through the winter, too. I really like her, but I suppose people don't want a seal sitting on their patio. I did sell most of the small carvings," she said. She took a sip of wine, which tasted surprisingly good.

"You'll be busy from now until Christmas, I guess."

"Yes. But they don't take very long to make." She wasn't going to tell anyone about Weldon Arnold until she decided what to do, but she desperately wanted to share her news with someone, and she hadn't had a chance to talk to Kim. "I did meet a contact."

"Oh? From the city?"

"Yes. He used to own a gallery in Union Square."

"Jesus, Cass, that's great." Paul swooped in for a quick kiss. "Tell all."

"Well, he bought two pieces for himself. He offered to make a few calls and introduce me, if I was interested." She tried to keep the excitement out of her voice and failed miserably.

"My God," he drawled. "Little bitsy Cassandra Parker might make the big time!" Then he smiled and his voice turned sincere. "I'm so proud of you. You deserve it."

"My inventory is a little thin right now, and I've already committed to the Christmas fair," she said. "And I may be out of my league."

119

"Don't be silly. You've never charged enough for your work. This would be a wonderful opportunity for you. Screw the Christmas fair."

"You know I can't do that. Kim would kill me."

"I would kill you for what?"

They both looked up as Kim shoved them out of the way and took the bottle of wine and poured a full glass. "I could have sold ten today, at least," she told Cassie. "You're right. I'll be doing abstracts all winter." She took a large swallow, then continued. "Kill you for what?"

"For skipping the Christmas fair," Paul supplied.

"*What?* Why?"

"I'm not skipping it," Cassie insisted.

"She got a better offer."

Cassie glared at Paul, who closed his mouth but couldn't keep the smile off his face.

"What's going on?"

"Nothing, Kim."

"Oh, please! You're such a chickenshit." Paul moved in front of Cassie and took Kim's arms dramatically. "She got an offer for Union Square."

Kim's eyes widened. "Oh my God!" she hissed. Then she shoved Paul out of the way. "You're joking?"

"I haven't even talked with him about it, Paul," Cassie said, wishing she had not even mentioned it.

"Who? Who?" Kim demanded.

"Some guy bought two pieces and offered to set her up," Paul continued.

"Well I'll be damned! Just like that?"

"Isn't it fabulous?"

"Hell, yes! When?"

They both turned to look at Cassie.

"I'm supposed to call him if I'm interested." Luke's supposed to call him, she corrected silently.

"Interested? Why wouldn't you be interested?" Kim demanded.

"We'll talk later, okay?"

"But this is great news, Cass."

"Yes. But I haven't even absorbed it yet. And I know I would be
a fool not to try, so I'll probably call him."

"I'm so proud of you," Kim said, wrapping both arms around
her. "Let me go tell Lisa."

"But no one else," Cassie called after her. Then she turned on
Paul. "Thanks a lot."

"It's great news, darling. Bask in it for awhile, why don't you."

She gave a silly grin. "Yeah, it is, isn't it?"

He refilled their glasses before offering a toast. "Here's to great
success."

"Thanks." She drank, then paused, wanting to turn the conversation away from herself. "How about Jeff? Did he do okay?"

"He was pleased, but I thought he overpriced some of them.
There was this guy from Petaluma, of all places, who had similar
sketches for a lot less," Paul said. "Not nearly as detailed as Jeff's
though," he added.

Cassie smiled at Paul's obvious bias. He was happy with Jeff,
that was perfectly clear, and she wished them well together. She
did, however, feel a twinge of envy. She had long ago given up
hope of someday having someone in her life to share things with.
She wasn't really surprised now when Luke came to mind,
although she doubted that would ever be a reality.

"Well, I've got to mingle," Paul said, disrupting her thoughts.
"I'm the host tonight, you know." He paused on the way out.
"Congratulations, Cass. I mean that."

"Thanks, sweetie."

Cassie followed him back into the living room, listening as
everyone seemed to be talking at once, each wanting to tell about
their success at the fair. She was glad she had come, and the wine
was helping her relax and forget her encounter with Weldon

Arnold. It was her first attempt at wine since the infamous party when she was certain she would never drink wine again.

Kim walked up behind her and squeezed her arm, startling her. "Lisa almost peed in her pants over your news."

"You didn't tell anyone else, did you? I'm not in the mood to answer a hundred questions tonight."

"This has really thrown you, huh?"

"Yes," Cassie admitted. "Scared shitless, actually. And I haven't even agreed to anything other than making contact with some guy at Lake Tahoe."

"Huh?"

"Weldon Arnold was his name. He's got a friend at Lake Tahoe that deals in woodcarvings. He's going to call him. That's all I agreed on for now."

"Of the Arnold-Birch Gallery?"

"I don't know. I didn't ask. All I know is that he sold the gallery and moved out to Russian River."

"It's been so long since I've been downtown, I'm not familiar with anything anymore," Kim said. "But honey, don't let this opportunity pass you by."

Cassie paused, then continued. "He's a friend of Luke Winston's, by the way," she said as casually as she could. "He saw the two eagles that she has and looked me up."

"Always good to have friends in high places, I guess." Then she paused. "Two eagles? When did she buy another one?"

Cassie bit her lower lip, wondering why she had not mentioned the second eagle before. This was Kim, her best friend. But she'd intentionally kept her friendship with Luke a secret and once you start a lie, it's hard to get out of it, she thought.

"I happened to mention to her about the eagle in flight. She came out to the house one time to take a look," Cassie said evasively. And it was true. There was no need to throw in boring details like the storm and spending the night at Luke's.

But Kim eyed her suspiciously.

"I'm surprised you never said anything."

"I thought I had."

"No."

Cassie shrugged, pretending it was no big deal and hating herself for not being able to confide in Kim. She knew she would have to eventually, but right now, later sounded better than sooner.

"Did you see her today?"

"Where? At the fair?"

"Yeah. I saw her walking with two guys. I mentioned the party to her. She said she might stop by."

Cassie forgot to breathe and nearly choked on her wine. *Luke? Here? Tonight?*

"Great. I need to thank her, anyway," Cassie murmured.

Kim motioned to the door. "I guess you'll get your chance."

Cassie let her eyes slide slowly across the room, stopping only when she met the dark ones looking back at her. With great difficulty, she managed to keep her composure as Luke walked purposefully toward them. Cassie let her eyes drop briefly, long enough to take in the loose jeans clinging to Luke's lean frame.

"Hello, ladies."

Cassie was surprised at the nervousness in Luke's voice, but it did little to calm her own nerves. She nodded and managed a mumbled hello before her throat closed completely.

"I'm really glad you could make it, Luke. Did you bring your friends?" Kim asked, apparently missing the tension between the two of them.

"No, they had to get back, but thanks for inviting us."

"Well, the party's been a tradition for years, and it's hardly limited to only artists, anyway," she said. "Can I get you some wine?"

Luke shook her head. "No, thanks. Nothing for me," she said and her eyes again found Cassie's. "I went by your booth, but you had quite a crowd," she said. "I didn't want to interrupt."

"I was . . . busy most of the day," Cassie said. She could not pull her eyes away. She knew that Kim was staring, but she was slowly

123

drowning in those dark depths. Right then she couldn't have cared less what Kim thought. Her mouth was dry, and she tried to swallow, finally bringing the trembling glass of wine to her lips.

"I guess I'll go find Lisa," Kim said. "You two have things to talk about, I'm sure," she added.

As soon as Kim was out of sight, Cassie relaxed.

Luke tilted her head and gave Cassie a lazy smile. "Miss me?"

Cassie grinned. "Yes, actually. When did you get back?"

"Last night. It was really late, and I probably should have stayed in the city until morning, but I wanted to get back." Luke leaned in closer, her voice low. "I missed you, too."

Cassie breathed deeply, Luke's now familiar scent sending shivers through her. Suddenly, they were back at Luke's house, on the floor, Luke pressed hard against her. Her shirt was gone and Luke's mouth feasted on her breast as her other hand moved slowly between her thighs . . .

"Cassie?"

"Hmmm?" She blushed, wondering if Luke had any idea the direction her thoughts had taken.

"How did it go at the fair?"

"Oh, yes. I need to thank you," Cassie said.

Luke raised her eyebrows in surprise. "For what?"

"Weldon Arnold came to see me yesterday," Cassie explained.

"I was hoping he would. I hope you don't mind, but I knew he would love your work. If you could see their patio, you'd understand."

"He also bought two pieces."

Luke nodded. "He tried to swipe my eagles from me."

"He told me. He also mentioned calling some of his contacts in Union Square. You didn't put him up to that, did you?"

Luke shook her head. "I've only known Weldon a few years. When he and Thomas were looking to sell the gallery and retire up here, he contacted me about doing their house. I went to their gallery twice, I think. He and Thomas were over for dinner one night, and they saw the eagles." Then she leaned closer, speaking softly. "Cassie, your carvings are great. Please don't think he's doing me a favor. I would never ask that of him. It wouldn't be fair to either of you."

"Well, thank you all the same. We'll see what happens."

There was an awkward silence between them, then Luke leaned closer, her eyes capturing Cassie's.

"Do you want to get together this week? Have dinner or something?"

Cassie nodded, wishing they could just leave the party and go somewhere right now. Alone. Cassie felt conspicuous here, talking to Luke. She could feel eyes on them, and she knew Kim had been watching.

"I really wish we could . . . go somewhere now . . . to talk."

Cassie's eyes dropped to Luke's mouth, watching as a ghost of a smile appeared. *Talk?* Had she said that? No, that's not what she wanted right now. Right now she wanted to taste those lips again. She raised her eyes, her breath catching at the desire she found in Luke's.

"Don't look at me like that," Luke warned.

"I can't help it," Cassie whispered. It was true. She had no control when it came to Luke. It was as if her very soul were on fire for this woman.

"Let's go . . . go talk somewhere."

Cassie couldn't even manage a nod. Luke took her hand and quickly led them down the hall, turning into one of the opened bedroom doors. She pulled Cassie inside and closed the door, drowning out the noise from the party.

Luke stepped closer to her, pressing Cassie back against the door. "Tell me what you want from me," she whispered. "I promised I'd go slow. But right now, that doesn't mean a whole lot."

Cassie opened her mouth to speak, then closed it again. Her eyes dropped to Luke's mouth and her own lips parted as she shuddered.

"Please," Cassie whispered, murmuring the only words in her mind. "Kiss me."

Then Luke was there, cupping her face, bringing Cassie to her waiting lips. The gentleness that she remembered from the first time vanished as soon as their lips touched. The fire ignited within her, and her mouth opened, gladly accepting Luke's tongue, pulling it into her mouth with an urgency that was foreign to her. Luke groaned and pressed her body hard against Cassie and Cassie's legs parted instinctively. She gasped when Luke pressed her thigh intimately against her.

I'm going to faint, Cassie thought crazily, and her hips moved toward Luke, pressing down hard on her thigh, trying to anchor herself. Then Luke's hands were there, pulling the shirt free from Cassie's jeans, buttons opening one by one. Cassie threw her head back when Luke's hands closed over her breasts.

"Yes, please," she murmured and Luke impatiently shoved her bra aside, easily cupping her breasts. Luke's mouth found hers again, and Cassie was not shy this time as her own tongue did battle with Luke's. Her hands cupped Luke's face, her fingers trembling as they moved through thick, dark hair. Luke drew back, their eyes locked, and Cassie saw desire unlike anything she could have ever imagined. She closed her own eyes and guided Luke to her breasts. She didn't try to stifle the moan that tore from her as Luke's warm mouth closed over one aching nipple. Cassie held Luke's mouth to her breast, her breath now nearly panting.

She had nothing to compare this to, this wonderful feeling of another woman at her breast. She groaned again when Luke moved to her other breast, her tongue swirling over the swollen tip. Cassie held Luke to her, her breasts aching for Luke's touch.

Her legs threatened to collapse when Luke finally left her breast and returned to her mouth, this time gentle. Cassie moaned from the tenderness of her kiss, and her arms slid around Luke's shoulders as she drew Luke to her, pressing her heated body against Luke.

"Please . . . Cassie, we've got to stop," Luke whispered. "I'm about to explode here."

Cassie nodded, wondering when her sanity had fled, knowing it was the instant their lips met.

"I can't remember the last time I wanted someone this much."

"I'm sorry," Cassie whispered.

"No, please don't be sorry. It's fantastic, this feeling. I didn't want to stop."

"And I didn't want you to stop," Cassie admitted.

Cassie pulled out of Luke's arms and tried to gather herself. With her back to Luke, she righted her bra, her nipples still taut and aching. She sighed heavily, part of her wishing they were alone and could finish what they started. But her rational side was glad they weren't. She knew, emotionally, she wasn't ready for this.

"I want to make love to you," Luke whispered.

Cassie shivered at her words and slowly turned to face her.

"I'm scared."

"I know. You're not ready."

Cassie nodded, feeling on the verge of tears again.

"Come here, sweetheart."

Luke gathered Cassie in her arms and held her. Cassie wrapped her own around Luke's waist and rested against her, the endearment still ringing in her ears.

"I'm going to head home," Luke said after awhile.

"You just got here."

"Yes, but I can't go out there and pretend we don't know each other. I don't want to spend the rest of the evening avoiding you."

Cassie nodded. She understood perfectly. Until she told Kim, it would be like this. Them pretending to be only casual acquaintances.

They pulled apart, and Luke bent and kissed her gently.

"We're not exactly going slow, huh?"

Cassie smiled and touched Luke's face, her thumb raking gently across her lips.

"With the direction my thoughts have been going lately, we're going very slowly," she said.

"Oh?" Luke grinned. "Gonna share?"

Cassie blushed. "No."

"Will you call me or are we going to go another week without seeing each other?"

"Yes, I'll call. And, no, I don't want to go a week without seeing you."

Luke slipped past her with only a quick squeeze on her arm, then she was gone. Cassie stood there for a long moment wondering if they were ever going to be able to be alone and not want to rip each other's clothes off?

She walked to the mirror and gasped. She looked well kissed, her lips red and swollen, her eyes still dark with passion. She raised a hand and tried to tame her hair, remembering Luke's fingers as they had threaded it, smoothed it. She met her own eyes in the mirror and smiled. After all these years of being dormant, she was going to have a hard time keeping her feelings in check now. In fact, had Luke not been the one to stop, Cassie would have gone willingly to the bed behind them.

But as Luke had told her, she wasn't ready. She knew that, of course. But that didn't stop her from wanting it.

Chapter Nineteen

"Where's Luke?"

Cassie avoided Kim's eyes and shrugged. "Don't know," she said. "Listen, I'm going to get out of here." She motioned to the door and was pleased with herself for holding her composure when she felt totally exposed.

"Already? We've barely gotten started," Kim complained. She grabbed Cassie's arm and turned her, her eyes widening as she looked at Cassie. "What happened to you?" she demanded. "What's wrong?"

"Nothing. I . . . I'm just tired and want to go home."

"Cass, what has she done to you? My God, *look* at you!"

Cassie shook her head slowly. She felt tears form and she looked away. How in the world would she be able to tell Kim about Luke after all these years of denial?

"I need to talk to you, Kim . . . but just not right now," she said. "Okay?" She knew her voice was trembling, but she could not stop it. "Please understand?" she begged.

"Oh, honey," Kim whispered. "Whatever you need, I'm here for you," she said. "Did she hurt you?"

Cassie grabbed both her arms and squeezed. "No. I'm okay, really," she said and she attempted a smile. "I just need some time to myself."

"Okay," she said. "Jesus . . ."

"Come over for coffee tomorrow morning?" Cassie pleaded.

Kim nodded. "I'll be there. Of course."

Cassie walked away, surprised at how confidently she had handled her discussion with Kim. Her insides were still all mixed up, and she tried desperately not to think about Luke's mouth as she walked across the room toward the door.

She sat in her van, calmly trying to rationalize her feelings, but when she remembered how she had guided Luke's mouth to her breast, wantonly throwing her head back in surrender as Luke feasted, she was nearly overcome with desire. And there was absolutely nothing rational about it. If there was any doubt left in her about her desires, it was squelched tonight. She wanted Luke . . . sexually, physically. Even if her mind tried to deny it, her body still ached for Luke's touch.

"But then what?" Cassie whispered out loud.

She drove home in a daze, her mind filled with images of Luke's soft hands on her, Luke's hot mouth as it closed over her breast, her own hips as they pressed intimately against Luke.

Too many years of celibacy, she thought. She still had enough of her humor intact that she nearly laughed. It was only then that she realized she was sitting in her own driveway, the engine still running.

"Take it slow, take it slow," she murmured. Her body wanted no such thing, but she firmly told herself it was for the best.

But her body spoke louder than her mind as she lay in bed. The sheets seemed to spark against her naked skin and if she closed her eyes, she could feel Luke's hands on her, smell her familiar scent as Luke's mouth moved from her lips to her aching breasts.

She moaned as she imagined Luke's hot, wet mouth closing

over her, sucking the taut nipple inside. Cassie's hands moved to where she needed Luke the most. Her hips rose instinctively, searching, and when she touched herself, she wasn't surprised at the wetness she found.

Oh, Luke.

Her hips arched, and she groaned as her fingers slid through wetness, her clit swollen and ready. She pictured Luke's fingers sliding into her, and her heels dug into the bed. Then Luke's mouth came to her, replacing her fingers, and Cassie cried out, her body on fire for another woman.

Her fingers stroked quickly, bringing herself to a shattering climax. She lay back, her breath hissing through parted lips, fingers still within her wetness. Then she buried her head in her pillow, knowing she was not really satisfied, knowing she never would be until Luke took her that way.

Was it wrong? Was it so wrong for her to desire another woman like this? Despite her father's teachings, she had long ago given up hope of finding a nice man someday. She had accepted the fact that it wasn't a man she wanted to be with. But at the same time, she had resolved herself to being alone, knowing she could never give in to her desires, could never openly be involved in a lesbian relationship. Despite all of that, she had been powerless to resist Luke Winston. Luke had come along and had been able to melt her resistance with that very first glance.

And now Luke had done something else. She had turned Cassie's cold, stone heart into a wildly racing, raging heart. She didn't want to think about what it meant. But she accepted her attraction to Luke, and she admitted that, yes, she wanted to make love with her.

Badly.

Chapter Twenty

Cassie clutched her coffee cup, ignoring Kim for the moment. She should just come right out and tell her. Kim had probably guessed most of it anyway.

"Luke and I . . . know each other better than you think," she started.

"I gathered as much," Kim said dryly.

Cassie took a deep breath, then continued, planning to tell her best friend everything that had happened. "We've had dinner a few times. And lunch," she added before turning around to face her. "And she bought the eagle in flight from me." When Kim would have spoken, Cassie raised her hand to stop her. She was afraid she wouldn't be able to get through it all. "The night of the storm, a few months back, I had a flat and she found me and took me to her house. I stayed the night with her."

"What?" Kim hissed.

"It was perfectly innocent," Cassie said. "I slept on the sofa. But it gave us a chance to get to know each other. The point is, we weren't exactly strangers last night."

"And that gave her the right to *attack* you in the back room?"

Cassie stared at her friend, knowing Kim was more hurt than anything that Cassie had intentionally kept all of this from her.

"She didn't attack me. I went willingly, Kim," Cassie said quietly. "I've denied it for years and lied to you along the way." Their eyes held for a long moment and Cassie's slowly filled with tears. "But I never lied to myself. I just couldn't accept it. I wouldn't accept it."

"I'm sorry. This is my fault," Kim stated. She pulled Cassie into a fierce hug. "I know I've pushed you—"

"No! I always knew, Kim, I just didn't want it to be true, you know. You always said it was, but I didn't want it to be. There was never a man that I was attracted to . . . and I wouldn't dare allow a woman to get close. I was so scared."

"Then why now?" Kim nearly whispered. "Why Luke Winston?"

Images of Luke, pieces of conversation, her own thoughts and feelings flashed fleetingly through her mind, none stopping long enough for her to grasp them. How could she possibly explain this to Kim? She barely understood it herself.

"She touched something inside me," Cassie finally said. She turned away, again staring out the window, seeing nothing. "From the first moment I saw her that day at the café, I knew," she whispered. "I don't know how I knew, but I did. I didn't seek her out. She didn't seek me out. It just happened." Cassie shrugged, then gave a small laugh. "If I didn't know better, I'd think a higher power was bringing us together."

But Kim didn't laugh. She turned Cassie around to face her.

"I'm worried about you. Yes, I've known all these years, and I kept pushing you, thinking you'd be happier if you could just accept this about yourself. But I also know from experience that you have to be ready to accept it. I was afraid you would never accept it, that you would end up spending your life alone, all because of some stupid shit you were brainwashed with as a kid. But I don't think Luke is the one for you."

"I don't know why you don't like her, Kim, but you don't know her. You've only been around her a couple of times and brief minutes at that."

"She just looks the type to—"

"But she's not. She's extremely kind and thoughtful. She's a nice person, Kim. And last night, in a stranger's bedroom, I wanted her to make love to me," she barely whispered. She looked up to meet Kim's eyes. "But she stopped. She stopped because she knows I'm not ready. Up here, anyway," she added and tapped her head.

Kim stared at her for the longest time, then finally nodded.

"Okay. So now what?"

It was Cassie's turn to stare. Now what?

"I don't know. She knows everything about my father, about my upbringing."

"You told her?"

Cassie nodded. "She knows about some things that I've never been able to tell even you."

"Cassie, you can tell me anything," Kim protested.

"You were too close. You already hated him."

Kim nodded. "Yes, I did. I do. Look what he's done to you," she said. "Why won't you see someone? A therapist could help you work through all of this," she suggested, not for the first time.

Cassie hugged her briefly. "I don't think I have that many years left," she said lightly. "And it would take a lot of years."

"Your father can't hurt you, Cass."

"I know that. He can only hurt me if I let him."

She walked to the sink and tossed out her long cold coffee. It wasn't so bad, she thought. If anyone, she knew that Kim would understand what she was going through.

"We're going to take it slow. At least, as slow as we can." She laughed. Last night, slow had not been in her vocabulary.

"But your hormones are in overdrive?" Kim supplied with just a hint of a smile.

"Off the scale to say the least."

Kim pulled her into another hug and they laughed, Cassie finally relaxing. It was a huge relief to have told Kim the truth. But now what? How much did Luke want from her? For that matter, how much could Cassie give? She had a lot of emotional baggage to sort through and she wondered if Luke would be able to deal with it, if Luke would even want to.

Chapter Twenty-one

Cassie sat on the floor of her workshop, a piece of driftwood positioned between her parted legs as she studied it. She ran her hands lightly over the smooth surface, trying to find something in it, trying to see what it would become.

She sighed heavily, a corner of her mouth lifting in a half-smile. She could see nothing but Luke. With each stroke of her hands, she saw nothing but the strong, athletic shape of Luke's body, a body she longed to touch.

It surprised her how easily she could admit this now. She had spent all of her adult life convincing herself that she was attracted to no one. It had been easy, really. She was not attracted to men in the least, and for the longest, she would not even consider the possibility of a woman. But then Luke Winston had come into her life and disrupted everything, without really even trying.

In a sense, Cassie felt freed. The constricting blanket she had placed on her life, her feelings, had been burned. And the woman who had set flames to it was but a phone call away.

Cassie had not yet dared to call her though. Oh, but that didn't stop her from dreaming of Luke's touch. She woke during the night, her body damp with perspiration—and desire. Her own hands touched herself where she longed for Luke to touch. It had only been two days. Two long days since she had confided in Kim. Two nights sleeping alone, dreaming of Luke's touch. She had awakened each morning with her body on fire, wet, a throbbing ache between her thighs, her pillow clutched tightly to her. And always the image of hands . . . dream hands . . . just leaving her.

Luke had not called and Cassie wondered if she herself never attempted to make contact, would Luke be the one to break down first and call? It wasn't that she didn't want to call her, didn't want to see her. She did. The truth was, she was scared. She wasn't strong enough to deny her feelings any longer.

The ringing of the phone startled her, disrupting her thoughts. She stood and reached for it nervously, afraid it would be Luke, hoping it would be Luke.

"It's me," Kim said. "Lisa said I should call you. It's been awhile since you've been over for dinner."

Cassie laughed. "New recipe, huh?"

"Eggplant," Kim said. "Don't make me do it alone."

Cassie laughed again. She needed a diversion, she knew. "Okay."

"Good." Then her voice softened. "How are you, honey?"

"I'm okay."

"Have you called her?"

"Not yet."

Kim knew not to press. "Come early and we'll catch up," she said.

Cassie left her workshop, the wood still untouched. Maybe tomorrow she would call Luke, she thought. Tonight she would escape in the company of her two closest friends.

While Lisa finished dinner, Cassie enjoyed looking at the paintings Kim had been doing, some completed, others just beginning.

"I've gotten so involved with these, I've had no inspiration for my usual seascapes," Kim explained.

"Maybe this is another phase in your career," Cassie said. "You can't continue to paint original seascapes without repeating some."

Kim looked at her for a moment. "Maybe you're right. But what about your work? I've seen you do eagles over and over again, yet they all manage to be unique in some way."

"All my animals have their own personalities," Cassie offered. "I sometimes forget they're only pieces of wood."

Lisa called them to dinner, and Kim linked a casual arm through Cassie's. "Lisa's already planning Thanksgiving dinner," Kim said. "Humor her."

"Any reason for her to cook." They laughed, and it felt good to Cassie. This was familiar to her and she knew she needed something familiar now that her life was about to change completely.

"I've been looking over these recipes for vegetable nut rolls," Lisa said as she scooped out generous helpings of the eggplant casserole for them. "A couple look promising."

"What was wrong with last year's recipe?" Kim asked, and she winked at Cassie.

"We can't always use the same one," Lisa explained. "Cassie, you can bring that wonderful squash casserole that you made last year." Then she looked up. "You are planning to join us?"

"Of course," Cassie said easily. "Don't I always?"

"You haven't heard from your father, have you?"

Cassie poured wine for them and carried all three glasses to the table. She gave Kim a blank stare.

"I can't remember the last time I've talked to him. I guess it was early summer." Lately, he hadn't been far from her mind, though.

"This is great, hon," Kim said around a mouthful.

Lisa ruffled Kim's hair as she walked past. She did the same to Cassie and they laughed.

"I'm glad you came over," she told Cassie.

"Thanks." She picked up her wineglass instead of her fork.

"Has she called?"

Cassie met Lisa's eyes, then glanced at Kim.

"No. And she won't. She left that up to me," Cassie said, downing the rest of her wine.

"She knows what you're going through, right?" Lisa got up for more wine. "I mean, obviously this is new to you."

Cassie was having a hard time discussing this with Kim and Lisa. They were her best friends, but still, she was embarrassed. After all the years of denying this part of herself, it was difficult to talk about it now.

"Yes, she knows. I think I may remind her of a previous relationship." Cassie took a swallow of wine before continuing. "She had an affair with a married woman for several years. Turned out, the woman was just playing with her, experimenting."

"And she thinks you might be doing the same?"

Cassie shrugged. "I wouldn't blame her if she did." In fact, the thought had crossed her mind several times, and she wondered if maybe that was why Luke was giving her time. She knew how badly Luke had been hurt before.

"I think you need to call her," Lisa said. "If nothing else, you should explain."

"Explain what? That I'm scared shitless by what I'm feeling? I think she knows that."

"Honey, I know this is hard." Kim gave her hand a squeeze. "We've all been there."

Cassie smiled, finally picking up her fork. "Let's just hope I don't run off and get married or something."

Kim laughed. "That was something, wasn't it? Talk about scared shitless."

"Did you even know what a lesbian was back then?" Lisa asked.

"Not until Jennifer explained to me why I wanted to touch her all the time."

"She was your first, right?"

Kim nodded. "Man, what a night. I had no idea what I was doing, I only knew I wanted to do it."

"How could you go and get married after that?"

"Lisa, you don't understand. I was completely alone. I didn't have anyone to turn to, except Cassie."

"And I wasn't a lot of help," Cassie added.

"It seemed the logical thing to do. I mean, all my life I'd been told I was going to get married and have kids. There was never any mention of falling in love with a woman." Kim reached for the wine and refilled everyone's glass, emptying the bottle.

"I was scared," Kim continued. "I went after the first guy I could find, just to prove I wasn't queer."

"More than one, if I recall," Cassie reminded her.

"Poor Richard. I practically roped him into the marriage, then made us both miserable for the next six months."

"Did he know about Jennifer?" Lisa asked.

"No. And I wish I hadn't told him at the end. We were both so young, and it wasn't his fault, but I'm sure it left a scar."

"No doubt," Cassie said. It was her turn to squeeze Kim's hand. "But he was a—"

"A jerk," Kim finished for her. "I know. But what do you expect when you're twenty-one years old and you find out your wife's a lesbian?"

"But you and Jennifer didn't last long," Lisa reminded them both.

"No. Once I found out what was out there, I was like a kid in a candy store," Kim said with a laugh. Then she turned to Cassie with a grin. "And you're too old to act like that. But just remember, Luke's not the only fish in the sea. I mean, you'll meet lots of people. Don't assume that just because she's the one to make you accept this, that she's the only one, you know?"

"But you like her?" Lisa asked gently.

140

"Yes. I really like her."

Cassie swallowed the last of her wine, and Lisa got up to open another bottle.

"You know, I really think you should call her."

Cassie smiled at them, wondering if they knew how they contradicted each other. Kim was overprotective, wanting her to find someone safe. Lisa was the romantic, pushing her to Luke because she could see the attraction.

"I don't think Kim likes her," Cassie said to Lisa. "She thinks Luke's too much for me."

"Honey, I just don't want her to take advantage of you," Kim said. "You're so innocent," she said quietly. "I don't want you to get hurt."

Cassie nodded, accepting the new glass of wine from Lisa. Innocent, yes. But that didn't mean she didn't know what she wanted. And she wanted Luke in the worst way.

"I've been afraid to see her," Cassie admitted. "That's why I haven't called her."

"You're afraid to be alone with her?" Lisa guessed.

"Terrified," Cassie whispered.

Chapter Twenty-two

It was nearly midnight, but Cassie was afraid if she waited until morning, she would lose her nerve again.

The phone was answered on the third ring.

"It's me."

There was a long pause.

"Are you okay?"

Luke's voice was heavy with sleep, and Cassie bit her bottom lip, wishing she had waited until morning.

"I'm sorry it's so late," she said. "I just . . . why don't I call tomorrow?"

"No, it's okay. I'm glad you called."

Cassie heard Luke turning in her bed, heard the rustling of covers. She imagined Luke was sitting up, perhaps leaning back against her pillow. The sheet would have slipped to her waist . . .

Cassie cleared her throat, words spilling out before she could stop them.

"Luke? What do you sleep in?"

A low chuckle sent shivers across her body. She covered her eyes with her free hand, wondering if she could be any more suggestive.

"I sleep in a bed," came the quiet response. "You?"

"Funny. A sense of humor, even at midnight."

Luke laughed, and Cassie's embarrassment eased somewhat, although she still didn't have an answer to her question. Did she need an answer?

"I was wondering if you had plans tomorrow. I thought maybe we could get together for lunch or something," Cassie offered.

"Can't tomorrow. I was up late finishing some designs. I've got to meet a client in Sacramento."

"Oh." Cassie tried not to sound disappointed. It was her own choice to wait four days to call. Luke had her own life, her own work and deadlines to meet. Did Cassie really think she had been sitting at home by the phone, waiting for Cassie to call?

"Why don't you come with me?" Luke suggested.

Cassie hesitated. She had work to do. She was already far behind her usual pace on the small carvings, the ones she would take to the Christmas fair. And if she ever wanted to call Weldon Arnold, she would need at least three more eagles to show.

"Please?" Luke's voice, still husky with sleep, whispered in her ear.

"Are you sure I won't be in the way?"

"Positive."

"Okay," Cassie agreed. She didn't know why she was hesitating anyway.

"Thanks. I'll pick you up about eight. Or is that too early?"

"No. But I better get to bed."

"Yes, you better do that."

Luke's low voice sent another shiver through her, and Cassie's mind raced, wishing she were crawling in beside Luke instead of her cold, lonely bed.

It was only then that she realized she had never slept with

anyone—a lover—overnight. On the two occasions she had attempted to find solace with a man, the one time in college, then right before she moved here, she had fled quickly afterward, wanting nothing more than to be alone. She had been too humiliated and disheartened the first time to even consider staying the night. The second time, with a man named Stephen, she simply could not stand his touch upon her and wanted to get as far away as possible.

It was after that night that she started wondering if it was only her father's words haunting her or if there was another reason she didn't want the touch of a man.

She had no doubt now, knowing she would be perfectly content to sleep snuggled in Luke's arms, safe and warm. She closed her eyes, wondering if the next time she and Luke were together, would she be able to make her stop. Would she want to make her stop?

Chapter Twenty-three

"You look very nice," Cassie said. She had debated over what to wear, finally settling on a newer pair of jeans and a long sleeved shirt. Luke, on the other hand, had shed her usual baggy jeans for a pair of neatly pressed black slacks and a deep maroon sweater.

"Thank you. My version of dressing up," Luke explained.

"Should I have . . .?"

"No, no, you're fine. It's just that I'm meeting him at his office. He's an attorney, and there'll be suits and ties and all."

They were quiet as they drove through town on their way to Santa Rosa and the interstate. Finally Cassie reached over and squeezed Luke's arm.

"I'm sorry I waited so long to call."

"I understand," Luke said and smiled. "Are you okay about the other night? I was afraid that it was too much, that you wouldn't want to see me for awhile."

"I told Kim," Cassie stated.

"You did? And how did she take it?"

Cassie laughed. "She wasn't really surprised. I mean, she's been telling me for years to look in the mirror. But she was worried about you. That you were forcing me into this, I think."

Luke nodded, then met Cassie's eyes for a moment.

"Is that what you think?"

"No! Of course not. It's just that, for so many years, I've denied this, at least to her. But I couldn't lie to myself any longer."

"Is it going to be hard to face people, friends? I mean to have professed to be straight and then suddenly show up with me?"

Cassie stared at the road for a long moment before answering.

"I don't really have a lot of close friends. I know them, of course, but only because of Kim and Lisa. I wouldn't exactly call them good friends of mine. And no, I really could care less what they think."

"You know, I find that so hard to believe. You're a very likable person, Cassie. Why haven't you let anyone get close?"

"I guess it was just easier to keep my distance." Cassie shrugged. "I never really had a lot of friends anyway. You know, my father and all."

Luke reached over and captured Cassie's hand and pulled it into her lap, holding it there as she drove. Cassie relaxed, giving into the gentle pressure as Luke's warm hand closed over hers.

"I'm glad you let me in," Luke said quietly. "You could have just as easily run from this, too."

"No. I couldn't. Believe me, I tried."

Luke brought Cassie's hand to her lips and kissed it gently before tucking it again in her lap.

"Actually, I tried, too."

"What do you mean?"

Luke smiled. "After the last time, I swore I would never get involved with anyone again. I didn't want to care about anyone like that again. I've had a handful of lovers over the years, but it was nothing more than casual, really. But with you, I don't want it to be casual. I very much want to get to know you better. And that scares me a little," Luke admitted. "I almost didn't recover from the last time."

Cassie squeezed Luke's hand before speaking.

"I can't promise I won't hurt you, Luke. This is just all so new, I'm . . ."

"Scared. I know."

Cassie nodded silently, wondering why she was scared. Physical intimacy was one thing, but after the other night, she knew once she was in Luke's arms, she would lose any inhibitions she may have. She suddenly blushed, remembering the way she had pulled Luke to her breast, shivering as she recalled the feel of Luke's warm mouth as it settled over her. No, that wasn't the problem.

The problem was her father. She could never tell him, she knew. That would be the end of any relationship they may have. But was she prepared to hide this? To blatantly lie to him? For all she knew, he thought she was still seeing Paul, the last name she had mentioned to him.

"Let's don't worry about it now," Luke said. "We'll have a good day. After my meeting, I'll take you to lunch. Then there are a couple of houses I want to show you."

"Ones that you designed?"

"Yes. One was years ago when I still worked for the company in San Francisco. The other was done just last year. There's a vast difference."

"Good. I've been curious as to what your designs are like. I mean, I love your house, but it's so unique. I imagine that's one of a kind."

"Definitely. It took me forever to design. I must have changed it ten times before I was satisfied. I originally had the office area enclosed. It was the only area with walls, but I just didn't want to be closed in."

"Why don't you have a spare bedroom? Are you never expecting company?"

Luke grinned. "Well, there is a spare room, an apartment really. It's above my workout room."

Cassie punched her playfully on the arm.

"And I got the sofa?"

"Actually, I just wanted you in the house with me," Luke said shyly.

147

"Really?"

"Well, I thought it was a bit soon to ask you to share my bed, especially since you had just told me you weren't gay."

They both laughed, and Cassie was secretly pleased that even then, Luke was feeling the attraction between them, too.

"I think I would have attempted to swim home if you'd suggested that."

"Yes, I know."

Cassie quickly leaned over between the seats and kissed Luke lightly on the cheek.

"I'm so glad you came into my life," she said quietly.

"I'm happy to be here."

Their conversation turned to lighter matters, and Cassie relaxed, glancing occasionally at their hands that remained entwined. In no time at all, they were crossing the Sacramento River and into the downtown area. Luke stopped at an office building within walking distance of the state capitol and paused before parking.

"You're welcome to come in with me or you can take the Lexus and explore a bit," Luke offered.

"Actually, I think I might wander over to the capitol and look around. But I can walk from here."

"Okay. If you want, we can go to an art museum later. The Crocker is one of the best in the state."

"You don't have to entertain me, you know," Cassie said. "I just wanted to be with you today."

The warmth in Luke's smile touched Cassie's heart, and she was surprised when Luke leaned over and kissed her on the mouth.

"Thank you. After lunch we can decide."

Cassie nodded, having to restrain herself from wrapping her arms around Luke's shoulder and pulling her back for another kiss.

"Do you want me to come find you when I'm through?" Luke asked.

"Or I can come back here. How long do you think you'll be?"

"Not more than an hour, I hope." Luke glanced at her watch

before guiding Cassie out of the parking garage with a light touch on her back. "There is a nice picnic area outside the capitol. Let's meet there. Then we can walk down Capitol Avenue. There's a really great Italian restaurant I think you would like."

Cassie agreed and watched Luke walk off, admiring her confident stride. She finally turned when she realized she was staring, and she walked off, alone with her thoughts. And they were simply filled with Luke.

She walked, unseeing, through the halls of the capitol, her shoes silent on the marble floors, staring absently at the paintings hung there. She couldn't seem to concentrate on anything, her thoughts continuously jumping back to Luke and the casual way she had kissed her. Suddenly her eyes widened.

"Oh my God," Cassie whispered. She put a hand to her chest and rubbed the spot over her heart slowly. She squeezed her eyes shut. "I think I'm in love with her," she whispered again.

She looked around quickly, realizing she had spoken the words out loud. Panic set in, and she found the nearest bench, sinking slowly down, wondering how on earth this could have happened. No, she told herself, I'm not in love with her. We barely know each other. She bent her head, grabbing the bridge of her nose with her fingers and squeezing. *Not in love.*

She sat for a few minutes, taking deep breaths as she tried to calm herself. It was just all so new, she told herself. That was all. They would get to know each other, take things slowly and then see what happened. Yes. That was all.

She smiled. *See, I'm not in love with her. That would just be crazy.*

An hour and ten minutes later, she saw Luke strolling across the lawn toward her. Her pulse quickened at the sight, and she rolled her eyes but couldn't keep the silly grin off her face.

Luke sat down next to her at the picnic table and casually took her hand.

"Miss me?"

"Of course not. Have you been gone?" Cassie teased.

A lazy smile appeared, and Cassie got lost in those dark eyes so close to her own. She dropped her glance to Luke's mouth, suddenly wishing they were alone.

"Cassie, don't look at me like that or I'll forget we're out in public," Luke threatened. "In Sacramento, no less!"

"I know. I'm sorry." She took a deep breath and moved back from Luke just a little. "How did it go?"

"Good. He liked the design. He only made a few changes, and that won't take me long to do."

"Do you contract out to build as well?" she asked.

"Sometimes. But usually closer to home. In this case, he's already got a builder."

Luke stood and pulled Cassie to her feet.

"Come on. If we hurry, we can beat the lunch crowd."

They walked out of Capitol Park and down Capitol Avenue, the sidewalk becoming more crowded as the noon hour approached. The avenue was lined with small shops and restaurants, and Luke stopped at one as the smell of Italian cooking drifted out to them.

"Smells good," Cassie said and her stomach agreed. She had skipped breakfast.

They only had to wait a few minutes before they were seated, and they stared at each other across the candlelit table.

"This is nice," Cassie finally murmured.

Luke raised one eyebrow. "Romantic?"

"Yes," Cassie said, unable to pull her eyes from Luke. Desire settled over her slowly, enveloping her like a warm glove on a cold winter's day.

"Cassie . . ." Luke warned.

"I want you," Cassie stated suddenly, without warning. Then, embarrassed, "I'm sorry."

"God, don't be sorry."

She watched, fascinated, as the pulse in Luke's neck throbbed. Her thoughts of earlier surfaced. In love? Did she even know what it felt like? But as she drifted into those dark eyes that held her captive, she knew exactly what it felt like.

"Ladies, how are we today?"

150

Cassie was the first to break their intense stare, and she looked away, again embarrassed. But it wasn't embarrassment that she saw in Luke's eyes at the interruption. It was regret.

"We're great, thank you," Luke said to their waiter who had materialized unnoticed.

"Good. Can I get you ladies a glass of wine before lunch?"

"I'll have apple cider, please. Cassie? Glass of wine?"

"Oh, apple cider is fine for me, too."

"Very good. A nice hot loaf of bread will be right out."

When they were alone again, Cassie dared to meet Luke's eyes. But they were warm and smiling, the earlier intensity gone for now.

"You could have a glass of wine, you know. I don't mind."

Cassie shook her head. "I like apple cider just fine."

A loaf of steaming Italian bread was placed between them. Luke poured garlic-flavored olive oil in small plates on the table and reached for the pepper mill, raising an eyebrow questioningly at Cassie.

"Yes, please."

During their meal, Luke told her about the house she was designing for the attorney, and Cassie was thankful Luke had turned the conversation to less personal matters.

"Why did you become an architect?" Cassie asked.

Luke shrugged. "I always loved to draw as a kid. I actually thought I'd be an artist," she said. "I just wasn't good enough. Neal is the one that suggested architecture."

"I really would love to see some of your paintings."

Luke laughed. "Probably not."

"They can't be that bad."

"Well, like I said before, if you're ever in my bedroom . . ."

Cassie blushed and Luke laughed again.

"You're terrible, you know that?"

"Yes, just terrible," Luke agreed, but the smile remained.

Chapter Twenty-four

The drive home was made in relative silence, one or the other occasionally attempting conversation. After lunch, Luke had taken her to the two homes she had designed. The first was an elaborate brick home not unlike most of its neighbors. The second, done only a few years ago, was a cedar home tucked between large trees. A three-tiered deck flowed on two sides, disappearing into a cluster of shrubs and trees separating it from the neighbors. Cassie loved the second home. She could see Luke's touch on it. She couldn't imagine the Luke she knew today having designed the first one.

The day had been pleasant, but now, as they headed back to Sebastopol, Cassie was unsure what was happening between them. Before they left Sacramento, Luke had leaned over and kissed Cassie. She had meant it to be brief, Cassie knew, but their desire stirred, and Cassie had captured Luke's lips, her mouth opening, inviting more. With the console between them, their kisses grew ardent, demanding. Both were gasping for breath when Luke finally pulled away, her eyes so dark with desire Cassie went back for one more kiss. But Luke had stopped her, instead, taking her hand and bringing it to her lips.

Then she had driven away without a word and now Cassie wasn't sure what to make of it. Their conversation had dwindled to nothing.

"Luke?"

"Hmm?"

"What's wrong?" she asked.

It was only then she noticed the tight grip Luke had on the wheel as her eyes stared straight ahead.

"Nothing."

But Cassie couldn't dismiss it that easily. She reached over and laid her hand on Luke's thigh, squeezing lightly. Luke tensed, and Cassie saw the way her breath caught.

"Please tell me."

Luke finally turned, meeting her eyes.

"I want to make love with you," she said quietly. "And every time I kiss you, it's harder and harder to stop, to give you the time you need."

"I didn't . . . I didn't want you to stop," Cassie whispered. Her hand relaxed and she rubbed the strong thigh beneath her fingers, feeling Luke tremble as she made her way up Luke's thigh, stopping only when she reached the crease in her jeans.

"Cassie, I'm going to drive us right off the road if you don't stop," Luke warned.

But Cassie didn't stop. Her hand slid intimately between Luke's thighs, feeling the heat between her legs. She gasped as Luke squeezed her thighs together, capturing Cassie's hand for a moment before opening them again.

"Jesus Christ, woman," Luke murmured.

Before Cassie knew what was happening, the Lexus pulled to a stop on the side of the road. Luke's eyes peered into hers for only a second, then her lips were there, covering her own, tongue demanding entry and Cassie opened gladly. Her heart was pounding so loudly in her ears, she didn't hear the traffic as it sped by them. Hands settled in Luke's dark hair and she groaned from the intensity of their kiss. She welcomed Luke's hands as they slid over her body, cupping her breasts, kneading gently as her thumbs raked over erect nipples. Cassie wanted to rip open her shirt, she wanted Luke's warm mouth on her, but Luke's hands left her breasts, sliding past her waist.

Luke's mouth pulled away, but Cassie guided her back, her moan mingling with Luke's as her tongue slipped inside Luke's mouth. Luke's hands slid to her thighs and Cassie's legs parted, her hips arching. When Luke's hand cupped her intimately, pressing the seam of her jeans against her aroused center, Cassie couldn't breathe. She leaned back against the seat, her chest heaving as if running. She felt her own wetness, and she pressed against Luke's hand, all control lost.

Finally, Luke eased the pressure, her hands moving from between her legs to rest on her thighs. Light kisses replaced the fervent ones of earlier.

"Don't stop," Cassie nearly whimpered.

"Yes," Luke whispered.

"No."

Luke brushed the hair off Cassie's forehead, then placed a light kiss there.

"Yes," Luke said again. "Our first time is not going to be in a car."

"Details," Cassie murmured, and Luke smiled.

"Do you know how badly I want to touch you? I could feel how wet you are," Luke whispered.

Cassie closed her eyes, her chest still heaving.

"Yes."

Complete silence settled over them as they drove slowly through Sebastopol. Luke's hand played upon Cassie's thigh, rubbing gently back and forth. Cassie's eyes were closed as she rested her head against the cool leather seats. Occasionally her own hand would cover Luke's, then slide up her arm, only to stop again when she realized how involuntary her touch had become.

When they pulled into Cassie's drive, her stomach rolled nervously. She wanted Luke to stay. But she wasn't certain Luke would.

In fact, Luke left the engine running, and they looked hesitantly at each other.

"I better go."

"I want you to stay."

"Cassie . . ."

"Please?"

It was only then that Cassie realized they were both breathing hard. She never imagined that she would have to be the one to lead this, but she took Luke's hand and held it between both of hers.

"I want this," Cassie whispered. In fact, she was surprised at how sure she was.

Luke's mouth parted, but still she hesitated.

"Please. Don't make me beg you."

Luke closed her eyes for a moment, then opened them to Cassie.

"I won't stop this time. I'm going to make love to you."

Cassie's eyes softened, and she reached out a hand to brush Luke's face.

"No. I don't want you to stop. I would take you into my bedroom, but I'm kinda new at this," she murmured, getting a half-smile from Luke. "I wouldn't know where to begin."

Luke raised an eyebrow, and this time Cassie was rewarded with that lazy smile she had grown to love. She didn't resist as Luke pulled her close and kissed her softly, but their kiss turned hungry. Luke pulled away first, her eyes once again questioning.

"Please come inside," Cassie said.

She didn't wait for an answer. She walked through the house and into her bedroom, turning to find Luke there. Cassie moved into her arms without speaking and they stood there, holding each other, feeling the rapid beating of each other's hearts.

Then soft lips moved over her neck and Cassie sighed, her head falling back in surrender. She was conscious enough to realize she wasn't afraid of this, then all thoughts fled as those same soft lips captured hers.

"We can still wait, you know," Luke murmured against her lips. "I want you to be sure."

Cassie didn't answer with words. She stepped back and pulled her shirt out of her pants, unbuttoning it slowly, watching as Luke's eyes darkened even more. She tossed it aside, reaching behind her to unhook her bra but Luke stopped her, her own hands releasing the clasp and exposing her breasts. Luke's hands were on her, cupping her swollen breasts as her hot mouth covered Cassie's. Cassie's mouth opened, letting Luke inside, taking her tongue, swallowing the moan that followed.

Luke's lips left Cassie's mouth, nipping at her neck and throat, moving with agonizing slowness to her breasts.

"Yes," Cassie murmured. Her hands dropped to Luke's waist, trying to reach under her sweater, wanting to touch her, but they stopped when she felt Luke's tongue graze her nipple. Her breath held as Luke's mouth closed over one tender breast, sucking the nipple inside. Cassie's head rolled back, eyes shut to the sensations ripping through her. "God, yes," she murmured again. *Finally.* She felt complete. She felt as if all the questions of her life were being answered . . . by this woman. This woman was what had been missing in her life.

She felt Luke's hands leave her breast, slide expertly past her waist and cup her hips, bringing Cassie flush against her. Cassie's thighs parted and the ache between her legs became nearly unbearable. Her hands reached for Luke, moving over strong shoulders, holding her near.

Luke's mouth left Cassie's breast and she raised her head, their eyes locking together, both their chests heaving as if they had been running.

Cassie's lips trembled, and she murmured, "Touch me."

Their eyes never wavered as Luke's hand moved to the button on her jeans, releasing it and the zipper in one quick motion.

Warm hands slid inside, under the waistband of her silk panties and pausing only once when they reached the soft triangle of hair. Their eyes still locked with each other, Luke moved again. Cassie's breath caught as Luke's fingers slid into her wetness for the first time. Cassie's eyes slammed shut as she tried to stifle the moan that escaped from her lips.

"Oh," she breathed. Her legs threatened to buckle as Luke pushed her jeans down, urging her to step out of them. Then they were on the bed, Luke still fully clothed as she settled her weight over Cassie's naked form.

"You're so beautiful," Luke whispered and captured her lips again. Her hands traveled over Cassie's body, igniting fires where they landed.

Oh God, *God*, Cassie thought as she felt Luke slide down her body, pausing only briefly at her breasts. When Luke's tongue wet a path across her stomach, Cassie's hips arched when she realized her intention and her hands at Luke's shoulders urged her down farther. Yes. She wanted Luke's mouth on her where she needed her the most, where no one else had ever been. The fire between her legs was too much, too much for her to bear even a second longer. Luke buried her face at Cassie's waist and Cassie held Luke to her for a moment, then gently pushed at her shoulders, telling Luke that it was okay, telling her that was what she wanted. All thought left her then as Luke kneeled before her, and her hands parted Cassie's thighs. When Luke's mouth touched her, Cassie screamed out her pleasure, unable to stop the sounds coming from her. She flung her head back, hands gripping Luke's shoulders as she tried to anchor herself, tried to hold on to her sanity.

"Oh, *God*," she breathed as Luke's tongue moved over her, into her. Then her thighs opened wider, her hands on Luke's head holding her there, pressing Luke harder against her. Luke's lips suckled her clit, tongue driving her mad as she felt her orgasm build, felt the first tremors threaten. She didn't want this to end, and her hands gripped Luke's shoulders harder as she tried to prolong her pleasure. But she couldn't stop the eruptions of her body, and her orgasm hit with such force, her hips lifted off the bed as her fingers dug into Luke's shoulders, and her breath hissed between her teeth as she screamed out her pleasure.

Her fingers relaxed their grip on Luke and her eyes squeezed shut as she tried to catch her breath. Luke's head rested on Cassie's thigh, and Cassie could feel Luke's rapid breathing against her leg.

"That was the most incredible thing I've ever experienced," Cassie finally murmured. "Come up here."

She pulled Luke to her, brushing the damp hair off her forehead. Her thumb touched Luke's lower lip as Luke sought her eyes.

"I'm sorry," Luke finally whispered.

"Shhh, shhh . . . no." It was her turn to capture Luke's eyes. "I wanted you, needed you like that. Don't you say you're sorry."

"Are you okay? I shouldn't have . . ."

"Yes. You're such a sweetheart, Luke, do you know that? You're the first person that's ever . . . made love to me like that."

Cassie's eyes softened, and she leaned forward, kissing Luke lightly, tasting herself on Luke's lips. Her mouth went back for more, her tongue grazing Luke's teeth before slipping inside her warm mouth. She felt surprisingly in control, and her hands had a will of their own as they boldly touched Luke's breasts for the first time, her thumbs rubbing over the taut nipples as they pressed against Luke's sweater.

Luke moaned into her mouth, and Cassie pushed her down on the bed, laying her naked body across Luke's still clothed one.

"Let me make love to you," Cassie whispered. Her eyes searched Luke's, trying to read them, seeing only desire as her mouth covered Luke's again. "Teach me."

She tried to tell herself that she didn't know what she was doing, that she had no idea how to please a woman, but her hands wouldn't wait. They pulled Luke's sweater over her head in one motion then eagerly touched soft, smooth skin. Luke's exquisite body unfolded before her, Luke's muscled frame surprisingly soft to her touch. With a groan, her mouth found Luke's breast, and her tongue danced over the swollen nipple before sucking it into her mouth.

Her body knew exactly what to do, even if she didn't, and her hands cupped Luke's small breasts, holding them for her greedy mouth as Luke's hands in her hair held her there.

Desire burned inside Cassie, and she fumbled with Luke's slacks, but the buttons refused to cooperate. She sat up, her mouth leaving Luke's breast, Luke's whimper sweet music to her ears.

"Please," Cassie begged. "Help me with these."

Luke's smile was gentle as she slowly unbuttoned them, but Cassie's eager hands pushed Luke's aside, and she shoved the slacks down Luke's legs, thin cotton briefs now her only barrier. She bit her lip and swallowed, wanting to tell Luke that she was scared, that she didn't know what to do. But Luke's eyes were closed, her hands moving to Cassie's face, urging her mouth back to Luke's breast.

While Cassie's mouth feasted, her hands moved over Luke's body, loving the way her velvet skin felt to her touch. Her hands moved down Luke's thighs then slowly back up again. She wanted so badly to touch Luke that her hands trembled when they touched soft cotton. Her lips moved back to Luke's mouth, groaning when Luke's tongue met her own. Then Luke's hands moved over her back, cupped her hips and brought Cassie intimately against her, the thin cotton barrier the only thing separating them. Cassie's hips surged against Luke, straining to touch her and their hips and pelvis rocked together and Cassie felt wetness flood her again. Without thinking, her hand moved between them, slipping past the offending barrier, her fingers sinking into warm wetness.

"Oh, Luke," she groaned. She couldn't have imagined this feeling, the wetness surrounding her fingers, hips rising up to meet her hand, warm flesh enveloping her, holding her captive. Her fingers moved through the wetness with ease, then, at Luke's urging, her fingers slipped inside, delving deep, meeting Luke's rising hips. Cassie's eyes were half-opened as she watched pleasure transform Luke's face.

Then Luke gently pulled Cassie from inside her, pressing Cassie's fingers against her, showing her the rhythm she needed as Cassie stroked her. Luke's hands left her, fists digging into the bedspread and Cassie's mouth covered her breast again as her fingers stroked Luke faster until Luke's hips surged up to meet her, and she heard her name gasped from Luke's lips again and again.

"Cassie," Luke breathed, and she gathered Cassie to her.

Cassie felt Luke's heart pounding beneath her ear, and she closed her eyes, hoping she had given Luke pleasure.

"I've wanted you for so long," Cassie murmured. "I had no idea it would feel this way."

Her last conscious thought before an exhausted sleep claimed her was Luke's lazy hand moving between her thighs . . . and her own mouth still at Luke's breast.

Chapter Twenty-five

Cassie woke slowly, disorientated. She was sleeping at the foot of the bed, the sheets and comforter a tangled mess on the floor. She sat up then, and a contented, exhausted smile warmed her. Every muscle in her body screamed as she rolled over, and she closed her eyes again, wanting to savor her night with Luke for a little longer. Her body quivered as she thought of Luke's fingers touching her, moving over her . . . and in her. They had done incredibly intimate things with one another last night, but Cassie felt none of the embarrassment that she had anticipated. She rolled onto her side and replayed the scenes from last night.

"Am I doing this right?"

"You're perfect."

Now she blushed as she remembered her uncertain question to Luke as her hands had spread Luke's thighs. And she blushed again as she remembered Luke's mouth on her body, Luke's lips and tongue taking her as she ripped the sheets from the bed.

"Jesus," she murmured, and she squeezed her legs tight. She was ready. She wanted Luke again.

Then she sat up. Where was Luke? The house was too quiet. She swung her legs over the edge of the bed and sighed, her body protesting. When she rubbed her face with her hands, Luke's scent assailed her, and she brought her fingers to her nose, feeling weak all over again. She wanted her mouth on Luke. She wanted to taste her . . . she had wanted it last night but she had not dared. She had felt clumsy, foolish, wanton. But now, the desire was too strong. She licked her lips, imagining Luke under her mouth, imagining her wetness, and she groaned again.

She had nothing to compare this want and need to. Perhaps it was just all these years of pent-up desires finally surfacing. She had a lot of time to make up for.

She reached for her robe and saw her clothes neatly folded on the chair beside the bed. Luke must have folded them. Her clothes had been where she had left them. In a forgotten heap by the bed.

In the kitchen, she saw the note. She was afraid to go to it, and she stood staring at the table for the longest time. It was good-bye, she knew. She was to have just one night. In her mind, she saw how inadequate she must have been. Luke had run. Cassie thought, perhaps foolishly, that Luke had enjoyed their lovemaking, that Luke had been . . . satisfied.

She wrapped her arms across her chest, then made herself walk to the table. The first sentence stilled her nerves a bit as she let out a sigh of relief.

"I didn't want to leave your arms this morning, Cass," Luke had written. "Last night was so incredible for me, I hope it was for you, too. I thought you might need some time to yourself. I won't force things. Call me when you're ready. And if you change your mind, I'll understand."

Cassie closed her eyes, clutching the note to her. *Change my mind?* God, after last night, was there any doubt? It was far too late for Cassie to change her mind. She read the note again, wondering if the last sentence was hard for Luke to write.

She made coffee in a daze, her mind never wandering far from

162

last night. She didn't know how she was supposed to feel this morning, and she couldn't seem to concentrate on anything. The scenes in her mind were like a motion picture, and she continued to rewind every one, over and over again.

She should be exhausted but she felt very much alive. And happy, she noted, as she smiled to herself. She felt . . . free. Finally.

She took a steaming cup of coffee and filled the bath, then slipped into the hot, bubbly water, enveloping her skin much like Luke's hands had done. A lazy smile covered her face, and shutting her eyes, she allowed Luke's hands to roam over her again.

Cassie could feel the change in herself. She wondered if it would show.

But she no longer cared, she realized. This newfound sense of freedom that she felt wasn't going to be easy to hide. Luke had set her spirit free and all Cassie felt like doing now was embracing her happiness, embracing her new life.

Embracing Luke.

Her body tingled as she toweled off, and her breasts ached. She wanted to go to Luke right now, she wanted to be in her arms, she wanted . . . to make love with her again.

She felt nearly insatiable, and she pulled on the first pair of jeans she found. She slipped an old sweatshirt on, shoved her sockless feet into her Nikes, and grabbed her keys.

She didn't stop to wonder if Luke would want to see her now, if Luke was even home. The only thing on her mind was having Luke's naked body in her arms.

As she stood by Luke's door, she realized she was trembling. She could hardly contain this want, this need, this burning desire to feel Luke's touch upon her, to have her own hands on Luke's body.

Luke answered her urgent knock quickly. Their eyes locked and held, and Cassie's chest heaved as relief . . . and desire flooded Luke's dark eyes.

Luke's hair was still damp from her shower and her T-shirt hid nothing as Cassie's eyes roamed over her body, locking on the erect nipples straining against Luke's shirt.

Cassie opened her mouth to speak, but there were no words to convey what she was feeling. Instead, she went to Luke, trembling arms sliding over strong shoulders. Luke's hands at her waist drew her closer. Their kiss was bruising, demanding, and Luke pinned her against the door.

Her body pressed hard against Luke, and her tongue shoved wildly into Luke's hot mouth. Luke cupped Cassie's hips and pulled her intimately against her, causing Cassie to groan loudly. Visions of last night flashed before her, and Cassie grew weak when Luke sucked her tongue deeper into her mouth.

Cassie shoved a knee between Luke's thighs, much like Luke had done to her that night of the party, her mouth covering Luke's breast, her tongue stroking the nipple through Luke's shirt.

"Bedroom," Luke murmured against her ear. "Now."

Cassie nodded, then lifted her arms as Luke pulled the sweatshirt over her head, dropping it unceremoniously on the floor. Luke's eyes, then hands found her breasts and Cassie was certain they would never make the bedroom. Then Luke collected herself and took Cassie's hand, pulling her toward the stairs.

They stopped halfway up, and Cassie slid her hands under Luke's T-shirt, moving over firm, warm skin. Her mouth would have gone to Luke's breast again, but Luke captured her lips instead, kissing her so thoroughly Cassie felt her legs threaten to buckle.

"Bedroom," Luke said again.

"Hurry."

At Cassie's urgent request, Luke turned and their eyes met, holding for a long moment, then identical smiles touched their lips followed by quiet laughter.

"Hurry, huh?" Luke teased.

Cassie nodded, only slightly embarrassed. She was far too aroused to be concerned with her lack of composure. She wanted to make love to Luke. She wanted her in the worst way.

Luke's mistake was stopping at the doorway to her bedroom and kissing Cassie. Cassie could take no more. Her body was on fire, and she pressed against Luke, hands sliding up her arms and over strong shoulders, pinning Luke against the wall. Then, in one swift motion, her hands yanked Luke's sweatpants down, and she touched warm flesh. Her mouth went to Luke's breast, unmindful of her T-shirt. Then she moved to Luke's mouth, wet and hard, and her hands slipped quickly inside white cotton. She grasped firm buttocks in both hands and squeezed. Her hands wouldn't still, and Cassie swallowed Luke's moan as her fingers slid quickly into Luke's wetness.

Cassie held Luke against the wall as her leg nudged Luke's thighs farther apart. Their tongues battled as Cassie's fingers delved deep inside Luke, pulling out slowly, only to dive back, deeper this time, meeting each thrust of Luke's hips.

Cassie's mouth again went back to Luke's breast, her shirt wet from Cassie's tongue, and Cassie's lips closed over an erect peak. Luke's hips thrust wildly against her hand, and her shoulders felt bruised as Luke gripped her hard, holding Cassie to her breast.

Luke's sharp gasps for breath thrilled Cassie, and her hand moved faster, plunging into Luke until she felt the first tremors shake Luke's body. Luke's hips surged once more against Cassie, and her cry was short and quick.

Cassie kept her fingers inside Luke and their eyes held, then Luke's mouth was soft on Cassie's as she slowly withdrew her wet fingers.

"Only in my dreams did I imagine this," Cassie murmured against Luke's mouth.

"You're a very quick learner," Luke teased.

Luke's hands slid up Cassie's body, warm fingers closing over her breasts and Cassie surrendered to Luke's demanding tongue as their mouths met yet again. Her knees felt weak, and she didn't protest when Luke pulled her to the carpet. Cassie guided Luke to her breast, holding her there as Luke's wet mouth covered her. Her legs locked around Luke's thigh and she arched into her, the ache between her legs greater than anything she could possibly comprehend.

Luke's hand cupped her intimately, the seam of her jeans pressing into her, arousing her even more. She wanted to feel Luke's fingers on her, inside of her.

"Luke . . . *please*." Cassie unbuttoned her jeans and took Luke's hand, shoving it quickly between her legs. She moaned loudly, her head thrashing when Luke moved through her wetness, slipping easily inside her.

Cassie kicked at her jeans, shoving them down around her knees. Luke spread Cassie's thighs even farther, and as her fingers moved in and out of her wetness, Luke bent down, her tongue licking at her intimately, joining her fingers as she sought to drive Cassie over the edge.

"Dear God!" Cassie's hips writhed beneath Luke, and she was blinded by the explosion that shook her body. *Too soon.* The scream tore from her, she shuddered, and tears streamed from her eyes.

"Luke." The word was barely a whisper and she gathered Luke in her arms.

Cassie lay there, her eyes still shut, and she let Luke kiss her tears away.

"It's just too much," Cassie finally whispered.

"What is?"

Cassie opened her eyes and found Luke's.

"The way you make me feel. Like I'm going to explode."

Luke kissed her hard. "I want you to explode."

Cassie rolled over, her weight now resting on Luke.

"Why is this T-shirt still on?"

She straddled Luke's legs and pulled her into a sitting position, tugging the shirt over her head. Her breath caught at the sight of Luke's perfect breasts, and she raised her eyes to Luke's.

"I don't think . . . I can get enough of you."

Their eyes held as Cassie's hands moved over Luke's breasts, her fingers raking across firm nipples. Then she pulled her eyes away and pushed Luke back, her mouth covering one breast, feasting as if it were the first time. Against her tongue, the nipple swelled even more ,and she sucked at it hungrily. She felt Luke's hips move against her and she shuddered.

Cassie's jeans were still tangled around one foot and Luke's sweatpants were only shoved down to her knees. Cassie kicked the offending jeans away and her hands peeled Luke's sweats off. Cassie again straddled Luke and knelt over her, their eyes locking as Cassie's hands moved over Luke's smooth skin, teasing her breasts before moving lower.

"I want . . . my mouth on you," Cassie whispered hoarsely.

She felt Luke tremble beneath her hands and as their eyes held, Cassie licked her lips, causing Luke to tremble even more.

"I don't know what to do," she admitted.

"Yes, you do."

She knelt between Luke's legs, her hands gently spreading Luke's thighs. Cassie moaned when she saw her, glistening wet and ready for her. She looked up again, but Luke's eyes were closed, her lips parted.

Cassie groaned in anticipation as Luke's scent drifted to her, then Luke's hands were there, gently urging her down, and she was nearly embarrassed by the sound that came from deep inside as her mouth settled over Luke. Her tongue moved through Luke's wetness, tasting another woman for the first time, and Cassie felt her own wetness flood her again.

Cassie stretched out full length on the floor and her arms wrapped around Luke's hips, pulling her more firmly against her mouth as if she had done this a thousand times before.

"Oh, God, Cassie . . . don't stop," Luke begged.

Cassie had no intention of stopping. Her tongue delved into her again, entering her, then her mouth closed over her swollen clit, sucking her hard into her mouth, and Luke's hips moved against her. Cassie held Luke tight, sucking harder until Luke gasped, her hips raised off the floor despite Cassie's effort to hold her there.

"Jesus!"

Cassie reluctantly pulled her mouth away, resting her cheek on Luke's smooth abdomen. She closed her eyes and listened as Luke's ragged breathing slowed, then she slid up next to Luke, one leg still pinning Luke beneath her.

"Okay?"

Cassie nodded at the whispered question. "I didn't want to stop," she said shyly. "I wanted you like that last night."

"Why didn't you?"

"I was afraid I wouldn't know what to do. I was afraid it wouldn't be enough."

"Enough?"

"I wanted you to be satisfied," she said shyly.

Luke let out a heavy sigh. "Oh, sweetheart, you're the best lover. I know all of this is new to you, but you have nothing to worry about." Then she grinned. "You know, I do have a bed."

They were standing together, silently touching, gently stroking each other, exploring soft skin beneath their fingers. Cassie's breathing felt labored, and she let her eyes travel lazily over Luke's body, finally meeting those dark, passion-filled eyes that locked with hers.

"You're so beautiful," Cassie murmured. "I love touching you."

If possible, Luke's eyes turned darker still, and she reached out a trembling hand to softly caress Cassie's face.

"You make me feel beautiful. I love the way you look at me."

Cassie turned and captured Luke's hand, pressing her lips into her palm, wetting it with her tongue. At Luke's soft moan, she brought the hand to her breast, watching as Luke's fingers closed over her. Then Luke's lips were there, claiming hers with a passion that ignited the flame in Cassie's soul.

Their eyes locked.

"Do you have any idea what you do to me?"

Cassie's whispered question echoed in the room and Luke's eyes softened. "And you have no idea what you do to me."

Cassie sunk onto the bed, pulling Luke after her, drawing her weight on top of her, loving the feel of Luke settling between her legs. There was no more time for words and their mouths met gently, softly, then with a hunger neither cared to suppress.

Chapter Twenty-six

"Do you have to get going right away?"

Luke was adding spinach to the onions and mushrooms already sautéing, and Cassie had just started the pasta.

"What do you mean?"

"Do you have work to do or can you spend the day?" Luke asked.

Cassie chuckled. "I always have work to do, but I'd love to spend the day with you."

"I thought maybe we could drive to Bodega Bay," Luke offered. "Maybe do a little hiking."

"Look for driftwood?" Cassie countered.

"And look for driftwood. It would almost be like working."

Cassie walked behind Luke, casually touching her as she peered into the pan. "Smells good. I'm starving."

"I wonder why?" Luke teased.

Cassie blushed crimson and moved away, but Luke reached out

and stopped her. "It was the best morning of my life," Luke said seriously.

"Mine, too," Cassie whispered.

Their passion of earlier was, for the time being, satiated, and their kiss was gentle, unhurried.

"I just don't want you to leave yet," Luke confessed.

A relieved smile crept onto Cassie's face as long arms pulled her close. She nestled her face against Luke's shoulder, wrapping her arms around Luke's waist and she sighed contentedly as lazy hands traced circles on her back.

"I'm not going anywhere."

She felt Luke kiss the top of her head, and the arms around Luke's waist squeezed in reflex. As Luke pulled away and went back to the stove, Cassie quietly fumbled with the feelings trying to explode inside her. *In love?*

Her cheeks flushed at her silent admission. Not that she had a lot of experience in the matter, but what she was feeling was certainly foreign to her. Maybe she was simply confusing her body's physical reaction to Luke, assuming she was in love with her, when perhaps it was only lust.

"Cassie?"

She looked up, startled. "Hmm?"

"Pasta," Luke prompted.

"Oh, sorry."

They finished preparing lunch, mostly in silence. Cassie thought that perhaps Luke was lost in her own thoughts. She must be wondering about Cassie's intentions, too. For that matter, Cassie wondered just how far Luke's feelings had gone.

"Weldon Arnold called me, by the way."

Cassie made room for Luke at the bar, accepting the plate piled high with pasta and vegetables.

"About me?" Cassie inquired. She hadn't given him a thought in days.

Luke nodded. "Some guy from Lake Tahoe is going to call you. Wants four pieces, if you've got them."

"Four? Sight unseen?"

"I'm sure he trusts Weldon. And Weldon wanted to know if you'd considered his offer of Union Square?"

Cassie finally picked up her fork, her hand slightly shaking. So, four pieces just like that. Her nerves got the better of her, and she put her fork down again.

"I'm not sure I'm ready for this," she admitted.

"What do you mean? You don't have four finished?"

Cassie nodded slowly. "Yes, I have seven completely finished, four others that still need some work. I mean, mentally, I don't think I'm prepared for this," she said vaguely.

"Are you afraid of success . . . or failure?" Luke asked gently.

Cassie sighed, knowing Luke had hit on the truth. "It's one thing to display my carvings at county fairs. People come by and look and if they like something enough, they'll buy it. If not, I wait for the next person."

"Displaying your work in a gallery is different how?"

"People who go to Union Square can afford my work. If they don't buy it, it's not because of the price, it's because they don't like it."

"Ah," Luke nodded. "And at the fair, if they don't buy it, you can blame it on the price?"

Cassie grinned. "Silly, I know. But it works for me."

Luke put her own fork down and squeezed Cassie's hand. "There are a lot of wealthy people around who would never dream of having me design a home for them. I don't take that to mean they dislike what I do, just that they don't like it for themselves. Sleek lines and steel beams aren't my style. And people who have homes like that wouldn't be interested in displaying one of your wood carvings, either."

"Thanks. I know you're right. This is just so sudden and unexpected," Cassie explained.

"I really wish you would give it a try, but it's your decision." Then she shrugged. "You're doing quite well the way things are anyway."

"Thanks to you. And Mr. Arnold," she added. "I'm going to send four to Lake Tahoe. I can start with that. Then, maybe in the spring, if I have enough pieces, I'll let Mr. Arnold make a few calls, if that's still an option."

"Good enough."

"And thank you for the encouragement. It means a lot to me."

Luke leaned over and kissed her. "You've got great talent. I just want you to be rewarded for it."

An hour later, they were headed for Bodega Bay. This late on a Saturday afternoon, it wouldn't be crowded, and Cassie looked forward to walking with Luke on the rocky shore. If they were lucky, they might see whales that were still migrating. Then she grinned. If they were really lucky, she might find a prized piece of driftwood.

"Why are you smiling?" Luke asked.

"I was picturing finding an awesome piece of driftwood and having you there to carry it back for me," she teased.

"Cheap labor, huh?"

"I'll make it worth your while," Cassie promised and was rewarded with a quick kiss from Luke.

But they had no such luck with driftwood. They passed several hikers on the trail, and twice Cassie wanted to accost them for the wood they carried. She watched with envy as they walked out of sight.

"Are you coveting their wood?" Luke asked as Cassie looked longingly after the hikers.

Cassie laughed good-naturedly and agreed. "Especially that last one. With the curve on it, I think I could have done another beaver similar to the one Weldon bought."

"Maybe we'll find something for you."

But the wood had been picked over, and Cassie was content to just enjoy her walk with Luke, although she did manage to find a few smaller pieces that she thought she could do something with. She was having a hard time dismissing her small carvings. She told Luke as much.

"Cassie, your art is as much a pleasure for you as it is a business.

You shouldn't give something up just because it won't make you as much money."

"I thought that I could stop and just do the large carvings, but I don't think I can," Cassie admitted. "The small ones don't take nearly as long, and it's almost therapy for me, you know. The large ones are work, but I love the finished product. The small ones are a hobby."

"At least you can sell your hobby, but I know what you mean about therapy. If I didn't take time to paint . . . or attempt to paint," she clarified. "I might very well take up drinking again. Sometimes, dealing with designs and demanding clients all day takes its toll."

"I wish you would let me see some of your paintings," Cassie said.

"No."

Luke's word was firm, and while Cassie wondered at her hesitation, she didn't press.

"They're not very good," Luke finally said. "But I do get enjoyment from doing them."

"I understand." Cassie also knew that artists were their own worst critics. They might not be commercial quality, but Cassie doubted they were as bad as Luke made them out to be.

It was only later, after a light dinner of salad and leftover pasta that Luke finally brought up the subject of their relationship. Cassie had secretly been dreading it. She didn't know what Luke wanted, and she was afraid of how quickly she was falling.

But as they sat together in companionable silence on Luke's sofa, their hands linked, Luke finally brought it up.

"Are you okay with everything?"

"Do I look like I'm not?"

"What about in here?" Luke asked, lightly tapping Cassie's head.

"Surprisingly, I feel great. I mean, I was so scared of what I was feeling, I was scared that I couldn't run from it. Every time I came near you . . ."

"What?"

"I wanted you," Cassie admitted. "But I kept hearing my father's voice, I kept hearing his words. I could see it as if it were yesterday, him holding his Bible over Kim, quoting from it, warning her of her fate." Cassie brought Luke's hand to her mouth and kissed it lightly. "None of that matters. That night of the party, what I really wanted you to do was throw me down on the bed and rip my clothes off," Cassie admitted shyly.

"I thought, maybe, that I had pushed too much, gone too far," Luke confessed. "I came home, took a giant bowl of ice cream with me and sat in the Jacuzzi for two hours, cursing myself. I didn't want to scare you. But I thought that once you were alone and had time to think about things, that you would hate yourself for what we did, for what we almost did."

Cassie nodded in understanding. "And then I didn't call you."

"Yes. And I couldn't bring myself to call. I was determined to let you make the decision."

"The real reason I didn't call was . . . I was afraid to be alone with you. I knew how much I wanted you. I'm thirty-three years old and here I was, trying to fight feelings that I had never had before."

"How long have you known you were gay?"

"I started considering the possibility the last time I slept with a man," Cassie admitted.

"How long ago was that?" Luke asked quietly.

Cassie shrugged. "Six, seven years ago."

Luke squeezed her hand. "I'm sorry. So many years of pretending," Luke said.

"Yes. I could never, ever acknowledge an attraction to a woman," she said. "I wouldn't let a woman get close. I was too scared." She shrugged. "Besides, I was introduced around here as Kim's straight friend. I've always been teased that I'm just the honorary lesbian in the group."

"And guys?" Luke prodded.

"I dated occasionally. A few kisses, nothing more." She turned

174

to Luke. "I didn't have any desire for sex. None." Cassie leaned over and kissed Luke on the mouth. "Then I saw you on the sidewalk that day, and I knew my life would never be the same. I knew that day, when you turned around and caught me staring, that I wanted you . . . sexually. I knew that at that very moment. I just couldn't accept it. And when I met you, feelings that I didn't even know were inside of me came out, and I couldn't handle it."

"What if I hadn't rescued you in the storm? We might never have become friends."

"You thought I was gay," Cassie reminded her.

Luke laughed. "You were!"

"Yes, but I wasn't nearly ready to admit it to anyone. Certainly not to you. I mean, you were the one causing me all this stress."

Their eyes were gentle on each other, and Luke brought Cassie's hand to her lips and kissed it.

"I didn't mean to cause you stress. I just couldn't stay away from you. I want to be with you. I want us to get to know each other better. But I'm not entirely certain what you want from this."

Cassie held her gaze, seeing uncertainty in her eyes. She wondered how a beautiful, strong woman like Luke could be insecure.

"Now that I've been with a woman, you think I might want to go out and sample the local gals? Make up for lost time?" Cassie asked lightly.

"Do you?" Luke asked weakly.

"Haven't you heard a word I've said?" She kissed Luke softly on the lips, then whispered, "There's only you." She smiled, her lips still pressed firmly against Luke. "I feel like I've been waiting for you my whole life."

Chapter Twenty-seven

Cassie drove home in a bit of a daze, her mind wandering back to the two days she had spent with Luke. She had come home only briefly on Sunday, to shower and change into clean clothes. Then she had gone back to Luke's, and they spent a lazy day exploring Luke's meadow and woods, then lounging on her deck, talking and sharing stories as if they were old friends. When the rain chased them indoors, they cooked an early dinner, far too much for the two of them, but they both found they enjoyed cooking together. They had gone to bed early, but they hardly slept, neither had wanted to. Now, the steady rain of the day before gave way to brilliant sunshine, and she fumbled in her backpack, looking for sunglasses.

Once again, her mind went back to the incredibly intimate night they had spent together. Her stomach rolled when she thought of them together and all they had done. Her lips were tender and swollen, and she thought that her passion was sated, but just the thought of making love with Luke brought back all of the heat and desire of last night. She felt her nipples harden and strain against the T-shirt she was wearing, Luke's T-shirt. Then she laughed. She looked a sight, she knew. They could not find her panties this morning, so she did without. And in her rush to get to Luke the day before, she had not bothered with a bra. Now her breasts were swollen, taut, still aching for Luke's hands and mouth. Even as she had left Luke this morning, Luke's hands were still touching her, her mouth still calling her.

And Cassie hadn't wanted to leave, but Luke had to make a trip to the city, and Cassie needed to work. She felt inspired, thank goodness. She had decided to do the Christmas fair after all, if only to bring the handful of smaller carvings that usually sold so well during the holidays. She shrugged. And the seal. Maybe someone would take a liking to her. The Christmas fair kicked off the week after Thanksgiving and was open every Saturday until Christmas. Because the costs of the booths were higher than the outdoor fairs, she and Kim always shared one, although she doubted she would have enough inventory to last that long.

The thought of telling Kim everything that had happened the last few days made her blush. Kim would want to know details. *Every detail.* She only hoped she wouldn't tease her too much. Especially on Thanksgiving, as she had invited Luke to share dinner with them. She knew Kim and Lisa wouldn't mind.

She drove into the driveway, her thoughts alternating between working and Luke's exquisite body when she slammed on her brakes.

"Oh . . . my . . . *God!*" Her pulse accelerated and her palms turned damp with nervousness. *Shit!*

There was her father, leaning against his old Ford, arms folded across his chest as he waited for her.

"Fuck! Shit!" She stopped her van next to his car and took a deep breath. What in the world was he doing here? And now, of all times.

"Well, Cassandra, I see you do still live here."

She slammed her door shut, and it took all of her courage to face him. He was an intimidating man, well over six feet tall. His hair had turned steel gray but his eyes were the same piercing blue that she remembered from her childhood.

"Hello, Father. What are you doing here?"

"It *is* Thanksgiving," he said pointedly.

She looked bewildered, wondering if her day and night with Luke had taken her around the clock more than once. "It's . . . Monday," she finally stammered.

"So it is." Then he frowned, his eyes piercing hers. "And where have you been?" he demanded.

"At a friend's," she said quietly. How dare he? How dare he show up here . . . at her house . . . and demand answers to her whereabouts?

"I called you all day yesterday. And late last night," he added. "I arrived here very early this morning. I was worried about you. It's been awhile since I've heard from you."

She swallowed with difficulty and averted her eyes. Once again, she was a child, and she stood to suffer the wrath of her father. It was very obvious that she wore no bra, and she resisted the urge to cover herself.

"Girl, you best not be living in sin!" he boomed. "I raised you better." His finger shook at her and she wondered why she was allowing him his say. "Now, out with it. What kind of man keeps a young girl out all night?"

She summoned all her courage and squared her shoulders, finally meeting his eyes. "I'm not a child. I'm a thirty-three-year-old woman, and I don't answer to you anymore."

"Nonsense! I'm still your father, and you are still my responsibility. When you take a husband, then he can watch over you."

His voice was raised, his finger shaking at her, and she couldn't take it another second.

"I am not your responsibility, and I don't need someone to watch over me! I have been on my own, supporting myself since the day I moved out of your house. *Jesus Christ!* You can't come here . . ."

"Don't speak to me like that! I'll not have it!" his voice boomed.

Cassie lowered her eyes, surprised at her outburst. "This is my home," she said quietly. "We haven't seen each other in two years. Must we start out with a fight?"

When he didn't answer, she asked, "Are you staying through Thanksgiving?"

"It is a time for family," he said, and his voice had calmed, too. "As you said, it's been two years. I thought we could spend some time together. I'm not getting any younger, you know. I waited for your invitation, but you never called. And when I couldn't reach you, I thought something was wrong. Apparently . . ."

"Don't start," she warned, cutting him off. She would not allow him to place guilt on her again. Jesus, what a way to spoil a perfectly wonderful day.

"Do you need help with your bag?" she offered.

"I can manage."

He lifted his worn suitcase from the trunk, then followed her to the house. "I don't want you to go to any trouble. I thought we could take in Thanksgiving dinner at one of the cafes in town."

"I already have plans . . . with Kim and Lisa," she said. *And Luke.* God, wouldn't this be fun.

"Kim? You still haven't come to your senses, girl?"

She kept her back to him as she opened the front door. "Kim is my best friend."

"She's a sinner," he spat.

"She's a lesbian," Cassie corrected, surprised how easily the word came out of her mouth.

"I'll not have you use that word in my presence!" his voice resounded.

She turned back to face him, her face red. "Why must you always come here and start a fight? Can't we have a normal father-daughter conversation for once?"

"I'm trying to save you, girl!"

"Well, I'll take my chances, thanks," she murmured.

"Don't let her bring you down, Cassandra," he continued.

"Whatever." She rubbed her temples. It was hard for her to believe that only an hour ago, she was still in Luke's arms.

Her father grabbed her arm and spun her around, towering over her as if she was a child again.

"She will suffer eternal damnation! Do not doubt my words. She is nothing but trouble."

Cassie opened her mouth to speak, then closed it again. What could she say to him? That Kim wasn't the only one in danger?

"Please," she begged. "I don't want to argue with you. If you plan to stay through Thanksgiving, I won't have this conversation with you." Then she straightened her shoulders. "If not, you can go right back to the city."

Her father released her arm, finally. "I pray for you," he whispered.

"Thanks," she said sarcastically. "That means a lot."

She wanted a cigarette.

Instead, she busied herself making coffee, cursing her weakness when it came to her father. She wasn't a child, for Christ's sake. And it wasn't as if she relied on him for support, emotional or otherwise. But a small part of her resisted severing that last tie between them. He was the only family she had.

"You haven't called me since summer."

She stiffened, but refused to turn to face him. Their last phone conversation had ended in an argument.

"I've been busy," she said vaguely.

"Oh, yes. With your *art*."

Cassie's eyes flashed. It was as if he enjoyed sparring with her over her chosen profession. She turned to face him, her eyes still shimmering with anger.

"It pays the bills."

"I don't know why you won't just get a real job."

"A real job, Father?"

"A respectable job."

Cassie managed to bring a quick smile to her face. "I am quite respected in my field, thanks. And I've long given up hope that you might someday be proud of me."

She brushed past him, satisfied to see that her words had hit their mark. The bridge between them had grown too large. She realized she no longer cared if she hurt him. It was like he was a stranger to her now.

It wasn't until she was standing under the hot spray of her shower that she allowed her thoughts to go to Luke. She shivered when she remembered Luke's hands and mouth on her and her own nearly insatiable desire to touch Luke.

And again she was angry with her father. How was she to explain to Luke that she couldn't see her tonight? Luke would never understand Cassie's fear of her father.

Well, she would have to deal with it soon enough. Luke was going to call her when she got back from the city. She planned to come over to Cassie's and they were going to cook a meal together. And after that, they would be in each other's arms again. Cassie didn't know what was better—going to sleep with Luke's arms wrapped around her, or waking with those same arms holding her.

And even though she was angry with her father, a part of her wondered if she had a right to be. He was getting older, and she was the only family he had. And it was Thanksgiving. She could make the sacrifice for a few days.

He did look older, she thought. And tired. She quickly calculated his age at sixty-six, but he looked years older than that.

When she went back into the living room, he was seated in her recliner, eyes closed, and she thought that he was sleeping. His voice startled her when he spoke.

"I don't want to keep you from anything."

"I was just going to go out to my workshop," she said.

"I've been admiring the squirrel you have here."

Again he surprised her. The small squirrel was perched on the table next to her recliner and by her own admission, it wasn't very good. But it was one of her earliest attempts, one she had done when she was still in college, and it had become special to her. A reminder of her innocence, perhaps, or how far she'd come as an artist.

"You're welcome to come out to my workshop and look around," she offered, clearly surprising him as well as herself.

They made the walk in silence, Cassie wracking her brain for a neutral topic, but nothing came. She was secretly pleased as his eyes widened when he saw her work, and she realized that this was the first time he had seen any of her carvings.

He walked slowly to one of the eagles, his hand tentatively reaching out to touch, then he stopped.

"It's okay to touch them," she said with a smile. "They won't bite."

"My goodness, it looks so real," he murmured. His eyes lifted to Cassie's, and she saw sadness there. "I never realized."

"Realized what?"

"That you were this . . . talented."

She swallowed the lump in her throat with difficulty. Despite everything that was between them, it meant so much to her to hear him utter those words, words she never would have believed he was capable of saying to her.

"Thank you."

"What would this cost?"

"Four thousand."

He literally gasped, and she grinned at the look on his face.

"I had no idea."

He cleared his throat and moved away from the eagle, quietly inspecting the other pieces she had before moving to the shelves that housed her smaller carvings. He gingerly picked up another squirrel and turned it over in his hands.

"You have a lot of squirrels," he said quietly.

She shrugged. She'd never thought about it really. Eagles, sure. They were her trademark, but as she surveyed the shelf, she noticed that she indeed did have a number of squirrels, all in different poses, with different expressions.

"Your mother loved squirrels," he said softly.

She felt her heart tighten. It was the first time he had mentioned her since she was a child.

"She used to feed them in the backyard," he continued. "You would sit on her lap and laugh as they ventured close. I remember the first time one ate out of your hand. You were barely four, and I was so afraid it would bite you, but she kept insisting you would be fine."

Cassie felt tears well in her eyes as she tried to remember her mother and her lost childhood. She wanted to ask a thousand questions, but he suddenly turned and hurried from the shop. She didn't stop him. Instead, she picked up the squirrel he had been holding and clutched it to her. She closed her eyes, trying to picture herself as a child, sitting on her mother's lap. She wondered if she looked like her mother. She certainly didn't resemble him. Only the eyes, she corrected. She had his blue eyes.

The ringing of the phone brought her back to the present.

"Where have you been?" Kim demanded.

Cassie sighed. "I'll start by saying I've been with Luke and end by saying my father's here."

"Good God! Are you joking? What's he doing there?" Then a pause. "Luke? You've seen her?"

"Yes. But it's far too much for the phone and now he's here for Thanksgiving."

"I take it this is unexpected? What happened with Luke?"

Cassie managed a laugh. "I went with her to Sacramento on Friday. I've been at her house all weekend." Then she lowered her voice. "He came into my workshop, Kim. He actually mentioned her."

"Luke?"

"*No*," Cassie hissed. "My mother."

Silence on the other end, then, "No shit?"

"No shit," Cassie murmured.

"What's up with that?"

Cassie rolled her eyes. Kim could be so difficult sometimes. "I've got a major problem here. Luke's supposed to come over tonight. Not only that, I invited her for Thanksgiving dinner."

"But that's great, Cass."

Cassie again rolled her eyes. "My father?"

Again silence. "I see. Well, you've got a problem all right."

"You're a big help."

"I would give you my opinion, but I doubt you'd like it."

"Go about my life and he can take it or leave?" she guessed.

"Pretty much. It's not like you're on good terms with him, Cass."

"But he's still . . ."

"Your father," Kim finished for her. "I know."

"He's the only family I have."

"Maybe the only blood family, but hardly your only family."

Cassie realized she had hurt Kim's feelings and Luke's words came back to her. Sometimes friends were better than family.

"I love you, Kim," Cassie said softly.

"I love you, too."

They both cleared their throats at the same time and Cassie chuckled. "So, are you up to seeing him? For Thanksgiving dinner, I mean?"

"Of course. But I won't promise I'll behave. If he starts on me . . ." she warned.

"I don't expect you to be anything less than who you are, Kim. He's the guest, not you."

"Okay." She sighed, then Cassie heard her amused chuckle. "Are you going to tell me about Luke now or make me wait?"

"Oh, I think I'll make you wait."

"Don't do this to me, Cassie. I've waited thirteen years for this moment."

"Have you, now?" Cassie teased. "Well, at least you know you were right. By the way, it was fabulous," she added before hanging up.

Chapter Twenty-eight

Cassie realized she was pacing. She had already had most of a bottle of Chardonnay and still Luke had not called. She glanced at the kitchen clock once again and feared Luke would just show up, expecting to surprise her.

Oh, it would be a surprise, all right.

Her father was in the living room, reading, waiting for dinner. She had a rice and bean casserole in the oven, hoping he wouldn't comment on her diet. It was something he had never understood and Cassie doubted he ever would.

She nearly dropped her wineglass when the phone rang, yanking it up on the first ring.

"Hi. Waiting for me?"

Despite the anxiety she was feeling over her father, that voice warmed her to her very soul.

"Are you running late?"

"Yes. I just want to shower. I'll be there in a few minutes," Luke said.

"Well, if you're tired, we can do dinner another night," Cassie offered lamely.

"I'm not tired," Luke stated. "It's still early enough for dinner, isn't it?"

"Oh, sure. I just didn't want you to have to rush over here, I mean, you've been driving all day and all."

Luke was silent for a moment, and Cassie could picture her raised eyebrow. "What's wrong?" she asked quietly.

Cassie closed her eyes. "My father is here," she whispered. "He was already here when I got home this morning."

"I see. And you'd rather he didn't meet me?"

Cassie heard the hurt that Luke tried to hide, and she realized she was being utterly ridiculous. She was no longer a teenager trying to please her father. She was a grown woman, used to being on her own, and there was no logical reason that she couldn't have Luke over to dinner like they'd planned.

"I'm sorry. Of course I want him to meet you. I was having a moment of panic, I'm afraid."

"No, I'm being unfair and very selfish," Luke said. "I understand if you're not ready to spring this on him."

Cassie swallowed. *Spring it on him?* She still had a hard time believing it herself. She wasn't nearly ready to confront her father with this. She wasn't sure she would ever be ready.

"I do want you to come over, Luke. But don't expect . . ."

"A kiss when I get there?" Luke finished for her.

"I know you don't understand. How could you? Your own mother brought you out, but this is different. I know him and what he would say and trust me, you don't want to be around for that."

"Okay, then let's don't do it. This is obviously upsetting you, Cass. Enjoy the evening with your father. We'll talk tomorrow, and just see what happens."

She was hurt, Cassie could tell. But this was for the best. Cassie just couldn't handle a scene with her father in front of Luke.

"Thanksgiving is still on, right?" Cassie asked.

"Are you sure?"

"Yes. Luke, just give me time to adjust to him being here. Please?"

"I missed you today," Luke said quietly.

"Me, too. I was looking forward to this evening with you."

"Well, there will be plenty of other evenings. I've got some work I can do anyway."

Cassie sighed, not liking the tone of their conversation. It was not at all how she pictured the evening. "I'm sorry," she whispered.

"It's okay, Cass. I understand. I really do. We'll talk later, okay?"

"Sure."

She hung up slowly and sighed yet again. Kim was right. She owed her father nothing. She should just go on about her life and not worry about his reaction. But she found she couldn't. She refilled her wineglass and stood staring out the window as darkness settled around her.

"So, people actually pay four thousand dollars for those carvings?" her father asked over dinner. He was on his second helping of her casserole, and she was genuinely pleased.

"Yes. Actually, I sold a rather large one awhile back, an eagle with a six foot wingspan, for twelve thousand."

He nearly spit his food out and she laughed.

"That was pretty much my reaction, too," she admitted.

"I guess you're not hurting for money, then."

She hesitated before answering. "I do okay. I'm not exactly a rich woman, but these last few months have been good." Since Luke walked into your life, she told herself silently, and she allowed a small smile to cross her face.

"I always worried that you'd be just scraping by, peddling your stuff on the streets just to pay your bills," he said quietly.

"You never took the time to find out," she countered. "You never showed even the slightest interest in my carvings."

He raised his eyes to hers, and she was surprised at the sadness there. She was so used to seeing disappointment . . . and contempt in them when he looked at her.

"I was a lousy father to you."

She opened her mouth to protest, but words wouldn't form. It was true. It was also the very last thing she expected to ever hear him say.

"I just wanted to protect you, to teach you what was right."

She couldn't stop the bitter laugh that followed. "Protect me? From what? *Life?*"

She stood quickly and took her unfinished plate to the sink. She stared out at the darkness, totally unprepared for the turn their conversation had taken. She was used to his chastising, to his preaching, to his belittling her.

"I grew up not knowing anything about the real world. Frankly, I'm surprised I was able to make it through college without going totally crazy. You always painted this picture of good and evil, but you never allowed for the gray area between them." She turned back to face him, gathering her courage before continuing. "Do you have any idea how it was to grow up alone, without being allowed to have friends, without being allowed to even go to the movies, or to the prom, or any of the other normal things kids do?"

"I was just trying to protect you," he said again. "Had you stayed with me, gotten more involved in my church, you would see . . ."

"That was your life. That was what you chose to do with it," she said. "I just wanted to be a kid. A normal kid."

"You wanted for nothing," he reminded her.

"I wanted friends," she countered. "But you were too afraid I might find out there was a life out there besides our little church community."

"I always hoped you would marry a nice man from the church, yes."

"How? You never let me date."

"You were too young," he said, his voice becoming hard.

"Eighteen is not too young. But you wouldn't even let me go to the prom alone. You insisted on taking us and picking us up."

"I didn't know what else to do. You weren't ready to go out alone."

"Because you never allowed me the chance to learn," she said loudly. "Don't you see? You never trusted me. You never trusted me to make the right decision on my own."

"I allowed you to go to a public college," he reminded her.

"Only because I threatened to leave home."

"And look where that has gotten you," he spat. "Living out here, alone. No husband, no children. There were plenty of nice men in the church who would have gladly taken you in."

"Taken me in?"

"Given you children. Made you a proper wife."

"Do you even hear what you're saying?" she asked. "What makes you think I wanted any of those men?"

"They would have made good husbands, a good home for you."

"I have a home here. I have a life here."

"Is that enough? Don't you want a family?"

She shook her head. "I'm happy here. I have great friends, and they can be better than family sometimes," she said, echoing Luke's words.

"It's not the same and you know it."

She sighed, wondering where this conversation would take them. "Kim is the best friend I could ever hope to have. She is always here when I need her, no matter what. I can't say that for family."

"Kim," he spat. "She was always the one to put these foolish thoughts into your head. If you had never met her, imagine what your life could be like."

"Yes. I shudder to think of it," she said sarcastically.

"Cassandra! She's brought you down. She's the reason you moved out here so far from your home, your family."

Cassie was surprised she could actually laugh at his statement. "She didn't bring me down. She brought me up. Don't you see? She showed me that there was this whole world out here," she said, spreading her arms. "A world I never even knew existed."

"Yes! A world of deviants and perverts."

She stared at him, waiting for one of the Bible quotes she knew was sure to follow. She was not disappointed.

"As Paul wrote to the Romans, 'Men abandoned *natural* relations with women and were inflamed with lust for one another. Men committed *indecent* acts with other men, and received the due penalty for their *perversion.*'"

"Oh, *excuse* me. And who was Paul?" she asked sarcastically. "Oh, right, he was the one who said women should not teach, should not speak in church, should not even cut their hair. We *do* follow all of his teachings, don't we?"

"It is not for you to question, child. Perversion is perversion, plain and simple. The Bible is very clear," he insisted. "And you were taught better than to associate with *those* people. Perhaps you need to spend a little more time in church and get reacquainted with God's word."

"Thank you, Reverend Parker," she said with a hint of sarcasm. "And here I thought I was having a discussion with my father."

She left without waiting for his reply and childishly slammed her bedroom door. It would never change between them, she realized, until she stood up to him and demanded that he treat her as an individual and an adult. Instead of the child he apparently still thought she was. Of course, running off and slamming the door hadn't helped her image any, she admitted with a humorless smile.

But did it matter? Did she really think she would ever win his acceptance, professionally or otherwise? No.

Chapter Twenty-nine

She was sitting on the floor of her workshop, the wood pulled between her thighs, carefully using a palm knife to carve around the hawk's head. This one had its beak open and Cassie could almost hear the scream of the red-tailed hawks that soared so effortlessly over her farm. The piece of wood was too small for an eagle but it had the look of a bird of prey, and she decided on a hawk, a red-tailed hawk with spread tail and all. The tail was all but finished, but the head still wasn't to her liking.

That was how her father found her, spread-legged on the floor. She glanced up to meet his eyes, then went back to her wood. They had not spoken since the night before when she'd finally ventured out to give him a blanket and pillow for the sofa.

"I wanted to apologize for yesterday," he started.

She nodded, but didn't speak. She would let him have his say.

"You were right. I keep forgetting that you're all grown up, capable of making your own decisions and choices now."

"Thank you. I hope you mean that," she said sincerely.

"Just so you understand that I don't necessarily agree with your choices."

"You don't have to. My life here isn't a reflection on you."

"No. But there are still members of the church that remember you and ask about you. I have a difficult time coming up with excuses for your absence."

She allowed a small smile. "You mean, you lie to them, Reverend?"

She was surprised that he smiled, too. "I may have stretched the truth a bit," he admitted.

"Surely you haven't said I'm married with four kids or something."

He didn't respond and she was afraid to know what he'd been telling people. But it really didn't matter to her. It was very unlikely she would ever see any of them again.

"Is there something I can do? Fix lunch?" he offered.

"I won't subject you to tofu. How about we drive into town?"

"Maybe get a burger?" he asked hopefully.

"And maybe get a burger," she agreed. "Give me about a half hour."

After he left, she realized that this was the most they had talked in years and the first time they had talked of anything personal. She wondered what was going on with him. Something had to have triggered his sudden need to see her. Last Thanksgiving, they had not even spoken on the phone, much less seen each other.

On the drive into town, she broached the subject of Thanksgiving dinner. He had never met Lisa and Cassie couldn't remember a time when she had mentioned her name. And then there was Luke. She didn't want him to think that it would just be Kim there. And honestly, she was afraid he was planning a preaching session.

"Dinner on Thanksgiving is at Kim's," she said. "It's become a tradition since I moved here."

"If you're worried I'll cause a scene, you can put your mind at rest. She is past saving."

She let out a heavy sigh, one he didn't miss, but she held her tongue. "Kim lives with someone. Lisa. And there'll be another

192

friend there. Luke." Just saying her name out loud caused Cassie to flush. She had not allowed her thoughts to go to Luke much and they had not spoken. She decided she would call her tonight, after she was settled for bed.

"Luke? Is he someone you're seeing?"

Cassie nearly drove off the road, and she coughed several times in panic. *He?*

"Actually, Luke is a woman friend. She bought a couple of my pieces awhile back. She's from the city and didn't have plans so we invited her to join us," she said in a rush.

"Is she . . . like Kim?" he finally asked.

"Like Kim?"

"You know perfectly well what I mean," he snapped.

She nodded. "Yes. Yes, she is. Is that going to be a problem?"

"Why you insist on hanging out with those people, I'll never know. Thick as thieves, I tell you! And you expect me to have *dinner* with them?"

"They're just people. And if you think you can't handle it, I'll recommend a good restaurant in town. You may prefer dinner alone instead of eating with *those people*."

"Cassandra, why? Don't you think people talk? They see you with them, don't you think they'll assume you're one of them, too?"

She laughed. "It's not like anybody cares, you know."

"Well they should care," he said, his voice deepening as if about to launch into a Sunday sermon. "It's sinful. Down right perverted!"

She refused to take the bait and get into an argument she could not win. "Old Towne is supposed to have a great Thanksgiving meal." Then she lowered her voice. "I refuse to let you ruin my Thanksgiving. Who I choose to spend it with is not your concern. You can either join us or eat alone," she threatened. But despite her brave words, her heart pounded nervously in her chest.

"I'll think about it," he said, not giving in easily.

Chapter Thirty

Cassie was disappointed later when Luke's machine picked up. She left only a brief message, telling her she could call later if she wanted. She did add a quick "I miss you" before hanging up, though.

She laid in bed for hours as sleep eluded her. She had hoped Luke would call, and she wondered if she had gone into the city or if she was out with someone.

She pushed the sudden stab of jealousy aside. Luke could go out if she wanted. It wasn't like they had a commitment or anything. *Did they?* She wondered what Luke really thought about Cassie's inability to deal with her father. Luke had been out so long, was openly gay with friends and family alike, probably out professionally, as well. Cassie didn't think Luke was the type to hide who she was from anyone. Maybe Luke had decided Thanksgiving dinner with Cassie's father would be too much for her. Maybe she had already made other plans.

But surely she would have called if she had. *Wouldn't she?* Cassie rolled over and punched at her pillow, mad at herself for being so weak when it came to her father. Was she willing to sacrifice her relationship with Luke to please a man she hardly spoke to, much less spent time with?

And how would Luke treat her at dinner? As a friend she hardly knew or as a lover?

A lover. The word caused all sorts of sensations in Cassie, and she realized just how much she missed Luke. The three nights they had spent together were still very vivid in her mind. Had she ever felt safer, sleeping with Luke's strong arms wrapped around her, holding her? Oh, and how Luke could snuggle. Cassie would never have thought that such an intimidating woman could turn into such a softie. She smiled, remembering how it felt to be loved by Luke, whose touch was as soft and gentle on her as a summer kiss.

She suddenly grabbed her pillow and held it to her, trying to ease the ache that hit her. Only in her dreams did she imagine a lover like Luke. Now that she'd found her, she admitted that she wasn't willing to let her go so easily. No matter what the cost.

Chapter Thirty-one

Cassie picked up the phone and shoved it between her shoulder and chin as she carved the hawk's eye.

"It's me."

Cassie nearly dropped the knife as Luke's voice purred in her ear.

"Hey." She clutched the phone tighter. "Oh, God, I miss you," she said, uttering the first words in her mind.

Luke chuckled. "Do you? I never would have imagined. My phone hasn't been ringing off the hook."

Cassie moved away from the hawk and sat with her back against the wall, knees drawn to her chest. She unconsciously picked at the wood chips clinging to her sweat pants. She had not talked to Luke since their brief phone conversation Monday evening. Here it was, Wednesday afternoon and all sorts of thoughts had been running through Cassie's mind. She had nearly convinced herself that Luke had run, that Luke couldn't handle being second in someone's life again. And it was sobering to acknowledge that she had put her father ahead of Luke. For that matter, she had put her father ahead of herself, too. She had simply abandoned the new life she was starting and reverted back to being the good little daughter, trying to please her father, knowing she never would.

"Can I . . . can I see you?" Cassie asked. "I need to see you," she added slowly.

"What's wrong?" Luke asked immediately.

"Nothing. Everything," she whispered. She felt tears form. She couldn't shake the feeling that she was losing Luke, that she was letting her slip away all because of this damn pretense for her father's sake.

"Luke, please don't give up on me," she whispered.

"Sweetheart, I'm not giving up on you. You said you needed some time."

"All the time in the world won't change anything. I really need to see you. I need to talk."

"You want to come over?" Luke offered.

"Yes. Do you mind?"

"Mind? Cassie, I want to see you just as much."

Cassie felt needy, clingy. Two words she would never have used to describe herself in the past. She was used to being alone, used to handling her father by herself. Now, she had someone to lean on, someone to talk to about her fears.

"Thank you. I'll be there in a few minutes."

"Okay. And please don't thank me. I'm being totally selfish when I say I want to see you."

Cassie smiled. "Well, thank you for that, too."

She found her father in the living room, asleep in the chair. He had a book opened, his fingers still curled around it on his lap. The Bible. Of course, she thought. Did he read anything else?

She quickly changed into jeans, debating whether to wake him or just leave a note. She decided a note would be easier. She would deal with his questions when she got back.

But as she walked to the kitchen, she heard him call to her.

"I didn't mean to wake you," she said when she went back. "I'm going over to a friend's for a little while. I'll be back before dinner," she explained.

"A friend?"

"Yes. I do have a few of them, you know."

He only nodded.

"Well, I'll be fine here. I've got a good book to read."

"Yes, I saw."

"Don't know if you've read it lately. Want me to leave it for you? I'm sure there are some chapters in here that you've forgotten."

She narrowed her eyes, wanting to let it go, as she would have in the past. Instead, she remembered with clarity the nights he would lock her in his study, dinner untouched on the table, all because she couldn't memorize a two-page chapter.

"No thanks. There were too many nights you fed me that book instead of dinner. I think I've had my fill."

"Cassandra! That was for your own good. You had an example to set for the other children in Sunday school. Do you know how embarrassing it was for me to have my own daughter unable to recite a passage?"

"My own good? You locked me in your study!"

"And a lot of good it did! Look at you. Throwing your life away up here, cavorting with sinners!"

"Stop it!" she yelled, finally losing her composure. "What you think means nothing to me. Nothing! Do you realize that? Stop wasting your breath. This is my life. Not yours."

"Cassandra . . ."

"No. I don't want to talk about it anymore. Like I said, I'm going to a friend's house. I'll be back in time for dinner," she said again.

Cassie turned and left without another word, but she was shaking with anger. She never intended to get into a screaming match with him.

Cassie raced over to Luke's. She simply needed to be with her.

Her hands were still tight on the steering wheel when she stopped, and she tried to make herself relax, but her hands were still shaking.

The door opened before she could knock. Luke's smile faded when she looked at Cassie, and Cassie moved into her arms without a word, just needing to be held.

"What's wrong?" Luke whispered into her ear.

Cassie shook her head, her face still buried against Luke's warm skin. She tightened her grip around Luke's waist and let the anger seep out of her.

"Tell me," Luke prompted.

Cassie finally pulled away, and Luke bent and lightly touched her lips with her own.

Cassie attempted a smile, but it faded quickly.

"My father is just being . . . my father. We had a small, heated discussion right before I left," she said.

Luke drew her inside and led her to the sofa.

"Sit."

Luke went into the kitchen and came back with two glasses of apple cider and settled next to Cassie.

"Now, tell me what's made you so upset. You were white as a sheet when you got here."

"I'm just so angry with him, Luke. I'm angry that he's here, I'm angry because of the words he says to me. I'm angry at myself for allowing him to talk to me the way he does. And I'm angry that I've allowed him to come between us."

Luke captured her hand and brought it to her lips, lightly kissing her.

"He's not come between us, Cassie. Not as far as I'm concerned, anyway. However you choose to deal with him, that's your business. I'll still be here."

"I don't like myself right now. I hate how I've bowed to him, I hate how I've put my life on hold because of him. Luke, he made some comment about me reading the Bible, and I reminded him of the times he used to lock me in his study." She raised eyes full of tears to Luke's and let them fall. "It didn't even faze him. He said it was for my own good, that he couldn't have his own daughter unable to recite a verse." She let Luke pull her into her arms and she let her tears fall. "Can you believe he said that?"

"No. No I can't," Luke murmured.

"I don't know if I can take another day like this. I've listened to sarcastic comments about Kim, about the *perverts* that live up here, about my lack of religious conviction, my lack of a husband and children, my art. I'm so frustrated, I just want to scream."

"Tell him."

"Tell him?"

"Tell him how he makes you feel. Tell him what you're thinking."

"It's not that easy. He has an answer for everything. Not that it would matter to him how I feel. Like I said, it didn't bother him in the least that locking me in his study was traumatic for me."

"Cassie, I'm not exactly an expert in this, but you're letting him control you. You are the only one that can make him stop. I can't even begin to understand this. You live your life separate from him, you hardly see him or talk to him, yet he comes here and takes over your life again, and you let him. Why?"

"I've always been alone. I've never had anyone. And a part of me is afraid that if I stand up to him, he'll disappear, and then I'll have no one. No family at all."

"I would think being alone would be better than this hell he brings to you. And you're not alone. You have Kim. You have me."

"Do I have you?" Cassie whispered.

"If you want me."

Cassie let her breath out slowly and smiled.

"I think I want you."

Chapter Thirty-two

"The casserole is in the oven," she told Kim.

"How is he?" she whispered.

"I don't think he can hear you through the phone, Kim."

"Well, I'm nervous as hell that he's coming, if that matters," she said.

"If it's any consolation, I think he's nervous, too. He's either out preparing his sermon or he's trying to convince himself that he won't be tarnished by spending time with *you people*," she said as lightly as she could.

"Very funny. I'm glad you can find humor in all of this. What does Luke think about it?"

"She doesn't understand why I allow him to come here and take over, I guess," Cassie answered honestly. "I saw her yesterday and we talked some. I was nearing a breakdown, I think."

"Is she still coming?"

"I hope so." It was Cassie's turn to whisper. "I'm sure she is."

Actually, they had not even mentioned Thanksgiving dinner. They talked, and Cassie was content to let Luke hold her while she gathered herself enough to return to her father.

"Well, what's up? Did she freak because your father was there?"

"Actually, I freaked," Cassie admitted. "I cancelled any plans we had. Yesterday was the first time I've really talked to her." She could picture Kim's expression, and she closed her eyes to the image and shook her head. "Don't start with me," she said quietly.

"I haven't said a word."

"No, but you want to," Cassie accused.

"Well, you could always see what David's doing today," she said sarcastically. "I'm sure the Reverend would love his Republican ass."

"Kim!"

"You simply amaze me. First of all, I don't even know what's going on with you and Luke, but I can imagine. It's not like you've filled me in."

"It's not like I've had a chance." Cassie rubbed her temple with her free hand, wishing Kim would save the lecture for later, but knowing she wouldn't.

"Okay. Let me just run it by you. Stop me anytime."

"Like I could," Cassie murmured.

"I'm thinking that since you rode with her to Sacramento and spent the weekend at her place . . . well, you know, you're no longer a virgin."

"*Kim!*" Cassie hissed.

"And you spent the next few days together enjoying each other."

"Will you stop?"

"And then dear old dad shows up, and you revert back to sainthood and blow Luke off for your father."

"You're being totally unfair here."

"Am I wrong?" Kim demanded.

"I didn't blow her off," Cassie insisted. "I explained to her that

I couldn't deal with him and her at the same time. She understood."

"And have you dealt with him? Or just cowered to him?"

"Kim, please," Cassie pleaded. "It'll be over soon. He's leaving first thing tomorrow."

"Until the next time. I'm sorry, but I don't know how you could jeopardize something like this because of him. What are you afraid of?"

"I honestly don't know," she said. "I guess a part of me still holds out hope that he will come around, and we can have a normal relationship. And if he finds out about Luke, I know that will be the end. I'll never see him again."

"Cassie, you don't even like the man."

"I know," she whispered. "But he's still my father. And there's no one else."

Kim was silent for the longest, then Cassie heard a weary sigh. "Okay. I'm sorry. I'm trying to understand. I forget that my parents didn't speak to me for two years."

"But they came around," Cassie reminded her.

"Do you honestly think your father could ever accept you as a lesbian?"

"Honestly? No. Never."

"Well, I guess you have to decide between them, then. Because I don't think Luke would take a back seat to him for very long."

No. Cassie didn't think Luke would. She was much too proud to pretend. But despite her breakdown yesterday, she still wasn't willing to tell her father everything. He would be gone soon, and she could get back to her life. And hopefully, she would go another two years before she had to face this again.

Chapter Thirty-three

"Please be nice," Cassie said for the third time.

"Will you quit worrying? I'll save my preaching for Sunday morning," he said. "Where people will listen," he added.

"Thank you."

They were a little early, but Cassie found all she was doing at her own house was pacing, and she thought she could do that just as well at Kim's. When she turned onto their street, her heart suddenly jumped into her throat. Luke's black Lexus was parked next to Lisa's car.

It was with shaky legs that she walked to their door. She had an uneasy feeling and knew in her heart that her father would not be able to hold his tongue for long. It would just all be too much for him. She glanced at him, noting the tight set of his jaw, the frown creasing his forehead.

"They're really nice people. I wish you'd give them a chance."

"Don't try to sell them to me, Cassandra. I know sinners when I see them."

"Stop it right now or I'll give you the keys, and you can go find a place in town to eat."

"I'll never understand you, child. Your choice of friends simply amazes me."

She stood at the door, about to knock, when she heard the sound of voices and laughter inside. If life were fair, she would already be inside, joining them, standing next to Luke, perhaps holding hands or Luke would have an arm casually draped over her shoulders. It was with a heavy heart that she reached up to knock. It was then she noticed the familiar CD playing. She wondered if Kim had chosen Melissa Etheridge just to piss off her father. Well, it would be a fine start to the day.

It was Lisa who answered her knock, and she stood there awkwardly for only a moment before flashing a charming smile.

"Come in, please. You must be Mr. Parker."

"*Reverend*," he corrected and Cassie rolled her eyes.

"Of course," Lisa said, and Cassie didn't miss the amusement in her eyes. "I'm Lisa Meyers."

For a moment, Cassie thought her father would refuse Lisa's offered hand, but he shook it briefly with a curt nod.

Lisa turned to Cassie and winked. "Hey, Cass. Happy Thanksgiving."

Cassie accepted her hug stiffly, conscious of her father's eyes on them.

"Happy Thanksgiving. It smells great in here."

"It does, doesn't it? Kim has been slaving over the turkey all morning."

"How much slaving does a tofu turkey take?" Cassie asked lightly.

"None. That's my point."

They both laughed, and again Cassie wished her father had not chosen this particular holiday to come back into her life. Movement in the living room caused her to look up, and she met Luke's eyes across the room. The familiar sight of her caused Cassie's heart to race, and she had a difficult time catching her breath. It felt like weeks had passed since she had seen her, since she had been in her arms and she allowed her eyes to feast, if only for a second. Luke looked very pretty in her burgundy sweater and tan pants. Then Luke gave her that lazy smile she loved and walked over.

"Hello. I'm Luke Winston," she said without even a hint of nervousness.

"Reverend Parker."

Their handshake was firm and fast, and it was only then that Cassie realized just how tall Luke really was. And confident. Her father would never be able to tower over Luke. Or intimidate her, Cassie thought.

"Happy Thanksgiving, Cassie."

Cassie felt her body melting into Luke's hug, and she realized just how much she had missed her the last few days. Yesterday, she had been too stressed to think about anything but the comfort Luke offered on the sofa. It was a quiet hour she needed, but still, it had been *days* since she and Luke had been intimate. She nearly laughed out loud. She had gone *years* before without being intimate with anyone. Now, with Luke, she was insatiable. She pulled away slowly, her eyes meeting Luke's for the briefest of seconds.

"Well, Mr. Parker, *so* good to see you again."

Kim's voice dripped with sarcasm, and Cassie knew she intentionally tried to provoke him. *Mr.?*

But her father didn't correct her as he had done Lisa.

"Kimberly. We meet again."

"Yes. Happy Thanksgiving."

He gave a humorless smile before speaking. "I'm surprised you actually celebrate this holiday."

"Why does that surprise you? I have a lot to be thankful for. A nice home, someone to share it with, great friends and a career I love. I couldn't be happier with my life."

"Well, enjoy this life, at least."

Kim opened her mouth to counter, but Cassie intervened, like she always had. Even before he found out that Kim was gay, they always found something to spar about.

"I love the flowers, Kim," Cassie said, linking arms with her and drawing her into the living room. "Everything looks great."

"I'm going to snap," Kim whispered.

"No, you're not," Cassie whispered back. "Don't let him get to you."

"He's already gotten to me, and he hasn't been here two minutes."

"Tell me about the turkey," Cassie said as she glanced over her shoulder at the others.

Kim forgot about her father for a moment and launched into a description of the basting technique.

"Paul gave me a recipe for a garlic and butter sauce that he bastes with. It smells really good, doesn't it?"

"It smells great." Then she lowered her voice. "Love your choice of music, by the way."

Kim grinned. "If I thought he knew who the Indigo Girls were, I'd have them on, too."

"Must you provoke him?"

"Yes. I must."

Cassie accepted a glass of wine from Lisa and was surprised when she produced a cider for Luke.

At Cassie's questioning glance, Luke said, "I brought my own."

Her father was seated in the living room, searching for a football game on TV, and Cassie relaxed for the first time since they arrived.

"I've missed you," she said quietly. "Yesterday was just so stressful, and there's so much I want to talk to you about. Thank you for being there yesterday."

Luke's eyes dropped to Cassie's lips for a moment, then captured her blue ones. "If I didn't know how badly you just needed to talk yesterday, I would have hauled you up to my bedroom." She motioned to her father with a toss of her head. "Don't think I'm going to let him chase me off."

Cassie blushed. "Maybe we should have skipped the talk. It seems like it's been forever since . . ."

"Yes, I know."

Their eyes held for a long moment, and the rest of the room faded as if it were only the two of them there. Cassie longed to go into her arms. The stress of the last few days was weighing heavy on her, and she wanted to dump that burden. She knew by the look in Luke's eyes that she would gladly accept it. And it was at that very moment, as she stared into Luke's eyes, that she realized how quickly love had come and captured her heart.

Luke finally broke the spell and looked toward her father. "How was it last night?"

"Bearable," she said. "But probably because we didn't really talk. Dinner was quiet and quick."

"That's good." Then her voice lowered, her words for Cassie's ears only. "Can we spend the weekend together?"

"I would really, really love that."

"I'll warn you now, I doubt I'll let you out of the bed."

Cassie blushed scarlet, but the look in Luke's eyes was completely serious. She wondered who would be keeping whom in bed.

"You're absolutely adorable when you blush."

Lisa chose that moment to walk up and refill Cassie's glass, and Cassie only briefly glanced at her, unable to keep her eyes from Luke for long.

Lisa cleared her throat and nudged Cassie with her elbow. "You're doing a great job of hiding your feelings, kid."

Cassie turned red from head to toe and realized just how close she and Luke were standing. She took a nervous step backward and rolled her eyes at Lisa. "Thanks a lot," she murmured.

"I think it's really cute, but your father may have a stroke," she said with a chuckle.

"I think I'll join him for football, anyway," Luke said. "Let me know if I can help with dinner."

"Is it that obvious?" Cassie asked Lisa when Luke was out of earshot.

"It's that obvious, sweetie. Have you told her?"

"Told her what?"

"That you're in love with her."

Cassie started to deny her accusation, but didn't. It was true, after all. She'd known for some time. She just wasn't sure she wanted to say it out loud. And when she did, she wanted Luke to be the first to hear it. Then she frowned. What if Luke didn't want to hear it? What if this was moving too fast for Luke? Oh, God, what if Luke only wanted a physical relationship with her?

"What's wrong?" Lisa asked, obviously seeing the many questions reflected in Cassie's eyes.

"I think I'm over my head here," Cassie admitted. "We haven't talked about anything. I don't know what Luke wants, how she feels."

Lisa squeezed her arm and grinned. "Honey, that woman absolutely adores you. She's not any better than you at hiding her feelings." Then she lowered her voice. "The way you two were looking at each other, I was afraid you would make a break for the bedroom. That's why I thought I should interrupt." She motioned to Cassie's father, who was engaged in conversation with Luke, apparently about the game. "He was watching you, too."

Cassie groaned. Why did it have to be so hard? Why was she still looking for and craving his acceptance? She wished she could be strong like Kim, who had told her parents immediately. They spent two years estranged, but now they accepted Lisa into the family without question. But she knew that her father would never, under any circumstance, accept Luke as Cassie's partner.

"Don't worry about it, Cass. Just get through the day and send him back home. Then you can get your life back to normal."

"I'm just so tired, Lisa. I'm tired of trying to win his acceptance. And what happens the next time I see him? What if Luke and I do make a life together? Do I go on pretending that we're just friends? Is that fair to her?"

"You have to decide what's fair and what's most important to you."

Cassie glanced at her father and Luke sitting on the sofa

together. Her father was nearly a stranger to her, but her eyes warmed as she watched Luke. She was surprised at how quickly Luke had become important to her, had become so necessary in her life. And she didn't think she was willing to give that up.

"Hey you two, help me set the table," Kim called.

"Come on. It'll give you something to do," Lisa said.

Cassie followed, only glancing once in the direction of Luke and her father, both still absorbed in the football game. She thought that, under different circumstances, Luke and her father might actually get along. And it made her sad to realize that day would never come.

"How are you holding up?" Kim asked.

"I'm okay," Cassie said. "This hardly seems like our normal Thanksgiving, though."

"No," Kim agreed. "We should all be in the kitchen drinking wine and cooking."

She followed Kim around the table, carefully arranging the silverware. Only two times a year did they set such a formal table. Kim had a beautiful fall flower arrangement in the center and her grandmother's crystal candleholders on either side.

As if reading her thoughts, Kim said, "I wonder why we only use the china during the holidays?"

"That's what makes it special."

"Yeah. But it seems a waste."

Cassie laughed. "The way you like to throw things in the dishwasher, they wouldn't last through the year."

"By the way, we had a nice visit with Luke before you got here."

Cassie glanced up. "And I thought we would be early. What time did she get here?"

"Nearly an hour before you. Why didn't you tell us she doesn't drink?"

Cassie shrugged. "It just never came up, I guess."

"Well, she's really nice. I know, at first, I thought she wasn't right for you," Kim said.

"Yes. She was just too experienced for me," Cassie said, repeating Kim's earlier words.

"With her looks and that body, I expected her to be conceited, pretentious and stuck on herself. But she's so unassuming and modest, almost. She's sweet."

Cassie laughed and glanced toward Luke. *Sweet?* She certainly was that, although she never would have thought to describe a nearly six-foot tall woman with lean muscle covering her frame that way. Looks could be deceiving, and she knew first-hand how sweet and gentle Luke could be.

"I think she's pretty hooked on you, Cass."

"Really?"

"Oh, like you don't know," Kim teased.

"I'm pretty hooked on her, too," Cassie admitted.

"I'm glad you found someone, Cassie. You deserve to have someone like Luke in your life."

But did Luke deserve to have someone like Cassie, with all the emotional baggage that came with her?

Chapter Thirty-four

Cassie and Kim exchanged glances as her father finished his Thanksgiving prayer before the meal. He only slightly stumbled over his words as he mentioned the joy of having good friends. At last, he lifted his head and addressed Kim.

"Would you like me to carve the . . . turkey?"

The tofu turkey sat proudly before him, and Cassie didn't miss his wry expression. No doubt he had never heard of tofu turkey, much less seen one.

"Probably should let me," Kim said. "They can be a bit tricky."

"Very well."

Cassie let out a heavy sigh as silence settled over the table as they passed around the dishes. She stole a glance at Luke, but she seemed perfectly at ease. Earlier, Cassie had gone into the living room, intending to rescue Luke from her father, but it appeared it was her father who needed rescuing. Luke was chatting away with him, and he seemed very uncomfortable in her presence. No doubt he was having a hard time disliking Luke. It was one thing to label faceless people as "deviants and perverts" but quite another to be sitting on a sofa, conversing and watching football with one of them.

"Everything looks wonderful. Lisa, you must be quite a cook," Luke complimented.

"Thanks for bringing the bread," Lisa said. "I've never actually known anyone who could really bake homemade bread."

"I learned it years ago from my Aunt Susan," she said, her eyes twinkling as she looked at Cassie. "She and Aunt Darlene taught the whole family to cook."

Cassie had a moment of panic, hoping Luke wouldn't describe life in the commune. She could only imagine how her father would react to that.

"Did you come from a big family?" her father asked, and Cassie rolled her eyes. *Of course he would ask.*

"Not immediate family, no. I was the only child. But I had a large, extended family growing up," Luke said and left it at that, much to Cassie's relief.

"Do you still see them?" Kim asked.

"Not as often. We have a reunion every year, and I try to make that, but holidays are pretty scattered."

"Your parents are still married?"

"No. They never married but they're still together."

"Never married?"

Cassie silently cursed her father for asking and held her breath as Luke answered.

"No. They were never much for the establishment. I always thought they might someday, if only for the tax breaks and what have you, but they never even brought it up."

"How odd," he said.

But Luke laughed. "Yes, but you'd have to know them to understand."

"And are you an . . . *artist*, too?"

Cassie thought it was time to put a stop to this line of question-

213

ing, but Luke seemed to be enjoying herself. Certainly Kim and Lisa seemed amused at the conversation.

"I should be so lucky," she said. "These ladies have tremendous, talent but my drawing tends to be a little more technical. I'm an architect."

Her father seemed genuinely surprised, Cassie noted. In his eyes, Luke was the only one with a real job. She wondered if his forced dislike of Luke was wavering.

Cassie watched him struggle with his first bite of the turkey and nearly laughed out loud. It was an acquired taste, and she met Kim's laughing eyes across from her. His expression was much more neutral on the vegetable roll, which to her, tasted just like the dressing she remembered from childhood.

The rest of the meal passed in silence, except for an occasional stray comment about the food. She was thankful when Lisa brought out another bottle of wine. She needed something to relax as the tension had built to an almost unbearable level. For the hundredth time, she regretted her father's presence. She thought back to last year, when the guests had been Lisa's brother and his two children and she missed the conversation and laughter that normally accompanied the meals with her friends.

"You were awfully quiet," Kim said later when they were clearing the table.

"I didn't know what to say. God, I wish he wasn't here," Cassie admitted.

"I know, but we survived."

"Survived, yeah, but it was hardly enjoyable."

"Not quite what I envisioned our Thanksgiving to be like, no. But at least he didn't launch into a sermon."

Cassie sighed. "Thank God. But we haven't had a chance to talk or visit like normal, and it shouldn't be this way," she complained.

"Honey, it is this way when you can't be yourself. Cassie, you're allowing him to dictate how you act. That's not his fault, it's yours," Kim said bluntly.

Their eyes locked for a moment and Cassie wanted to be angry, but it was the truth. She was the one choosing to act differently because her father was here. And she'd hardly spoken to Luke except for the brief exchange when she'd first gotten there. Now Luke and Lisa were both in the living room with her father, and Cassie was very aware of the silence in the room.

"He can't even bring himself to carry on a conversation with them."

"No, he can't. He's not even trying," Kim said. "It's like he's made up his mind that he won't like them, no matter what."

"Exactly." But what could she do about it?

"Look, let's just get through it. We'll finish the wine, then make coffee and serve dessert. Then you can take him home. Tomorrow is another day."

They piled the plates on the counter, and Kim busied herself putting the leftovers away while Cassie started washing.

"Why don't you go out and save them," Cassie suggested. "I'll finish up in here."

"I'd rather do dishes," Kim said.

"You hate doing dishes. Go on," Cassie urged. "Make conversation."

"You owe me," Kim said as she walked out.

Cassie tried to remember a time when she'd felt as depressed as she did now and couldn't. The beginning of the week had been so promising. She had probably spent the best two days of her life with Luke, and she had so been looking forward to the holiday and sharing that time with Luke and her friends. She wanted Kim and Lisa to get to know Luke. She knew they would like her. She envisioned the four of them spending many good times together. Cassie had been the tag-along with them for so long, the fifth wheel, and she had looked forward to having someone of her own so that Kim and Lisa didn't feel the need to constantly entertain her and include her in everything. With Luke, she could have a partner, someone to share secret glances with, much like Kim and Lisa did. But not tonight, she conceded. Not as long as her father was here.

When the kitchen door opened, she expected Kim. But Luke stood there, her weight shifted slightly on one leg, empty wine-glass in her hand. Their eyes locked, and Cassie very nearly dropped the plate in her hand.

"Hey."

"Empty?"

"An excuse," Luke said.

She finally moved, walking slowly toward Cassie, never breaking eye contact.

"This has been the longest day of my life," Luke said when she stopped just inches from Cassie.

"Mine, too," Cassie agreed. "I'm so sorry."

"It's a little strained out there," she said. "We've all tried talking to him."

Cassie dried her hands on the towel then tossed it on the counter with a sigh.

"This was a mistake. I should have just taken him into town for a meal and been done with it. It was stupid of me to think that he might actually like everyone if he spent time around here. Instead, I've ruined Thanksgiving for everyone else."

"Cassie, his hatred is very deep. You can't change someone who believes the way he does. He's been teaching for years that we're nothing but a bunch of sinners."

"But it's so unfair. How can I make him see that?"

"You can't, honey."

Cassie was taken aback by the sincerity of the endearment and her heart melted. She took the empty glass from Luke and blindly set it on the counter, moving into her arms without thinking.

"Hold me," she whispered.

Luke's strong arms folded around her, pulling her close, and she nestled her head against Luke's soft sweater, finally finding peace.

"God, I've missed this," Luke murmured into her ear.

Cassie's arms tightened around Luke's waist and she pressed her face into the softness of Luke's neck.

"I wanted this day to be special for us," Cassie finally admitted.

"Sweetheart, it has been special. Just you inviting me here, despite your father, means so much to me."

"We've hardly had a chance to talk, Luke. It's like we're strangers."

Luke pulled back and cupped Cassie's face with both hands. "We'll have time. I understand your need to keep a distance with your father. You're not ready to tell him."

"But I hate this," Cassie said. "I just wanted to be with you today."

Luke smiled. "Well, we'll shoot for this weekend, huh?"

Cassie reached up and touched Luke's face. "You really are a very sweet woman, you know that?"

"Sweet?"

"Yeah. Sweet," Cassie whispered, and she locked eyes with Luke, watching as they turned dark with desire.

"I've missed you," Luke whispered as she lowered her mouth to Cassie's.

Cassie didn't hesitate as her mouth opened to Luke, accepting her kiss without a second thought. Their bodies molded together, pressing intimately against each other as they lost themselves in their desire.

Cassie's tongue found its way into Luke's warm mouth, swallowing Luke's moan along with her own and she pressed her body closer still, her thighs tight against Luke's lean form. She let their passion rage and neither heard the door open or the gasp that followed.

"Good God in heaven!" he bellowed. "Take your hands off of my daughter!"

Cassie pulled away blindly, her eyes wide as she looked at the angry face of her father.

"Cassandra! What has she done to you?"

"It's not . . . like it looks," she stammered, hating herself for being so weak. She felt Luke move away from her, and the quick glance between them was enough for Cassie's heart to break. Luke's eyes were begging Cassie to tell him the truth.

"It looked like this *pervert* was forcing herself on you," he spat.

"Of course not! Don't be ridiculous."

Cassie was only slightly aware of Kim and Lisa standing in the doorway, silently watching the exchange.

Luke faced her father, her shoulders square. "I'm sorry, this is my fault, although I take offense to being called a pervert. You know nothing about me or my life."

"I know your kind, and you will all suffer God's wrath, but you're not taking my daughter with you. She will be saved!"

His voice had changed, deep and threatening, and Cassie was taken back to her childhood when she would sit in the first row at church, frightened more by the sound of his voice than the words he spoke. But she shook herself. She wasn't a little girl anymore.

The moment seemed to unfold before her in slow motion. Her father's face was red with anger but Luke's had turned passive, easily dismissing his words. Cassie found all eyes on her and she knew, in that moment, that she would have to make a life decision. Right now. There would be no more skirting the issue, no turning back. She could either try to make a life with Luke, a life without her father in it, or she could try to rebuild the relationship with her father, a relationship that could never include Luke.

Cassie turned to meet Luke's eyes, seeing love and understanding crowding out the hurt.

"I'm sorry," Luke murmured.

She started to turn, but Cassie grabbed her arm, letting her fingers slide down to entwine with Luke's.

"No, Luke. I'm sorry."

"Child, what are you doing?"

Her father's voice shook her but Luke's hand tightened, giving her the strength she needed.

She raised her head high and met her father's angry stare.

"I'm not a child. Luke is much more than a friend to me, Father. I'll not have you speak to her that way."

"You're *sick*. You don't know what you're saying."

"I know exactly what I'm saying. Luke and I are . . ." She turned to Luke for help, stumbling over the words.

"Tell him."

"Luke and I are lovers."

His gasp became a growl, and he clutched at his chest.

"My God, look what they've done to you." Then he turned on Kim, pointing angrily at her. "You! This is all your fault. You should be locked away somewhere."

Cassie grabbed his arm. "No, Father, this is not Kim's fault."

He turned quickly and slapped her hard across the face, causing her to stumble back into Luke's arms. She stared at him in disbelief. He had never once struck her, but seeing the rage in his eyes now, she had no doubt he would do it again.

Luke stepped between them, a dangerous glint in her eyes as she faced him.

"Don't you *ever* hit her again." When he would have spoken, Luke raised her hand and pointed at him. "No, you listen to me. Cassie is one of the kindest, gentlest people I've ever met. She wouldn't dream of hurting another living thing. Now that I've met you, it's a wonder she has any spirit left. It's not Kim's fault. It's not my fault. It's not even Cassie's fault. She is who she is. It's as simple as that."

They all stood in stunned silence, but he found his voice first.

"You will all rot in hell," he spat.

"For what? For loving someone?" Luke asked. "You are so filled with hate, if I were you, I'd be worrying about my own soul."

He looked as if he wanted to strike Luke, but she stood her ground. Instead, he turned to Cassie.

"Cassandra, you will come home with me this instant. We can get you help. You can still be saved."

Cassie finally found her voice. "No. This is who I am. And I feel like I have been saved."

"Then you are no longer a daughter of mine. You'll have no family now."

Kim spoke for the first time. "When have you ever treated her like a daughter? Cassie's tried to please you her entire life, but what did she get from you in return? A father who despised her? A father who wouldn't even let her contact her own mother?"

He gasped at her words, and his cold stare caused Kim to take a step backward, but she didn't lower her eyes. Cassie wondered if anyone had ever spoken to him like Luke and Kim just had.

They all stood there in stunned silence, looking from one to the other, questions lingering in everyone's eyes.

"It is certainly none of your business. And I will not discuss this here," he said, his voice quieting. He glanced at Cassie briefly. "I think I'd like you to take me back now."

Cassie had never seen him this resigned before. His voice was quiet, submissive almost, and she very nearly felt very sorry for him, but she wasn't willing to give in. She may have lost him, but that was his choice. Like Luke said, his hatred was very deep.

"Okay. I'll take you back."

"I'll be waiting outside. I don't want to spend another minute in this house of sin."

He left them standing in the kitchen and their eyes went from one to the other slowly. It was Kim who finally broke the tension.

"I'd say that went pretty well. At least no one's in the hospital."

Cassie's relieved chuckle turned into an outright laugh.

"I love you guys," she said. "Thanks for sticking up for me." She took Luke's hand and pulled her into a hug. "This probably isn't the best time to tell you this, but . . . I'm in love with you," she whispered into her ear.

She pulled away before Luke could comment, mostly out of fear of what her reaction would be. Luke stood silently, stunned, as Cassie hugged both Kim and Lisa.

"Are you sure you're going to be okay with him?" Kim asked.

"I'll be fine. I doubt he's going to lock me in his trunk and haul me to the nearest mental hospital."

"But maybe Luke should go with you," Lisa suggested. "Just in case things get ugly."

"I'll be fine," Cassie said. "I think it would be worse if Luke were there."

"I'd feel better if you'd let me come."

Cassie met Luke's eyes, and she trembled at all she saw there. She walked over to her and kissed her softly on the mouth.

"Thank you. But I need to be able to do this. I've spent too many years cowering to him. If he decides he wants nothing to do with me after this, then that's his choice. I've got my own life to live."

She let her eyes linger on Luke's, memorizing them, drawing strength from the love she saw there.

Chapter Thirty-five

The ride home was made in complete silence, and Cassie glanced several times in his direction, but his gaze was focused only on the road. Twice she opened her mouth to speak only to close it again. She could not find the words to begin, and she thought it might be safer in the comfort of her own home.

When she pulled to a stop, they both sat there for a moment, then he opened the door and got out, slamming it just a little too hard, she noticed. She halfway expected him to pack his things and leave right then, but he was waiting for her in the living room.

"I've been thinking maybe you're doing this to punish me in some way," he started.

"I know you can't possibly understand this. You won't even allow yourself to try."

"Understand? It's *unnatural*," he hissed.

"Do you think I wanted this?" she asked. "Don't you think I fought these desires?"

"The Devil's temptation."

"No. That's what you taught me to believe, but no."

"It is against God's will," he stated.

"How can you say that? For the first time in my life I feel something for someone. All these years, I've dated men, but I was never attracted to them. But because of your teachings, I would never consider that it was because I was attracted to women instead. Because you taught me it was wrong."

"It is wrong," he insisted.

"You would rather I spend my life alone? Miserable, like you?"

"It would be better than the hell you've invited."

Cassie paced across the floor, wondering how she could explain to him how she was feeling, wondering if it would even do any good.

"I've fallen in love for the first time in my life. I'm thirty-three years old, and I've never known such joy before. Luke makes me feel things I always thought were for others to have, not me. Am I to deny myself these wonderful feelings because you say they're not God's way? Are you saying it's God's way that I feel miserable and depressed and alone again? This happiness I'm feeling surely is a gift from God."

"She's a woman! Have you no shame?"

"Shame? For what? For loving someone?" She walked to him, desperately wanting him to understand. "Don't you see? For the first time in my life, I feel complete. I'm sorry that some man couldn't make me feel this. But I've accepted who I am and what I am. I'm not going to run from this, no matter what you say. And if you feel like you don't want me in your life, just because of this, then that's your choice. If you can't accept this about me, if you can't accept Luke in my life, then there's no point in us even trying to maintain any kind of a relationship."

He stared at her for the longest time then let out a heavy breath. He closed his eyes briefly, as if fighting with himself.

"I can't accept this," he stated quietly.

"So be it," Cassie said, turning away from him.

"Your mother left us for a woman," he finally murmured. "And I tried my whole life to protect you from that."

"*What?*" His words were like a blow to her, so unexpected. She sunk down onto the sofa without looking, dazed beyond belief. Her mother? A *lesbian*?

"That's why you hate so?" she whispered.

"Your mother was an . . . artist, too. She painted, started taking classes. That's where she met her."

So much made sense to Cassie now. Just a few words from him, and she understood a lifetime of hate. His hatred of gays. His hatred of artists. His position in the church just gave him an excuse for his preaching when all along it had been so very personal for him.

"I'm sorry. I can only imagine your hurt," she said quietly. "But you had no right to keep me from her. She was still my mother."

"I didn't want her to poison you with her beliefs."

"Instead, you poisoned me with yours," she said before she could stop herself.

"You never had any contact with her at all, yet you turned out exactly like she did."

"Where is she?" Cassie whispered. "What happened to her?"

She didn't expect him to answer. She wasn't sure he even knew. She watched as conflicting emotions crossed his face and he abruptly turned and left, leaving the front door standing open.

When he returned, he had a bundle in his hands, an assortment of letters bound by rubber bands.

"The last one came about five years ago. From Seattle. Then Saturday, I got another one."

He silently handed them over to her and with shaking hands she took them. Tears flooded her eyes as she flipped through the envelopes, all unopened, all addressed to her.

All these years, her mother had been writing to her. And getting nothing in return. Cassie let out a great sob and brought the letters to her chest. Her mother hadn't forgotten about her after all.

"Why?"

He frowned, shaking his head, not knowing what to say.

"All these years, I thought she had deserted me. I thought she never tried to contact me. Do you know how hard it was for a child, a teenager, to live with the thought that her mother didn't want to know her?" Cassie's sobs shook her body. "How could you do that to a child?"

"At first, you were too young," he explained. "Then later, we never talked about her. I wasn't sure you even remembered her. By the time you were a teenager, it just never seemed to be the right time. And I was scared," he said.

"Scared of what?"

"Scared that you would leave me. I was afraid of what the letters said. I was afraid she would ask you to come to her and subject you to her perverted lifestyle."

He moved away from her when she didn't reply. "I know, after everything that's happened, you probably don't care one way or the other if I'm in your life or not. I guess I always feared this day would come. I knew, with you hanging out with Kim and her kind, that she would influence you. And I knew that one day, I was going to have to give you those letters."

Cassie wiped her eyes, trying to compose herself. She had no idea how to respond to him. "First of all, my sexuality is not an issue to discuss. It wasn't a choice I made to get back at you, as you seem to think. In fact, because of you, I fought this for so long. But like I said, Luke makes me happy. And if you want to make me choose between the two of you, you're going to lose, so it's really your decision."

He turned his back to her for a moment, as if collecting himself. "I cannot, as a good Christian, accept this. I don't know that I can ever accept it. In my eyes, what you're doing is wrong. A sin. And honestly, I don't know what you could possibly have with this woman."

"Have? You mean sexually?" Cassie asked.

"I don't even want to think about that, Cassandra. No, I mean, what do you hope to have with her? What kind of life?"

"I guess I don't understand. A relationship is a relationship, regardless of the sex of the partners. I guess I want what Kim and Lisa have. A home together, a life together."

"And why can't you have that with a man, Cassandra? Why must you go against God?"

She let out a heavy sigh, not knowing how to make him understand. "It's not just sexual, although that is a big part of it. I just connect with Luke, on all levels. Emotionally, she gives me what I need. And if things don't work out with Luke, I still wouldn't want a life with a man."

"All these years, I've tried to think of what I did wrong with your mother. Was it was something I did to make her change? She never asked for much, but when she did, I gave it to her. She seemed to enjoy the life we had in the church. But I think back, she didn't have many friends." He paced slowly across her living room, head bent down as he spoke. "When we would have couples over for dinner, she was always distant with them. Polite, but distant. I think she would have rather been in the kitchen taking care of you than entertaining with me."

Cassie felt his need to tell her what happened all those years ago, his version anyway, so she let him talk, not wanting to interrupt with her own thoughts on what had happened.

"She always sketched. It was the one thing she seemed to find genuine joy in. When she asked if she could take a class to learn to paint, I agreed without hesitation. I felt she was getting restless. I thought she needed something of her own, something other than the church and the friendships we had established there. I saw the change in her right away. She would pack you up along with all of her painting stuff and go to a park or to the bay, often coming home just in time to start dinner." He cleared his throat before continuing. "And that's when she stopped being interested in me. It was as if she couldn't stand my touch anymore. I had no idea what was going on with her. She wouldn't talk to me. I found her many times in the backyard, holding you and crying."

Cassie could imagine the turmoil a young mother and wife would

226

be going through nearly thirty years ago, with no one to help her, no support groups. No one for her to talk to about it. Except maybe the woman she had met. The woman she had left them for.

"I remember so clearly the day she told me. She said she had met someone, said that she had fallen in love. She said she was going to leave and take you with her. It was such a shock, so totally unexpected. Divorce was not something that happened often back then, and certainly not in our church. My first thought was how it would look to the members of the church. My second thought was that she was taking you with her, to have some other man raise you. I pleaded with her, I threatened her, begged her to give us another chance. Then she told me it wasn't a man. She didn't understand it anymore than I did, but she was in love with this woman, and she didn't want me anymore."

Cassie heard the agony in his voice, even after all these years. And it dawned on her that he'd had no one to talk to either. He couldn't very well have gone to one of his friends or anyone from his church. No one could have sympathized or understood. He would have been condemned right along with her mother. He had suffered through it all alone.

"I told her to get out. To go live her perverted life, if she wanted, but there was no way she was taking my daughter with her. No way she was going to expose you to that kind of life."

"I'm sorry," Cassie whispered. She had no words to console him, and she wished with all her heart that he would have had the courage to tell her all this years ago.

His shoulders sagged, but his voice hardened.

"She left with nothing but her clothes. I wouldn't even let her take your baby pictures. I watched from the window and . . . that woman picked her up on the corner. I never saw her again. But I had saved you. Or so I thought."

Cassie could imagine his hurt back then, watching as his wife walked out of his life for good. She could also imagine the grief a young mother would be feeling, walking away from a safe, secure life . . . her child, all for the sake of love. She understood, at that very moment, the power of love. But that understanding did nothing to take away her own hurt.

"I'm only telling you this because I thought you deserved to know. Perhaps it might explain my actions when you were a child. Apparently, her influence was too strong, even at your young age."

"I deserved to know all of this years ago. I deserved the opportunity to know my mother."

"You have the letters. I'm sure anything you need to know will be answered there."

"Why did you keep them?"

"I honestly don't know."

"Guilt, perhaps?"

His eyes flashed at her. "I have nothing to feel guilty about. I'm not the one that willingly left behind a spouse and child for a life of sin." He began throwing his few things into the suitcase.

"But you're leaving now?" she asked.

"Yes. I am going back to my church. And I will pray for you. But I will never accept this. If you choose to destroy your life, I'll not be a part of it."

Cassie nodded. She knew it would come to this and strangely, she didn't feel sad. She felt relieved. He would no longer be there to criticize her, to belittle her. She could live her life in happiness and not worry about offending him or disappointing him. It was truly her life now.

"I hope you're happy now."

Cassie laughed. "No you don't. You want me to be miserable, like you've been. I've wasted enough years of my life trying to please you. Now, I'm going to please myself."

"Well, it's your choice not to have your own father in your life. You have to live with that."

"No, no. You're not laying that guilt on me. It's *your* choice."

"Don't you see? You leave me no other option."

"As you wish," Cassie whispered.

Chapter Thirty-six

Cassie sat quietly on her patio, the pre-dawn light just beginning to hint of the sunrise soon to come. She pulled the blanket closer around her to ward off the morning chill and closed her eyes. She didn't know how many hours she had been sitting out here, replaying scenes from the previous day, and scenes from her childhood.

Her father had simply driven off without another word and Cassie had sunk into her chair, listening to the sounds of his car fading as he drove out of her life. The emptiness that she expected never came. And it was with a sense of guilt that she felt relief.

She had called Kim. Luke had just left there, so she waited a few minutes before calling her house. Luke had wanted to come over, but Cassie needed some time alone, and she hoped Luke understood.

She stared at the bundle of letters for the longest time, wondering why she was hesitating opening them. It was just too much for one day, she decided. But she couldn't sleep. She finally crawled out of bed and poured a glass of wine, taking it with her to the patio. Thunderstorms were flashing in the distance, and she could smell the rain. She probably should have gone to Luke's, crawled into bed beside her, and slept. But she was still too wound up to sleep. She would let the new day break, then she would go to Luke's. They would talk. And Luke would hold her.

Cassie nodded, holding the coffee cup that had replaced the wine of earlier. Yes, Luke would hold her and everything would be okay. She leaned her head back, watching the fading stars as the sun rose and chased them from the sky. It was peaceful. She stretched her legs out, a feeling of contented bliss so strong it actually made her laugh. But again, the slight sense of guilt sobered her. Her father was gone from her life, most likely forever. But she had a whole new life to start with Luke. And possibly with her mother.

She sat for another half-hour, long enough for the sun to warm her. But someone else beckoned, and she stood and stretched, feeling a growing urgency to go to Luke.

Cassie was slightly nervous as she drove to Luke's. Their brief conversation on the phone last night had not touched on the 'I think I'm in love with you' statement that Cassie had blurted out. She had been so preoccupied with her father that she hadn't even thought about her admission of love to Luke.

But now, alone, they would have time to talk. Luke would want to know what had happened with her father, yes, but they had their own issues to discuss. She wondered if Luke would bring up Cassie's profession of love. Maybe Luke would dismiss it as just a fleeting emotion brought on by the stress of the night. She shook her head, no. Perhaps the stress of the evening had caused her to blurt it out like she had, but it was no fleeting emotion. Cassie felt it deep in her soul. Luke was the one she had been waiting for all of her life.

The door opened before Cassie could knock. Luke stood there in her T-shirt and ever-present faded jeans, bare feet sticking out. Then the lazy smile Cassie loved transformed her face as their eyes held.

"Hi, sweetheart."

Cassie's eyes slid closed at the soft endearment and she fell into Luke's waiting arms, wrapping her own securely around Luke's waist and burying her face into Luke's neck. Strong arms held her as Cassie relaxed in Luke's warmth, feeling calmness settle over her. Gentle lips kissed her forehead and she sighed, breathing in Luke's scent.

"Are you okay?" Luke finally whispered.

Cassie nodded. "I just need you to hold me for a minute."

"I've got you, for as long as you like."

Yes, you've got me. For the rest of my life, I hope. She gave Luke a squeeze before pulling out of her arms.

Luke's kiss was gentle, unhurried, hiding the passion that Cassie saw simmering in her eyes.

"Do you want to talk?"

Cassie met her eyes. *Talk?* "Just for a minute. Then I want to be in your arms."

Luke's hand found hers, and their fingers entwined, then Luke pulled Cassie after her, slowly mounting the stairs to the loft.

They lay down sideways on the bed, both fully clothed. Cassie curled up at Luke's side, slipping one arm over her waist and resting her head on Luke's breast, sighing contentedly.

Luke waited patiently for Cassie to speak, simply stroking her back with a lazy hand.

"I found out why my father has so much hatred," she started. "My mother left him for another woman, an artist."

Luke's hand stilled.

"Jesus. No wonder," she said quietly. "So much makes sense now. I was really afraid he was going to convince you to run from me, from this. That once he got you alone . . ."

"No, Luke. I told him not to make me choose between the two

of you, because he would lose. I got a few things off of my chest before he left," she said.

"I'm sorry."

"I'm not. I can finally see him for what he is. A pathetic, lonely old man filled with hatred. And I know that it's his choice. But he shed some light about my mother, and he gave me a bunch of letters that she'd been sending all these years."

"You're kidding. Why did he have them?"

"I don't know why he kept them. He wouldn't say. I don't know why he had them in his car, either. Maybe he couldn't bear to have them in his house."

"What did they say?" Luke asked.

Cassie's hand traced circles on Luke's shirt, finally slipping underneath to meet warm skin.

"I haven't opened them yet."

Luke seemed to understand her hesitation. Cassie felt lips kiss the top of her head and felt Luke's arm tighten around her.

"There's plenty of time for that. You've had a lot happen in the last few days."

"Yes," Cassie murmured, letting her hand slide dangerously close to Luke's bare breasts. She smiled as she felt Luke's sharp intake of breath at her touch.

"Cassie?"

"Hmm?"

"Did you mean . . . what you said?"

Cassie watched Luke, but her eyes were closed, waiting. There was no need to pretend. She knew exactly what Luke was referring to. Cassie, too, closed her eyes for a moment, then slid her hand the few inches to completely capture Luke's breast.

"Yes," she whispered. "I'm in love with you."

Luke opened her eyes then, finding Cassie looking back at her. Cassie waited, watching silently as different emotions crossed Luke's face. Finally, Luke's eyes closed again.

"I'm very glad." Then, a soft smile. "I didn't want to be the only one who felt this way, you know."

"You don't think it's too soon, do you?"

"Too soon?" Luke's eyes fluttered open. "I fell in love with you months ago."

Luke pulled Cassie on top of her, finding her mouth, kissing her passionately, possessively. "I couldn't sleep last night at all. I kept hearing your words over and over again, until I was certain I had only imagined them."

"No, you didn't imagine anything." Cassie pressed her hips intimately against Luke, feeling the now familiar sensations rock her body. "I never thought I could feel this way for someone."

Luke's hands cupped her hips, sliding over rounded buttocks to press Cassie closer against her. Their kiss was slow, lips touching lips, tongues reacquainting themselves until their passion wouldn't allow a leisurely pace. Cassie moaned when Luke rolled them over and settled her weight on Cassie. Cassie's hands slid under Luke's T-shirt, softly caressing her smooth back.

"I love you," Luke whispered into her mouth before claiming her soundly.

The stress of the last few days washed away as Cassie closed her mind to everything except Luke and the hands now molding her body. She didn't protest when Luke sat up and pulled first her own, then Cassie's shirt off and tossed them on the floor. Cassie's hands cupped small, firm breasts, then guided Luke over her, her mouth hungry as she feasted. She trembled as the nipple swelled in her mouth, and she let her tongue lick the rounded bud until Luke pressed her breast harder against Cassie's mouth and she opened again, sucking more of Luke inside.

"Yes, harder," Luke murmured.

Cassie moaned too, as her fingers rubbed Luke's other breast before turning her attention back to Luke's mouth, taking the offered tongue inside. Her legs parted, and Luke settled between them, jeans hindering their desire to be close. Luke rolled away in frustration, quickly shedding her jeans before tackling Cassie's. Cassie kicked them away impatiently and pulled Luke down to her naked body, sighing contentedly as she wrapped arms and legs around Luke.

"I can't get close enough," Luke whispered into her ear.

"I know. I want you inside me."

Their eyes held, then Luke shifted her weight slightly, allowing room for her hand to move between them. Her touch was soft on Cassie's heated flesh, but Cassie wanted her to hurry. Her hips surged up to meet Luke's hand, but Luke's hand continued down her thigh, gently caressing, teasing.

"Please," Cassie begged.

Luke smiled against her mouth, rubbing her tongue seductively across Cassie's lips. "Always in a hurry, aren't you?"

Cassie growled deep in her throat, then rolled them over. She straddled Luke's thigh, rubbing her wetness against Luke, pressing her throbbing center hard against Luke.

"Oh, Cassie," Luke whispered, and she cupped Cassie's hips and held her.

"Do you feel me? Do you feel how wet I am?"

Cassie lowered her mouth to Luke's breast, her tongue raking lightly over the swollen tip before taking it inside. Luke groaned and grasped Cassie's head, holding her there, pressing Cassie's mouth harder against her.

Cassie used her knee to urge Luke's legs farther apart, then she settled between them, lowering herself until they touched. Luke arched into her, hips rocking against hips as they strained to touch, to get as close as possible.

"Please, go inside me," Luke whispered hoarsely.

Cassie lifted slightly and slid her hand between them, moaning loudly as the silky wetness enveloped her fingers. She easily slipped fingers inside Luke, feeling Luke's muscles close around her. With her hips, she drove herself deeper inside Luke, only to pull out slowly before pushing in again. Her hips set the pace as she pulled in and out of Luke and she lost herself in the sensation of being inside her. Luke's hips rose to meet each thrust, and Cassie rocked against her, faster and faster, until she felt Luke's contractions against her fingers, heard the guttural sounds Luke couldn't suppress. She let go then, let her own orgasm overtake her, and they cried out in unison at their mutual climax.

Cassie lay limp upon Luke, her fingers still within her wetness. Her skin was damp with perspiration, as she tried to catch her breath.

"Okay?" Luke murmured.

Cassie smiled. "Perfect."

She felt Luke's arms fold around her, and she snuggled deeper, gently nuzzling Luke's neck, too spent to go any further.

Cassie felt herself slipping into a peaceful sleep as Luke's hands slowly caressed her back, relaxing her totally.

Chapter Thirty-seven

Cassie settled on the steps of Luke's deck with her coffee. The sun was barely over the horizon and the morning air was cool, but Cassie wanted to savor this time alone. She had slipped out of Luke's arms, leaving her lover sleeping peacefully in bed. They had finally fallen into an exhausted sleep in the early morning hours. They talked a lot, had taken time for a light lunch and a late dinner, but mostly had spent their time loving each other. Cassie blushed when she remembered begging Luke to skip dinner and make love to her yet again. By the time they finally made it downstairs, Cassie was ravenous.

She sighed contentedly, wondering how her life could have changed so quickly. If anyone had told her three months ago that she would be madly in love with a woman . . . and that same woman madly in love with her, she would have laughed and dismissed the comment with the ease she had dismissed Kim all these years. And if that same person would have told her that she would finally stand up to her father, Cassie would have told them to seek therapy quickly. But not only had that happened, the real possibility existed of finally contacting her mother.

She glanced at the letters beside her. That is, if she could find the courage to open them and seek her out.

She shivered slightly and sipped from her coffee, absently watching the storm clouds forming, moving in from the Pacific. It would rain soon, she knew. She could smell it in the air.

She was still sitting on the steps when Luke came out nearly an hour later, two cups of coffee in her hand. Cassie turned at the sound of her footsteps, and their eyes locked.

"Hey."

Luke's voice was quiet and in that one word, Cassie heard the love of her life calling. Luke's eyes were full of concern and compassion . . . and love. Mostly love. Cassie knew then that nothing else really mattered.

"Hey yourself." Cassie scooted over to make room for her. Luke folded her long frame next to Cassie and handed her the hot cup of coffee. Cassie bumped Luke's shoulder playfully and was rewarded with that smile she loved so.

"Everything okay?"

"Perfect," Cassie said. "Absolutely perfect."

Luke nodded and they both sipped from their coffee, eyes still locked.

"You have the letters out. Are you ready to open them?"

Cassie shook her head. "Not just yet. But soon."

They were quiet, both looking out over the meadow.

"Going to rain today," Luke said.

"Yes."

"Maybe we could put on a pot of chili, have a fire," Luke suggested.

"Like that first time?"

Luke smiled. "Yes, just like that first time."

"I'll really glad it stormed that night."

"Me, too." Then Luke's eyes turned serious. "You know, you

could always bring some clothes and things over . . . to leave here . . . just in case."

"Just in case?" Cassie smiled at the light blush that crept up Luke's face.

"Nothing. It's too soon. I'm sorry."

Cassie slipped her hand inside Luke's arm, rubbing lightly against her skin. "Tell me."

"It's just, I like . . . sleeping with you, waking up with you." Luke met her eyes, albeit, a bit shyly. "I mean, I know it's too soon to talk about moving in together, but maybe, you know, occasionally . . . oh, hell."

Cassie squeezed her arm, totally charmed by Luke's embarrassment. "I love you, Luke. And I think it would be great if you could spare me some room in your closet."

"Yeah? You do?"

"I want to be with you, too," she whispered.

"Good. Because I want to be here for you, whatever you need. When you open those letters, I want to share that with you. If you decide to contact your mother, I want to be right beside you. If you decide to have a showing at Union Square, I want to be there supporting you." Luke took Cassie's hand and placed it over her breast. "I never thought I'd trust anyone with my heart again, you know. But I love you very much, Cass. I think we have something really, really special between us."

Cassie blinked the tears away and circled Luke's shoulders with one arm, laying her head against her. She had finally found her rock, the partner and companion she was certain she would never find.

"I love you," Cassie whispered. "You're so *damn* sweet."

They sat that way, quietly, until the first raindrops chased them inside. Cassie casually tossed the bundle of letters on the sofa. Maybe later, with a fire going and chili simmering . . . and Luke by her side, she would open them.

Maybe.

Publications from
BELLA BOOKS, INC.
The best in contemporary lesbian fiction

P.O. Box 10543, Tallahassee, FL 32302
Phone: 800-729-4992
www.bellabooks.com

BELL, BOOK & DYKE: NEW EXPLOITS OF MAGICAL LESBIANS by Kallmaker, Watts, Johnson and Szymanski. 320 pp. Reluctant witches, tempting spells, and skyclad beauties—delve into the mysteries of love, lust and power in this quartet of novellas.
1-59493-023-6 $14.95

ARTIST'S DREAM by Gerri Hill. 320 pp. When Cassie meets Luke Winston, she can no longer deny her attraction to women . . .   1-59493-042-2 $12.95

NO EVIDENCE by Nancy Sanra. 240 pp. Private Investigator Tally McGinnis once again returns to the horror filled world of a serial killer.   1-59493-043-04 $12.95

WHEN LOVE FINDS A HOME by Megan Carter. 280 pp. What will it take for Anna and Rona to find their way back to each other again?   1-59493-041-4 $12.95

MEMORIES TO DIE FOR by Adrian Gold. 240 pp. Rachel attempts to avoid her attraction to the charms of Anna Sigurdson . . .   1-59493-038-4 $12.95

SILENT HEART by Claire McNab. 280 pp. Exotic lesbian romance.
1-59493-044-9 $12.95

MIDNIGHT RAIN by Peggy J. Herring. 240 pp. Bridget McBee is determined to find the woman who saved her life.   1-59493-021-X $12.95

THE MISSING PAGE A Brenda Strange Mystery by Patty G. Henderson. 240 pp. Brenda investigates her client's murder . . .   1-59493-004-X $12.95

WHISPERS ON THE WIND by Frankie J. Jones. 240 pp. Dixon thinks she and her best friend, Elizabeth Colter, would make the perfect couple . . . 1-59493-037-6 $12.95

CALL OF THE DARK: EROTIC LESBIAN TALES OF THE SUPERNATURAL edited by Therese Szymanski—from Bella After Dark. 320 pp.   1-59493-040-6 $14.95

A TIME TO CAST AWAY A Helen Black Mystery by Pat Welch. 240 pp. Helen stops by Alice's apartment—only to find the woman dead . . .   1-59493-036-8 $12.95

DESERT OF THE HEART by Jane Rule. 224 pp. The book that launched the most popular lesbian movie of all time is back.   1-1-59493-035-X $12.95

THE NEXT WORLD by Ursula Steck. 240 pp. Anna's friend Mido is threatened and eventually disappears . . .   1-59493-024-4 $12.95

CALL SHOTGUN by Jaime Clevenger. 240 pp. Kelly gets pulled back into the world of private investigation . . .   1-59493-016-3 $12.95

52 PICKUP by Bonnie J. Morris and E.B. Casey. 240 pp. 52 hot, romantic tales—one for every Saturday night of the year.   1-59493-026-0 $12.95

GOLD FEVER by Lyn Denison. 240 pp. Kate's first love, Ashley, returns to their home town, where Kate now lives . . .   1-1-59493-039-2 $12.95

RISKY INVESTMENT by Beth Moore. 240 pp. Lynn's best friend and roommate needs her to pretend Chris is his fiancé. But nothing is ever easy.   1-59493-019-8 $12.95

HUNTER'S WAY by Gerri Hill. 240 pp. Homicide detective Tori Hunter is forced to team up with the hot-tempered Samantha Kennedy.   1-59493-018-X $12.95

CAR POOL by Karin Kallmaker. 240 pp. Soft shoulders, merging traffic and slippery when wet . . . Anthea and Shay find love in the car pool.   1-59493-013-9 $12.95

NO SISTER OF MINE by Jeanne G'Fellers. 240 pp. Telepathic women fight to coexist with a patriarchal society that wishes their eradication.   ISBN 1-59493-017-1 $12.95

ON THE WINGS OF LOVE by Megan Carter. 240 pp. Stacie's reporting career is on the rocks. She has to interview bestselling author Cheryl, or else! ISBN 1-59493-027-9 $12.95

WICKED GOOD TIME by Diana Tremain Braund. 224 pp. Does Christina need Miki as a protector . . . or want her as a lover?   ISBN 1-59493-031-7 $12.95

THOSE WHO WAIT by Peggy J. Herring. 240 pp. Two brilliant sisters—in love with the same woman!   ISBN 1-59493-032-5 $12.95

ABBY'S PASSION by Jackie Calhoun. 240 pp. Abby's bipolar sister helps turn her world upside down, so she must decide what's most important.   ISBN 1-59493-014-7 $12.95

PICTURE PERFECT by Jane Vollbrecht. 240 pp. Kate is reintroduced to Casey, the daughter of an old friend. Can they withstand Kate's career? ISBN 1-59493-015-5 $12.95

PAPERBACK ROMANCE by Karin Kallmaker. 240 pp. Carolyn falls for tall, dark and . . . female . . . in this classic lesbian romance.   ISBN 1-59493-033-3 $12.95

DAWN OF CHANGE by Gerri Hill. 240 pp. Susan ran away to find peace in remote Kings Canyon—then she met Shawn . . .   ISBN 1-59493-011-2 $12.95

DOWN THE RABBIT HOLE by Lynne Jamneck. 240 pp. Is a killer holding a grudge against FBI Agent Samantha Skellar?   ISBN 1-59493-012-0 $12.95

SEASONS OF THE HEART by Jackie Calhoun. 240 pp. Overwhelmed, Sara saw only one way out—leaving . . .   ISBN 1-59493-030-9 $12.95

TURNING THE TABLES by Jessica Thomas. 240 pp. The 2nd Alex Peres Mystery. *From ghosties and ghoulies and long leggity beasties* . . .   ISBN 1-59493-009-0 $12.95

FOR EVERY SEASON by Frankie Jones. 240 pp. Andi, who is investigating a 65-year-old murder, meets Janice, a charming district attorney . . .   ISBN 1-59493-010-4 $12.95

LOVE ON THE LINE by Laura DeHart Young. 240 pp. Kay leaves a younger woman behind to go on a mission to Alaska . . . will she regret it?   ISBN 1-59493-008-2 $12.95

UNDER THE SOUTHERN CROSS by Claire McNab. 200 pp. Lee, an American travel agent, goes down under and meets Australian Alex, and the sparks fly under the Southern Cross.   ISBN 1-59493-029-5 $12.95

SUGAR by Karin Kallmaker. 240 pp. Three women want sugar from Sugar, who can't make up her mind.   ISBN 1-59493-001-5 $12.95

FALL GUY by Claire McNab. 200 pp. 16th Detective Inspector Carol Ashton Mystery.   ISBN 1-59493-000-7 $12.95

ONE SUMMER NIGHT by Gerri Hill. 232 pp. Johanna swore to never fall in love again— but then she met the charming Kelly . . .   ISBN 1-59493-007-4 $12.95

TALK OF THE TOWN TOO by Saxon Bennett. 181 pp. Second in the series about wild and fun loving friends.   ISBN 1-931513-77-5 $12.95

LOVE SPEAKS HER NAME by Laura DeHart Young. 170 pp. Love and friendship, desire and intrigue, spark this exciting sequel to *Forever and the Night*.
                                                                ISBN 1-59493-002-3 $12.95

TO HAVE AND TO HOLD by Peggy J. Herring. 184 pp. By finally letting down her defenses, will Dorian be opening herself to a devastating betrayal?
                                                                ISBN 1-59493-005-8 $12.95

WILD THINGS by Karin Kallmaker. 228 pp. Dutiful daughter Faith has met the perfect man. There's just one problem: she's in love with his sister.   ISBN 1-931513-64-3 $12.95

SHARED WINDS by Kenna White. 216 pp. Can Emma rebuild more than just Lanny's marina?   ISBN 1-59493-006-6 $12.95

THE UNKNOWN MILE by Jaime Clevenger. 253 pp. Kelly's world is getting more and more complicated every moment.   ISBN 1-931513-57-0 $12.95

TREASURED PAST by Linda Hill. 189 pp. A shared passion for antiques leads to love.
                                                                ISBN 1-59493-003-1 $12.95

SIERRA CITY by Gerri Hill. 284 pp. Chris and Jesse cannot deny their growing attraction . . .   ISBN 1-931513-98-8 $12.95

ALL THE WRONG PLACES by Karin Kallmaker. 174 pp. Sex and the single girl—Brandy is looking for love and usually she finds it. Karin Kallmaker's first *After Dark* erotic novel.
                                                                ISBN 1-931513-76-7 $12.95

WHEN THE CORPSE LIES A Motor City Thriller by Therese Szymanski. 328 pp. Butch bad-girl Brett Higgins is used to waking up next to beautiful women she hardly knows. Problem is, this one's dead.   ISBN 1-931513-74-0 $12.95

GUARDED HEARTS by Hannah Rickard. 240 pp. Someone's reminding Alyssa about her secret past, and then she becomes the suspect in a series of burglaries.
                                                                ISBN 1-931513-99-6 $12.95

ONCE MORE WITH FEELING by Peggy J. Herring. 184 pp. Lighthearted, loving, romantic adventure.   ISBN 1-931513-60-0 $12.95

TANGLED AND DARK A Brenda Strange Mystery by Patty G. Henderson. 240 pp. When investigating a local death, Brenda finds two possible killers—one diagnosed with Multiple Personality Disorder.   ISBN 1-931513-75-9 $12.95

WHITE LACE AND PROMISES by Peggy J. Herring. 240 pp. Maxine and Betina realize sex may not be the most important thing in their lives.   ISBN 1-931513-73-2 $12.95

UNFORGETTABLE by Karin Kallmaker. 288 pp. Can Rett find love with the cheerleader who broke her heart so many years ago?   ISBN 1-931513-63-5 $12.95

HIGHER GROUND by Saxon Bennett. 280 pp. A delightfully complex reflection of the successful, high society lives of a small group of women.   ISBN 1-931513-69-4 $12.95

LAST CALL A Detective Franco Mystery by Baxter Clare. 240 pp. Frank overlooks all else to try to solve a cold case of two murdered children . . .   ISBN 1-931513-70-8 $12.95

ONCE UPON A DYKE: NEW EXPLOITS OF FAIRY-TALE LESBIANS by Karin Kallmaker, Julia Watts, Barbara Johnson & Therese Szymanski. 320 pp. You've never read fairy tales like these before! From Bella After Dark.   ISBN 1-931513-71-6 $14.95

FINEST KIND OF LOVE by Diana Tremain Braund. 224 pp. Can Molly and Carolyn stop clashing long enough to see beyond their differences?   ISBN 1-931513-68-6 $12.95

DREAM LOVER by Lyn Denison. 188 pp. A soft, sensuous, romantic fantasy.
                                                                                                        ISBN 1-931513-96-1 $12.95

NEVER SAY NEVER by Linda Hill. 224 pp. A classic love story . . . where rules aren't the only things broken.   ISBN 1-931513-67-8 $12.95

PAINTED MOON by Karin Kallmaker. 214 pp. Stranded together in a snowbound cabin, Jackie and Leah's lives will never be the same.   ISBN 1-931513-53-8 $12.95

WIZARD OF ISIS by Jean Stewart. 240 pp. Fifth in the exciting Isis series.
                                                                                                        ISBN 1-931513-71-4 $12.95

WOMAN IN THE MIRROR by Jackie Calhoun. 216 pp. Josey learns to love again, while her niece is learning to love women for the first time.   ISBN 1-931513-78-3 $12.95

SUBSTITUTE FOR LOVE by Karin Kallmaker. 200 pp. When Holly and Reyna meet the combination adds up to pure passion. But what about tomorrow?   ISBN 1-931513-62-7 $12.95

GULF BREEZE by Gerri Hill. 288 pp. Could Carly really be the woman Pat has always been searching for?   ISBN 1-931513-97-X $12.95

THE TOMSTOWN INCIDENT by Penny Hayes. 184 pp. Caught between two worlds, Eloise must make a decision that will change her life forever.   ISBN 1-931513-56-2 $12.95

MAKING UP FOR LOST TIME by Karin Kallmaker. 240 pp. Discover delicious recipes for romance by the undisputed mistress.   ISBN 1-931513-61-9 $12.95

THE WAY LIFE SHOULD BE by Diana Tremain Braund. 173 pp. With which woman will Jennifer find the true meaning of love?   ISBN 1-931513-66-X $12.95

BACK TO BASICS: A BUTCH/FEMME ANTHOLOGY edited by Therese Szymanski— from Bella After Dark. 324 pp.   ISBN 1-931513-35-X $14.95

SURVIVAL OF LOVE by Frankie J. Jones. 236 pp. What will Jody do when she falls in love with her best friend's daughter?   ISBN 1-931513-55-4 $12.95

LESSONS IN MURDER by Claire McNab. 184 pp. 1st Detective Inspector Carol Ashton Mystery.   ISBN 1-931513-65-1 $12.95

DEATH BY DEATH by Claire McNab. 167 pp. 5th Denise Cleever Thriller.
                                                                                                        ISBN 1-931513-34-1 $12.95

CAUGHT IN THE NET by Jessica Thomas. 188 pp. A wickedly observant story of mystery, danger, and love in Provincetown.   ISBN 1-931513-54-6 $12.95

DREAMS FOUND by Lyn Denison. Australian Riley embarks on a journey to meet her birth mother . . . and gains not just a family, but the love of her life.   ISBN 1-931513-58-9 $12.95

A MOMENT'S INDISCRETION by Peggy J. Herring. 154 pp. Jackie is torn between her better judgment and the overwhelming attraction she feels for Valerie.
                                                                                                        ISBN 1-931513-59-7 $12.95

IN EVERY PORT by Karin Kallmaker. 224 pp. Jessica has a woman in every port. Will meeting Cat change all that?   ISBN 1-931513-36-8 $12.95

TOUCHWOOD by Karin Kallmaker. 240 pp. Rayann loves Louisa. Louisa loves Rayann. Can the decades between their ages keep them apart?   ISBN 1-931513-37-6 $12.95

WATERMARK by Karin Kallmaker. 248 pp. Teresa wants a future with a woman whose heart has been frozen by loss. Sequel to *Touchwood*.   ISBN 1-931513-38-4 $12.95